THE
HAUNTED
BOOKSTORE
Gateway to a
Parallel Universe

Wagaya wa Kakuriyo no kashihonya san Novel 6
©Shinobumaru (Story)
This edition originally published in Japan in 2021 by
MICRO MAGAZINE, INC., Tokyo.
English translation rights arranged with
MICRO MAGAZINE, INC., Tokyo.

Seven Seas press and purchase enquiries can be sent to
Marketing Manager Lianne Sentar at press@gomanga.com.
Information regarding the distribution and purchase of
digital editions is available from Digital Manager CK Russell
at digital@gomanga.com.

Follow Seven Seas Entertainment online at
sevenseasentertainment.com.

TRANSLATION: Mimi Wang
ADAPTATION: Jack Hamm
COVER DESIGN: Nicky Lim
LOGO DESIGN: George Panella
INTERIOR LAYOUT & DESIGN: Clay Gardner
COPY EDITOR: Jade Gardner
LIGHT NOVEL EDITOR: Laurel Ashgrove
PREPRESS TECHNICIAN: Melanie Ujimori, Jules Valera
EDITOR-IN-CHIEF: Julie Davis
ASSOCIATE PUBLISHER: Adam Arnold
PUBLISHER: Jason DeAngelis

ISBN: 978-1-68579-631-0
Printed in Canada
First Printing: July 2023
10 9 8 7 6 5 4 3 2 1

THE HAUNTED BOOKSTORE

Gateway to a Parallel Universe

VOLUME 6
The Inimitable Father-Daughter
Pair's Eternal Promise

WRITTEN BY
Shinobumaru

TRANSLATED BY
Mimi Wang

Airship

Seven Seas Entertainment

TABLE OF
Contents

That Fated Day

AS I LAY on a small hill on the outskirts of the town in the spirit realm, I watched the starry sky twinkling above and thought about all the conversations I'd had with my father.

I was ignorant in my earliest days, before I knew just how wide the world was. But, because of that ignorance, I thought I could become anything I wanted. As I spent my days with my smiling father, I thought he was cooler and stronger than any hero in any story, and I held just one wish in my heart: that I could become a real daughter to the adoptive father I loved so much.

More than anything, I was terrified because we were not related by blood. What if my "real" parents came one day and I was handed over to them? The possibility always frightened me. I couldn't bear to leave the one who had shown me so much kindness and joy. My heart just couldn't take it.

I knew that no matter how hard I tried, I would never become a "real" daughter to him. I did everything I could to distance myself from that reality.

I was such a child in those days.

There was no way Shinonome-san would have cast me aside like that.

But that fear was a matter of life and death to me then. I remembered once, trying to keep him by my side, I said to him with great conviction, "I'll help you be anything you want, if you find something you want to be."

He smiled back at me with traces of tears welling in his eyes and replied, "Sure. The moment I find something I want to be, I'll be sure to come to you." His grin accentuated the many folds that wrinkled in the corners of his eyes, and he stroked his stubble to try and hide his blush. He could be quite scary when he was mad, but his bashfulness made him seem no older than a teenage boy.

Even now, I could still remember that expression clear as day.

I wondered to myself whether I would ever be able to do for Shinonome-san what he had done for me. And was I really worth the time and effort he had put into raising me?

No doubt these were common questions that children often asked.

Shinonome-san... Are you proud of the person you raised?

I didn't know the answer to that question.

I was in the dark, and I would continue to be, all the way until this fateful day crept up on me.

On another night, when the sky of the spirit realm was dyed a clear green, a gentle breeze caressed my cheek. Below the winking stars, I stood upon a hill that was covered by nemophilas on one side. With every whisper of the wind, the flowers waved like the ocean, and even the sound they made when they brushed up against the surrounding grass sounded like the crashing you'd hear on a beach.

Countless spirits carrying glimmerfly lanterns wove between them as they headed for the peak of the hill. Some had taken human forms while others retained their beastly features, but all of them were wearing black. Slowly, slowly, their faint light trailed through the sea of flowers.

It was a beautiful view, one that could only be seen in the spirit realm. I was so taken by its phantasmic allure that the grasp of time was beginning to slowly slip away from me. It was hard to believe that it was real and not pulled from someone's imagination.

But no, this *was* real. That was the undeniable truth.

Suddenly, my heart was gripped by a painful pang. I took a deep breath and exhaled. Then I clenched my jaw and tried my best to not give in to the sadness.

I don't think I'm ever going to forget what I'm seeing, I thought to myself.

"Kaori!" a voice called out to me. I whipped around to see who it was and spotted Shinonome-san and Noname. I felt a damp heat prickling in my eyes, but I couldn't let myself cry. Not yet.

I smiled at the two, and Shinonome-san immediately deepened his frown. He could probably sense that I was forcing myself to be positive. I wasn't exactly trying to lie to him, but...I just didn't want to reveal my true feelings yet.

"Surprise! Thanks for coming out here," I greeted them.

"Tell me what's going on," my adoptive father replied without trying to hide his displeasure. I smiled wryly at him and straightened my clothes, then began to walk through the spread of blue flowers. I could imagine that my spotless white attire looked like a brilliant moonbeam on a dark night, standing out brightly among the nemophilas.

I began to think about the events leading up to this day.

It all started last autumn, the chilly season of whispering dried fall leaves, on a day that seemed no different from the rest.

CHAPTER 1

My Adoptive Father

AS THE AUTUMN WIND rattled the window relentlessly, a red spark crackled and burst forth from the burning wood. Shivering and shrunken from the chilly draft, I added more wood to the brazier. The freezing wind had been blowing all day, but it wasn't quite at the level of winter, so I didn't want to get out the kotatsu just yet.

That was why I decided to sneak into Shinonome-san's room, like I always did on days like this.

His room was small, just under seven square meters. It had a built-in closet, a bookshelf against one wall, and a humble writing desk. His business documents and his failed manuscripts were scattered across the floor.

It wasn't the neatest room in the world, but it was the right size for one single brazier to heat it up quickly and easily. That was exactly why I liked to spend time in there when it was cold. We weren't exactly made of money, so I did what I could to be frugal.

Well, at least we wouldn't be struggling as much as last year.

I looked at the family budget planner I was holding and smiled. Glancing behind me, I could see Shinonome-san concentrating silently on his writing.

He'd been acting differently recently. The biggest change was that he'd stopped drinking his favorite alcohol. He'd also started taking his writing a lot more seriously. He used to take his own sweet time until his deadline was too close to ignore, but now he would work on his manuscripts whenever he had time to spare. He'd also started being firmer with rental prices when it was his time to man the store. Thanks to that, we'd been seeing better profits and probably wouldn't have to stress as much as last year about what the new year had in store for us.

What had spurred such change in him...?

The catalyst that made the most sense to me was the passing of his best friend during the summer. Tamaki-san, the shifty man who always wore round sunglasses, a gaudy haori, and a fedora, had been Shinonome-san's friend from way back when he came to the spirit realm. The two of them had even teamed up to publish *Selected Memoirs from the Spirit Realm*, an anthology of tales from spirits that lived in this realm. They had found a niche that needed filling, and thus, the book was born.

Spirits didn't have a tradition of writing stories or creating written records because there was never a need for them to do so. Humans were the ones who did the writing, and spirits were only characters in their tales at best. They took the spotlight in many artworks and stories created by humans, and one of those creators was Tamaki-san, back when he was Toriyama Sekien. A famous artist who illustrated countless spirits, he was best known for publishing *The Illustrated Demon Horde's Night Parade* back during the Edo period.

However, times have changed. With the advancement of technology, humans and spirits essentially ceased contact. The darkness in which the spirits dwelled had been completely flooded with the light of science, and their mystifying existence justified with logic and reason. This was the spirit equivalent of having their records burned. It seemed as though spirits would eventually fade away and disappear without anyone ever knowing their stories. Saddened by this fact, Shinonome-san and his friends decided to publish their own book to preserve the spirits' lore.

When their first volume was published, Shinonome-san spoke excitedly about writing another one, and I remembered Tamaki-san had been enthusiastic about it too. *Selected Memoirs from the Spirit Realm* had become a mission that they needed to complete at all costs. However, Tamaki-san passed away before the second volume could be published. Perhaps Shinonome-san's newfound motivation sprang from his desire to carry on the wishes of his late friend.

He worked tirelessly through the days and nights. I had to do whatever I could to support him as his daughter.

But what? I thought.

I was completely useless when it came to writing, so I had to help him in other ways. I glanced at the clock and saw that it was the perfect time for tea.

"Right!" I said and rushed to the kitchen. After rummaging through the cupboards, I hurried back to Shinonome-san's room and placed a metal mesh across the top of the brazier. I laid a few orange bars, three or four centimeters long, above the fire. They were dried sweet potato sticks, the perfect snack for the cold season.

To do good work, you must have good nutrients. And when your brain is feeling sluggish, you need sugar. These little things were packed full of both, and they also filled you up pretty well. Plus, their texture would provide good stimulation for your mind as you chewed on them. They're the best treat to have when you're writing!

I rolled up my sleeves and braced myself. It was time for Operation Support Shinonome-san. *May he have the tasty treat he needs to keep up his writing!*

Well, even so, all I would be doing was toasting the sweet potato sticks.

If I had some Western-style sweets, maybe I could have arranged them into something cuter, I thought to myself with a laugh.

As the heat of the fire crackled and roasted the sticks, a sweet scent not unlike honey began to drift from the sweet potatoes.

Oooh, it smells sooo sweet! I broke out into a smile as I flipped them with a pair of cooking chopsticks. They had turned a lovely golden brown on the outside and looked to be just about done, ready for eating.

And, of course, I had a drink ready to go for Shinonome-san as well: a nice, cold glass of milk! It's truly the perfect companion for roasted sweet potato sticks, and nothing can change my mind about that. To each their own, but I'm right about this.

I loaded a tray with the glass of milk and the plate of sweet potatoes and carried it over to my adoptive father.

"...Shinonome-san?" I called out. I tried to take a peek at him, but he didn't give me so much as a single glance back. He was probably concentrating so heavily that he didn't even realize I had approached him. He had the tendency to shut himself off from the world like a clam in the deep ocean every time he picked up his brush. He would just write and write and write without eating, drinking, or saying a single word.

And then he would suddenly run out of energy the next day and collapse, sleeping the hours away like a dead man. That was how it usually went.

I grumbled a little. I had to make him eat somehow, or my toasty sweet potato sticks would all go to waste!

I couldn't just interrupt him, though. That would be so inconsiderate.

A small idea popped into my head.

I stabbed a piece of sweet potato with a toothpick and blew gently on it to cool it down. Then I poked Shinonome-san's mouth with it...and he ate it.

"Ooh," I murmured. It worked! He continued to stare at his manuscript, chewing as he wrote. I smiled with satisfaction and approached his mouth again with the straw in the glass of milk.

"Oooh," I whispered again. Another success! He took the glass and began to slurp up the liquid in great, unconscious gulps.

Seeing that he had drained half the glass in a few seconds, I grinned.

It kind of felt like I was feeding a small animal of some sort, like when I'd had to feed Kinme and Ginme, back when we first found them. The first time I gave them food was such an emotional moment for me.

While I thought about the time when my childhood friends were baby chicks, I offered another piece of sweet potato to Shinonome-san. Sure enough, he took it and chewed in silence, showing no reaction.

"Um..."

I was getting a little worried. Was he even noticing the taste of what he was eating? The snacks were from Noname, so Shinonome-san probably didn't *hate* them, but...

I snuck myself a piece as a taste test.

I immediately puckered my mouth and let some of the hot steam escape.

"Yep, it tastes good," I said with a nod and a smile to myself. The fire had done a good job of toasting it until it was crispy on the surface while keeping the inside soft and moist. Its sweetness was like syrup, its richness a dominant presence in my mouth.

Oh, this is really good. I gotta roast some more for myself later.

"But wow, he must be concentrating really hard if he doesn't even notice that he's eating something this delicious," I whispered as I gave him more sweet potato and milk. Hardly a moment later, the plate and cup were completely empty.

This plan had gone pretty well. Maybe I could even give him dinner the same way. I'd have to cook something that could be eaten with a spoon then, like fried rice.

I carried the tray back to the kitchen, and when I peeked into his room again, I could see his broad back hunched over.

I paused in thought, then walked over to the bookshelf and picked out one of my favorite books. I carried a cushion over to Shinonome-san and sat behind him, leaning against his back. I could feel the warmth radiating from him, and it made me feel closer to him.

"Good luck with your writing," I whispered. He stopped for just a moment and resumed a second later, as if responding to my small encouragement. I giggled to myself and opened my book.

The fire continued to spark and crackle, and the window rattled on with every gust of the autumn wind. The only other sounds in the room were the *fwip* as I turned the pages and the *skritch skritch* from Shinonome-san occasionally scratching his head.

The afternoon continued its comfortable, quiet lull...but not for long.

"HELLOOO THERE!" a voice burst in, shattering the peaceful atmosphere.

"Whoa! Toochika-san?!" I yelled. The kappa, who was Shinonome-san's other best friend, had flung open the sliding door and entered wearing an expensive, brand-name suit.

"Hey, hey! How've you been?" The well-dressed spirit greeted me with vigor. Before I could answer, he began shouting some orders to someone behind him.

"Come on, bring them over here. Hey, be careful there! Gently, gently!" he barked.

"Oh, I'm so glad we're finally here! Toochika, this is way too heavy!"

"Why did you make me do this? I'm not strong and buff like Ginme is..."

The ones behind the kappa were Kinme and Ginme, the Tengu twins. They both panted and huffed as they stumbled into the room with huge, heavy cardboard boxes in their arms.

"Are you guys okay?" I asked in concern. "What's all that, anyway? That looks like...a lot."

"Ask Toochika... I can't do this anymore. I'm gonna die... Kaori...tea, please."

"M-me too... And make it cold, if you can..."

"Yeah, sure. Take a seat, you two!" I said to the twins. They were drenched in sweat, wheezing for breath, and stooped over in exhaustion.

Compared to them, however, Toochika-san was bursting with energy. He sped over to Shinonome-san and started slapping his back with great force.

"Wh... Toochika-san!" I cried, watching in horror as the kappa tried to break the concentration that Shinonome-san had sunk into. However, now that he was in the zone, there was nothing much that could snap him out of it. Toochika-san's next words, though, seemed to be strong enough to hoist my adoptive father out of the depths of his mind.

"Shinonome! They're here! The new books have finished printing!"

"...What?" Shinonome-san said after having been speechless for so many hours. He blinked and stared back at his friend's face. The kappa nodded back while Shinonome-san's eyes glittered.

"Really?"

"Yeah! I'm serious!"

Shinonome-san immediately flew to the cardboard boxes and scrambled to tear them open, completely ignoring the twins and me while we watched him with surprise. As he reached a hand into the space within, his face flushed red.

"The second volume of *Selected Memoirs from the Spirit Realm*...!" he gasped as he flipped through its pages, his eyes darting about as they scanned the writing within. When he reached the final page, he turned to the cover and paused to soak in the exquisitely drawn illustration of a spirit adorning it.

"So Tamaki did finish it..." he whispered, his eyes growing wet with emotion.

This sequel would be Shinonome-san and Tamaki-san's last collaborative work.

I hadn't realized it was this close to being finished. My heart squeezed, and I felt like I could start crying at any moment too.

"I think it came out really well," Toochika-san said cheerily. Shinonome-san's face crumpled, and he smiled as he wiped his tears away and sniffled.

"We have to go and thank him," he said.

"Yeah," the kappa agreed.

They solemnly nodded to each other.

"Are you going out now?" I asked.

Shinonome-san nodded. "Yeah. We should at least say hi to him after he gave us so many stories."

That reminded me of how, a few days after the first volume came out, he'd made the journey to give his thanks as well.

I'd have to start helping him pack, then. The weather was cold, so he'd at least need his haoris and scarves, and maybe even a coat.

As I racked my brain on what to pack for Shinonome-san, he surprised me by saying, "Kaori, you should come too."

"What?" I blinked, stunned. "But what about the store? Are we closing up?"

We were open seven days a week, and we rarely ever left the store unattended because we wanted as many spirits as possible to borrow our books.

"I guess," he answered. He took a piece of paper and began to write an explanation of why the store was closed.

I tilted my head, confused by the unexpected response. Suddenly, the twins began to fuss.

"What? Kaori, are you going on a trip? I wanna come!" Ginme cried.

"If Ginme's going, then I want to go too!" Kinme followed up.

"No," Shinonome-san said. "You two have to stay for your training. Stop whining."

"Boooooo!" the brothers shouted.

"Oh, quiet, or I'll tell the Sojobo!"

As the three argued on, I cast a glance at Toochika-san. When our eyes met, I couldn't help but give him a wry chuckle.

A few days later, I was at the front of the store locking the door and putting up the notice of closure. I carried a large travel bag in one hand, filled with everything I would need for an overnight stay at the place where Shinonome-san was going to conduct some interviews.

"I'm going to go lock up in back," Shinonome-san said.

"Oh, yes please," I replied. I watched him as he turned and headed behind the house, clad in an Inverness cape. I sniffled and shifted my gaze to the front of the shop, following the crisp leaves that were being blown about by the wind. The day was cold enough that my lungs felt like they were freezing with each breath. The spirits passing by also seemed sluggish in their steps, all wrapped up in thick layers. It truly felt like winter was on our doorstep.

However, I wasn't very bothered by the weather right now. I had bigger things to worry about instead.

I looked around me uneasily. When I realized that the person I had hoped to see still wasn't here, my shoulders dropped. I fidgeted aimlessly and kicked at a rock on the ground with my boots. I tried to adjust my beanie and started to wish for a mirror when I realized that it was messing with my hair.

"Can you calm down? You're making *me* anxious too," said an annoyed voice.

I grumbled and pouted. "But... But..."

"No buts. Get a hold of yourself, and firmly!"

I looked down and saw a cheeky black cat staring back at me. She was Nyaa-san, a Kasha spirit and my best friend. Her three tails tapped at the ground impatiently, and she darted up my leg, worming into my coat. When she reached my collar, she poked her head out. I panicked and tried to support her so she wouldn't fall, and she twitched her ears contentedly when I caught her. This was her way of being friendly with me, although her words were still as blunt as ever.

"There's no need to be nervous," she said. "All that's changed is that you two are now mates."

"Wh-what?! No! It's not like we got married or anything!" I blushed in protest, but all Nyaa-san did was turn the other way.

"I don't get you humans. You like each other, so just go and have some children already. Doesn't matter if you're boyfriend and girlfriend or mates, it's a pretty normal thing to do," she said.

"That's still waaay off the table!" I said in a loud and flustered squeal. "We're not cats, you know!"

The cat spirit just began to groom herself, pretending not to hear. I exhaled slowly, trying to dispel some of the heat that was rising in my cheeks. Why did I get so worked up so easily?

Well, there was only one answer, and it didn't even need to be said. It was because of Shirai Suimei, the ex-exorcist who was two years my junior.

He was coming with us on our trip too, and I'd only found out that morning. Shinonome-san came to me and just dropped

"The boy's coming with us too," so suddenly that I was still trying to mentally prepare myself.

And could you blame me? This was going to be an overnight trip with my boyfriend, with my adoptive father in tow...

Conflicted, I looked up at the sky of the spirit realm. My head was full of anxiety, and I prayed that nothing would happen.

After I confessed to Suimei, it had taken a nerve-racking amount of time before he could tell me his feelings. But one summer's day on Awaji Island, he told me that he also liked me, and so we officially began to date. Our relationship had been smooth sailing for two months now, with no notable fights and plenty of opportunities to go out together.

The only thing was, I hadn't told Shinonome-san about our relationship yet.

I sighed, watching my white breath disappear into the air. I still hadn't mustered up enough courage to tell him. He was overprotective and tended to become very tunnel-visioned when it came to me, so I knew that the news would shock him at the very least. I didn't want this to shake him out of the focus he'd finally developed for his work.

"Maybe I'm just trying to make excuses, though," I sighed and shook my head.

For as long as I could remember, Shinonome-san had always been the most important man in my life, but that was beginning to change. I knew that romantic love and parental love were two different things, but my heart and mind couldn't keep up with the evolution that was happening within me.

Part of me knew that getting a boyfriend meant that an inevitable distance would grow between Shinonome-san and me, and I was still too clingy to bear leaving my adoptive father's side.

Aaaaaagh. I'm too much of a daddy's girl... I thought.

Realizing my love for Suimei also brought my love for Shinonome-san to the forefront, along with more trouble and less knowledge of what to do about it. I was stuck at a crossroads; if I accidentally let slip that I was dating Suimei during the trip, no doubt Shinonome-san would explode. One option, then, was to come clean before any fuses were lit.

But that still...kind of...

"Kaori?"

I jumped as a voice pulled me out of my worries. I felt my chest grow warm, and I turned around slowly, meeting the gaze of a pair of light caramel eyes. Before me stood a boy whose soft white hair fluttered in the autumn breeze. He had glowing pale skin, a sculpted nose, and lips thin like the petals on a flower. He was the very image of a storybook prince, and he was also surrounded by several glimmerflies. The presence of these phosphorescent insects proved that he was human.

Suimei.

I swallowed and tried to stop my heart from leaping out of my chest. *Is my face red? Did I pick a cute outfit today?* A storm of questions raced through my mind, but I shoved them away and opened my mouth to greet him.

"Morning," I mumbled.

Suimei's face broke into a relaxed smile. "Good morning," he replied.

Oh God, that smile...! I thought and darted my eyes away. My heart was beating much too loudly for my liking.

Back when we first met, Suimei barely made any expressions. Coming from a family of exorcists, he had practiced that as a necessity for his job. Having a blank face was just the norm for him. I wondered how he felt about it now. Every time we saw each other, I could feel that he was getting more and more expressive. I couldn't help but stare at his every move and return his gaze, so full of a kindness that drove me wild.

As small as every single one of his changes was, they built upon each other to create something that held so much impact.

"U-um, I just heard this morning that you were coming with us," I said, hurriedly trying to start a conversation that would direct our attention away from my embarrassment. I gathered my courage and looked at him again, but what I saw almost made me spit all over him.

There was a face wrapped up in his duffel coat, and its eyes were peeking at me from underneath his chin.

"Kaori! And the black cat! Good morning! Wow, we match!"

That black fur with red spots... It was Kuro, the Inugami. He seemed to be having the time of his life being bundled up with his beloved partner. The hem of Suimei's coat began to shake. Kuro's tail was probably wagging at record speed underneath.

"It's cold, huh? Super cold! I thought my nose was going to freeze solid! And the ground is like ice. It felt like my toe beans were gonna get frostbite and fall off! But when I told Suimei, he let me sit in his coat!"

"O-oh, that's nice."

"Heh heh heh," Kuro grinned. "Suimei is sooo nice. He's the best partner in the world! You look pretty warm too, black cat. Good for you! Kaori is sooo nice too! Not as nice as Suimei, though!"

Nyaa-san seemed to dislike the Inugami's smugness. "Listen to yourself, yap-yap-yapping at this early hour. Pipe down, or I'll maul you."

"What?!" Kuro yelped.

The cat returned an apathetic stare. "Are you stupid? How can you even compare anyone to our Kaori? *She's* the best in the world, duh."

"I-I'm not stupid! And nuh-uh, Suimei's the best!"

"Still yapping? You really want to get mauled, huh?"

"What?! No!"

The black cat scoffed at the horrified Inugami and turned her nose up at him.

I was told that Nyaa-san had been asked by my late mother to watch over me, and she was every bit as overprotective as Shinonome-san was. Kuro had crossed a line that she would defend with her life, and her rarely seen stubborn side was not having any of it.

"Aw, go easy on him, Nyaa-san," I said.

"I didn't do anything," she said. "Go tell the mutt if you've got a problem."

I gave Nyaa-san a defeated pat on the head and saw that Suimei was desperately trying to soothe Kuro's quivering. He treated the dog very dearly, perhaps because they'd been raised together.

"There's no point in fighting them, Kuro," he said. "You'll only get hurt, and for what?"

"B-but, Suiiimeeeiii..."

"Don't cry, or she's going to call you a mutt again."

"Waaaaaahhh...! B-but... But I'm right...!"

As Kuro sobbed, Suimei continued to gently calm him. They were truly more like siblings than partners. While I was thinking about the two, Suimei caught my eyes, and suddenly we both became extremely aware of how strange we must have looked with animals in our coats. We blinked at each other and burst into laughter. I'd been doing such a good job of not laughing, but I couldn't hold it in anymore.

"Ah ha ha ha! What are we doing?!"

"Seriously!"

While we were beside ourselves, Shinonome-san returned.

"What are you two up to?" he asked, puzzled, and I showed him how we both had animals bundled in our coats. It was too much for him, and he chuckled.

"Pfft! You look so silly!" he said. I couldn't help but feel happy at how cheerful he looked. But Suimei blushed, a little embarrassed that Shinonome-san was laughing at him.

"Well, Kuro said he was cold! What else was I supposed to do?" he huffed.

"Don't spoil him too much or you're going to end up carrying him everywhere forever," Shinonome-san advised.

"Urk... I'll keep that in mind."

Judging from their friendly expressions, they seemed to be getting along. Suimei looked the same as always when he talked to my adoptive father, so maybe it was just me, but this seemed... different somehow, in a good way.

I giggled to myself, realizing that I had been worrying for nothing. If I didn't let my relationship slip, great. If I wanted to tell Shinonome-san about it, then I wanted to do it properly. I decided to stop worrying so much about the trip.

"By the way, where are we going? Will it be far?" I asked.

Traveling from the spirit realm to the human world didn't take very long. We had a network of hells in the spirit realm that was well connected to different spots all over Japan, so we usually only had to make a day trip when we traveled. It was actually quite rare for us to have to make advance preparations to stay overnight. Maybe we would be going to a remote island, or something like that...?

Hearing my question, Shinonome-san rubbed his stubbled chin. A devilish grin began to stretch across his face.

"Yes, you could say that. We'll be visiting a hidden village."

"A hidden village...?" Suimei and I asked, looking at each other in confusion.

The bookstore had a lot of customers who would deal only with Shinonome-san. This was because he'd expanded his business with personal visits to spirits who lived in secluded, hidden corners of the human world rather than the spirit realm. However, they felt no desire to connect with mortal society, and they would often shut themselves away in their homes, rarely if ever making contact with the outside.

Shinonome-san would trek all over Japan to deliver tales to these spirits, fueled by his strong belief that everybody needed stories. And today, we would be meeting one such customer.

We passed through the hells and arrived in the human world, exiting from the hollow of a gigantic tree. The autumn sky was clear and bright, and the scent of the fallen leaves was thick enough for me to feel it in the back of my throat. We were deep in the mountains, far from the rest of civilization, dappled by the sunlight drifting down through the trees. The leaves whispered with every breath of the wind.

The presence of the sun made it much less cold here than in the spirit realm. Nyaa-san leaped out of my coat and allowed herself a big stretch. Kuro had also left Suimei's coat, and he approached the cat.

"Where are we?" I asked Shinonome-san.

"The Kunisaki Peninsula in Oita Prefecture," he answered simply as he began to walk. I hurried after him.

Looking up, I could see more foliage than sky. Seeing all the giant trees growing from the earth, I could think of one word to describe this mountain: *grand*. But as remote as this place was, there were still traces of man-made efforts. A short distance from the hollow, we came across some mossy stairs made with natural, uneven pieces of stone that were fitted with a set of railings. The steps did not, by any stretch, look easy to climb.

"The Kumano magaibutsu are at the top of these stairs," Shinonome-san said.

Magaibutsu were Buddhist relief statues carved straight into the stone of a mountain wall. These particular ones were said to have been created during the late Heian period, and they were recognized by the Japanese government as Important Cultural Properties.

"There are no records in the human world that say exactly who made them, but one theory says that Ninmon Bosatsu was responsible."

I felt like I had heard about the Kumano magaibutsu somewhere before... And then it hit me.

"Oh! There's a legend that says these stone steps were built in one night by an oni, right?" I said.

"That's right. They didn't do a very good job of it, though. Maybe they panicked when Kumano Gongen gave the order."

I stared at the stairs, taking the sight of them in. The legend said that, long ago, an evil oni lived here. To right their wrongs, Kumano Gongen, the deity of the Kumano shrines, ordered them to build the stone stairs in one night. Hearing that this would free them of their sins, the oni rushed to finish the job. As we imagined the sight of a hulking oni stacking the stones with the best of their efforts, Suimei nodded deeply beside me.

"Wow, the Kunisaki Peninsula sure has a lot of legends involving oni," he said.

"There's more?" I asked.

"I don't know too much about them, but when I was still training to be an exorcist back home, a lot of the elders told me that the peninsula had a deep history with oni. Oni are usually hated and feared by humans, but here, the people were raised to look at them differently."

One of the main examples would be the Shujo Onie festival, where oni and fire came together in one big celebration. Monks would dress themselves up as oni for the festivities, something which usually would be quite ironic, but not in the Kunisaki Peninsula. Oni were considered sacred, and people prayed to them for good harvest and health, even inviting them into their homes after the festival with offerings of alcohol. To the people here, oni were not necessarily evil.

"The elders would also go on and on about not targeting any of the oni here," Suimei said.

"That's so interesting!" I said, thinking about my oni acquaintance. "I'm kinda glad the folks here don't hate oni. They seem like nice people."

Suimei chuckled. "That's so you. Well, I guess you'd be right... No, I'd say they lean closer to being open-minded. It makes sense that they'd be more accepting of outside ideas and influences, since this is where Shinto-Buddhist syncretism started."

Shinto-Buddhist syncretism came about when local religion combined with Buddhist teachings, creating a new faith altogether. The Kunisaki Peninsula was home to a unique culture called Rokugo Manzan that was born from merging Shugendo, the worship of the deity Hachiman, with practices from the Tendai sect of Buddhism.

"Come to think of it, the first Japanese person to become a Christian priest in Rome was also from here. Petro Kasui Kibe, right?" I said.

All these pieces made a lot of sense. Shinonome-san, who had been listening intently to Suimei, gave a hearty laugh.

"You sure know a lot! Been studying up, eh?"

"...Not really. It's not a big deal, anyway. It's all common knowledge for an exorcist," Suimei said. He obviously felt awkward at Shinonome-san's praise and was trying to hide his embarrassment. "So, are we really going to the Kumano magaibutsu? Are we meeting an oni today?"

The spirit shook his head. "No, this is just our starting point. We won't be staying."

He stretched his body and his ankles in a rotating motion.

I blinked. It seemed like he was psyching himself up a bit too much for climbing some stairs.

"You seem pumped," I commented.

"Well, of course I am. We're going to a hidden village. We can't just waltz in, you know."

"What do you mean...?"

"Hey, you animals, let's go!" Shinonome-san cried to the cat and dog, both of whom were sniffing around. "Nyaa, let Kaori ride on your back."

He took some wooden tags with half-finished designs on them out from his robes. With a breath, he made some arrow and sun-like symbols appear on them and grinned boldly.

"Suimei was right about the culture here being open to outside influences. Not that it accepted everything and anything, but given enough time, it would take in a lot. This is the perfect place for outcasts who need somewhere to call home."

He looked to the top of the stone steps and stared, then took a huge step in his wooden geta.

"Watch closely now, Kaori. As long as you follow everything carefully, you'll have no trouble opening the gate to the hidden village. We're going to cross a whole bunch of lost relics," he said and bolted up the stairs with great speed.

"Wh... Shinonome-san! What relics?!" I shouted after him.

"Get on, Kaori!" Nyaa-san cried.

"O-okay!" I said as I scrambled atop her. She had grown more than tenfold in size. We followed after Shinonome-san, with Nyaa-san accelerating so fast that I thought I was going to be flung off. I clung to her neck for dear life, but we didn't seem to be getting any closer to the other spirit, who had blue-white lightning crackling around his feet as he practically flew up the stairs.

I narrowed my eyes at my adoptive father. "Jeez, why couldn't you have explained all this beforehand?! Then we wouldn't have to rush like this!" I yelled, accidentally letting my thoughts slip.

Suimei, who was keeping pace with Nyaa-san and me, raised an eyebrow. "Rich coming from you, considering you never explain anything to me."

"Urk!"

"The apple really doesn't fall far from the tree, huh?"

"Heh heh heh!" I giggled. "Yeah, I guess."

"That wasn't a compliment!"

I laughed wryly at Suimei's brutal honestly. Then, in a flash, we reached the top of the oni-made stairs, and I caught sight of an eight-meter-tall statue.

It was the magaibutsu of the Wisdom King. He was usually depicted as wielding a jeweled sword with a fearsome expression, but he looked peaceful in the one here. I was a little taken aback by how friendly he seemed, as if he had not one single angry bone in his body. Shinonome-san snapped me out of it, though.

"Shugendo still prospers here in the Kunisaki Peninsula, and once every decade, they host a Mineiri pilgrimage that stretches through the mountains, starting right here!"

Then he charged straight for the maigaibutsu without slowing down even a little.

"Shi...!" I cried, but I was so shocked that the rest of his name would not follow. When it seemed like he was about to crash into the statue, he passed through it like it was a completely normal thing to do.

"Wh-what the... AAAAAAHHH!"

Before I knew what was happening, I came face-to-face with the Wisdom King. He was getting closer, and fast!

I froze in terror.

I'm going to hit it! I'm going to slam straight into it!

I was so scared that I flinched on instinct and accidentally released my grip on Nyaa-san.

"Aah!" I gasped.

"You idiot! Don't let go!"

I could feel someone holding and supporting me from behind. It was Suimei, who had hopped onto Nyaa-san's back out of worry for me.

"S-Suimei! Thank you... Eep!" I yelped.

I could only relax for a second before I was faced with the Wisdom King again. I squeezed my eyes shut, ready for the inevitable impact.

But it never came. Instead, I was enveloped by a strange sensation that I can only describe as like passing through layers of warm air. When I slowly opened my eyes, I was greeted with a complete change in scenery all around me.

Did we just...teleport?! I thought, gobsmacked.

I tried to grapple with my confusion, my mind racing as I attempted to work out what had just happened.

The first thing I spotted was an old stone torii gate. Next, I saw two Nio statues on either side of a path that most likely led up to a temple. I couldn't spot one anywhere, though. They just stood there in silence, covered in the gold of the fallen leaves.

"Shinonome-san! Where are we?!" I cried when I realized that he was now keeping pace with Nyaa-san and me.

"In a place called Kunimimachi," he answered, "where the old Sento-ji used to be."

"Wait, so we're in the ruins of an old temple?"

"That's right! The first of the Rokugo Manzan temples, to be exact. The story goes that a Christian daimyo called Otomo Sorin burned it to the ground during the Warring States period and put it completely out of commission. It used to be so thriving that it earned the nickname of 'Mount Koya of the West.' A new temple was built elsewhere during the Meiji era, but I suppose its former glory could never be recaptured. These Nio statues really are something. And look at the size of the land here! It makes you wonder how busy it was during its heyday."

We passed between the two statues and sped deeper into the grounds.

"Whoa, look at all this! It's so cool!" Kuro said excitedly from behind Shinonome-san.

The cedar-laden path was covered with stone pagodas—gorinto, to be exact. Each of the five segments of these pagodas represented an element, and they started being used as gravestones and memorial towers at the end of the Heian era. Even with one glance over the path, I could tell that there had to be thousands of gorinto here. They had not seen any cleaning or care in a very, very long time, and they were covered in leaves and moss.

It hit me that this place had well and truly lost its purpose.

"Whose graves are these?" I wondered. "Whoever is resting here, they must have all had their own loved ones once upon a time."

However, there was no one left to offer them any prayers. And after the temple burned down, did the people left behind have a chance to mourn properly? I could only hope that all the souls here were able to rest in peace, but there was no way to know for sure.

I felt a sense of melancholy looking at the stone pagodas, and my heart filled with forlorn sadness.

Suddenly, lights began to shine from between them.

"Huh?" I squinted. My thoughts went to fireflies at first, but then I realized that wasn't possible because it was autumn. As I pondered what it could be, the couple of lights began to grow and multiply until the brightness was so intense that I had to close my eyes.

"All right, we're just going to borrow a bit of power from these prayers of old and keep going," Shinonome-san said.

Is that what the lights are for? I thought, but my mind was already overwhelmed trying to keep up with how fast everything was being thrown at me.

I felt like I was passing through layers of warm air again, and in an instant we had been taken to yet another mountain. I blinked, taking in the megaliths that now stood around us. Each of them must have been two or three meters tall. They gave off a mysterious vibe, lining up and exposed to the elements.

"What is this stone circle...?" I asked.

"It reminds me of Stonehenge, but smaller," Suimei said as we turned to catch each other's glances.

Shinonome-san said that we were now in the city of Usa, somewhere southwest of Mount Komekami.

"These are the Sada-kyoishi," he explained. "The popular explanation is that they are the remains of an ancient ritual site.

Humans have theorized that these were torii prototypes or that they were used to inscribe sutras long ago, but no one knows the truth for sure. I guess you could say that this is another place that has lost its original purpose."

There was sorrow in his words as he shared this with us. But why? Was there something lurking deeper beneath the surface?

I opened my mouth to ask, but specks of light similar to what we'd just seen started appearing in the shadows of the megaliths. I closed my mouth as the light began to enclose us. My vision turned a searing white as it consumed Shinonome-san and the sadness on his face.

When the light eventually faded, we found ourselves in a different place again, this time in the shadowy gloom of a forest. The trees grew dense and thick, and red leaves were drifting down to scatter all over the ground. The sky had already begun to set into a vibrant crimson, even though we had left early in the morning. We had spent quite a lot of time getting here, and I was sure that this was our final stop.

I could sense that from the two figures who were waiting for us.

"We've been expecting you."

The two of them put their hands together and bowed at the same time. They were each wearing a peculiar mask, with one horn sprouting from a face that looked like it was part monkey and part monster. It had a black base with red and white patterns painted all over it, and although it had all the elements of a terrifying design, it made me feel no such emotion. Perhaps it was mitigated by the smile that it bore.

"Hey, that looks like a mask that they use during Shujo Onie," Suimei whispered. I stared, trying to figure out if the two figures were oni.

One of them wore old-fashioned suikan robes with a quiver hanging from his waist and a large bow over his shoulder. The other seemed to fit in better with the mountain: His torso was covered by a vest made of animal hide, and his pants were sewn from hemp. Wrapped around his feet were straw sandals, and he appeared slightly scruffier than his companion. The only thing they seemed to have in common was the identical mask that they sported.

They both stood quietly beside the giant stones in the forest, emanating a strange aura. I braced myself, but Shinonome-san stepped forward to the one in the pelt and held out the wooden tags he had prepared earlier.

"We're finally here. This is the entrance to the hidden village," he said.

The man pulled out his own tag and touched it to Shinonome-san's. The moment they met, I sensed a growing glow coming from the stones. It was soft and felt different from the prayer-created light that had guided us previously.

What is that? I thought as some odd markings appeared on one of the stones. I approached it to inspect the pattern. No, they were words. Words with a primitive form, winding like snakes and adorned with markings that resembled the sun. I had no clue what they said, but I could sense that there was some sort of message behind them.

Suimei seemed curious about the carvings too. His eyebrows were furrowed in thought.

"What kind of writing is this?" he pondered. "Oracle bone script...? No, I feel like they're closer to hieroglyphs."

"In Japan? Why would we have ancient Egyptian writing here?" I pointed out.

"Dunno," he shrugged.

As we tried to guess what it could be, Shinonome-san shook his head.

"It's from neither China nor Egypt. It's called Toyokuni moji, a script that was supposedly used by nomads," he said.

He continued to explain that Toyokuni moji were used before the Japanese script we use today was developed and that they belonged to a larger group of ancient scripts called Jindai moji.

"Having said that, many researchers believe these to be fake. It's unknown whether these scripts really did exist in ancient times. No one has left any record of the origin of these stones, after all."

Oh.

Something clicked in my head. I finally understood what all the places we'd visited had in common.

We'd gone from the Kumano magaibutsu, whose sculptor was unknown to the former Sento-ji and were ruins which had lost their purpose as a place of prayer, to the Sada-kyoishi, whose truth remained lost even though we could still infer its old role as a ritual site. And finally, these stones with the carvings of the fascinating but dubious Jindai moji... There was little to no hope of ever uncovering their truths or seeing them in their prime again. To be more precise, it would be impossible no matter how hard we wished for it, because everything this process required—information, architecture, belief—was lost.

But it may have been a different story if there remained any credible records.

A light bulb went on in my head. Perhaps this was related to why my adoptive father had taken up writing and publishing.

Was he trying to show me something…?

I cast a glance at him. It was definitely possible. He wasn't the best with words, so he preferred taking action over speaking.

When he noticed I was watching him, he rubbed his chin.

"Just a little bit more, now. Let's go into the village. Our guest is waiting," he said.

He patted my head lightly, and then the giant stone shone with a bright light.

It was so dazzling that I winced. Once it subsided, I saw that we were now in the middle of a large grassy plain.

I blinked, trying to orient myself. We had been transported from a quiet forest into the midst of lively pipes and taiko drums mingled with the sounds of laughter. Past the waving sea of grass, I could see a thick forest and a settlement. It must have been close to dinnertime for them because I could smell the smoke from their cooking even from this distance. Near the settlement, a group of children were playing and dancing with musical instruments in their hands. They must have been the source of the joyous laughter.

"Allow us to guide you to our village now," the masked men said as they began to lead us.

"Let's go, Kaori," Shinonome-san said.

"W-wait!" I said. I was trying to keep up with him, but I couldn't stop staring at the scenery around me.

The sky seemed even higher than usual, and the air was clean and crisp. Birds fluttered above us, and there were even rabbits and other small critters hopping around in the grass. Alongside the settlement, there was a wide spread of farmed land. The season was prime for harvesting, and indeed there were numerous people with sickles in their hands toiling among the golden stalks that sprouted from the ground. The trees that surrounded the village were all drooping heavily with ripe fruit. Citrus was in season, and its refreshing scent filled the air.

There was plenty of variety to be found in the clothes worn by the people here too. A man in a head wrap and untreated hemp kanto top, the very picture of a peasant from ancient times, could be spotted near a graceful woman absorbed in the composition of a poem. She was robed in the luxurious layers of a junihitoe and had a crowd of female attendants, as if she were a noblewoman from the Heian era. Beside her was another lady, smiling and laughing, dressed in an extravagant uchikake kimono like a princess of the Edo period.

There was even someone in the uniform of the Japanese Empire and another who was dressed just like me. As different as they all looked, they clearly felt a connection with each other in some way. Their faces were free of worry, and they all seemed happy and satisfied.

It felt like a storybook utopia.

"Where are we...?" I asked as I stared at the one-story, straw-thatched houses and shinden-zukuri mansions built near each other.

"AH!" Kuro yelped excitedly. "Look, look! Doesn't this look like that magaibutsu we saw?"

He was motioning toward a magaibutsu of towering height.

"Oh, you're right," I replied.

Giant stone Buddhas resembling Nio statues were lined up in a row. They were not exactly the same as the Kumano magaibutsu we had seen atop the oni stairs, but they gave off a very similar vibe, so much so that you could very easily convince me they were by the same sculptor.

When I glanced away for a moment, I realized that there were stone pillars erected throughout the village. At their bases, there were piles of offerings and flowers of all colors, along with a crowd engaged in eager worship.

This...kind of reminds me of the Sada-kyoishi...?

"Thank you for making the journey out here, Shinonome-sama," said a voice. I turned and saw an elderly man with a head of white hair grinning cheerfully at us.

He must be the guest that Shinonome-san had referred to. He wore a haori with a geometric pattern woven through its fabric with dyed hemp yarn. His wrinkled hands and fingers, wrapped around a wooden staff, were like the branches of a withered tree. A necklace made of bones strung together hung from his neck. The word "shaman" popped into my head when I saw him, and I caught myself staring for a little too long.

"And thank you for coming out here to meet us," Shinonome-san greeted the other man and shook his hand. "How's your hip? Did the medicine help?"

"It's doing fine," the man answered, and Shinonome-san broke out into a happy smile. They seemed to be very familiar and friendly with each other.

I approached my adoptive father, who was still chatting. When the old man noticed me, he smiled. I gave him a small bow in return.

"Hi, it's a pleasure to meet you. I'm Kaori," I greeted him. "Thanks for all the generosity you've shown my father here. Hey, Shinonome-san, introduce your friend to us. What kind of spirit is he?"

Shinonome-san pursed his lips and looked away, humming as a distraction. "Oh, didn't I say?" he bluffed. He scratched his head with guilty absentmindedness.

He placed a hand on the elderly man's shoulder and said, "He's not a spirit. He's human."

"What?" I blurted out in surprise. It was all I could manage.

Shinonome-san laughed. "A lot of humans who become unable to live in the human world for one reason or another end up here in this hidden village. Well, maybe it would be more accurate to call this their refuge. This place gives these people the chance to put down some roots and live out the rest of their lives. Toochika and I come here to deliver goods for their day-to-day lives and books for their entertainment."

Two girls ran past us, one wearing a kanto top and the other in a white dress. As mismatched as they looked, their smiles were both equally adorable.

This place was so unique, like someone had taken a bunch of different time periods and blended them together...

Just like the spirit realm! I laughed as the sense of familiarity struck me.

As I watched the two girls run off, Shinonome-san continued:

"The people here can pass down their histories in a way that matches their experiences more accurately."

He spoke keenly about how the citizens there could have their voices heard properly, without having their histories altered by those who had the advantage of power. This, he said, was a precious thing that had to be protected at all costs.

"I want to help those who were rejected by society preserve their stories, not just spirits. That's why I started conducting interviews alongside my book-lending," he said.

Hearing his words, I had a sudden epiphany. Maybe we could even find the sculptor of the magaibutsu and the truths behind the other sites here.

I scanned my eyes over the settlement again and marveled at how well the magaibutsu there blended into the scenery. Flowers grew all over them like decorations, just as the offerings placed by the people served as adornments for the pillars. These stone structures were not objects of mystery to the villagers here, but rather an everyday focus of their religious faith.

"That makes sense... I never knew," I said in reply to Shinonome-san.

I was quite surprised to hear that he felt so strongly about this for humans as well as the spirits. At the same time, I felt very proud of him.

"That's pretty cool of you," I smiled.

He chuckled, embarrassed. "I know, right? Ain't your dad such an awesome guy?" He grinned toothily and cheekily, but then he winced at how big his head was getting. Trying to laugh it off and apologize, he watched me carefully.

"I brought you here because I wanted you to see the kind of work I'm doing," he said.

I blinked in surprise. He'd never done this sort of thing before, so why now?

However, before I could voice my curiosity, Shinonome-san ruffled my hair as one would do to a child.

"You must be tired, huh?" he said. "We've been traveling a lot today. The people here are going to host a feast for us tonight. Take a little time to relax before then."

"...All right," I nodded back, and he smiled at me like he always did.

Shinonome-san's work, huh...? I thought as I watched my adoptive father turn back toward our elderly guide.

Skree, skree, ka-lunk. Skree, skree, ka-lunk.

The sounds of weaving looms at work rang through the sunset-dyed village. Suimei, Kuro, Nyaa-san, and I were taking a leisurely walk around to kill time before the banquet.

"Wow, look over there, black cat!" Kuro cried. "It's so pretty! Let's go there!"

"Can you shut up for once?" Nyaa-san grumbled. "I'm not going *anywhere* with you."

"Whaaaaaat?!" Kuro gasped. "Then where *will* you go?"

"Some place without you," the cat said.

Kuro whimpered. "But I wanna hang out with you! How come you're so mean?"

"No fighting, you two!" I warned.

"Nothing ever gets Kuro down, huh?" Suimei sighed as he raised an eyebrow at the two spirits carrying on.

The hidden village was a lot bigger than I'd expected. It apparently existed in a sort of rift between the human world and the spirit realm. It had stable weather all year round and was very suited to growing produce. Radishes and different kinds of freshwater fish hung from the eaves of aged houses with straw roofs. The men toiled in the fields and hunted, and the women wove with looms and crafted things from all sorts of materials. No one seemed surprised at our sudden visit, and they all greeted us with warm smiles. The children regarded us with curiosity and followed us around in a big crowd. The entire place was filled with a peaceful atmosphere, and it felt like time itself had stopped.

"It's nice here, isn't it?" said Kinui, our guide. He was one of the men we had met at the large stones before we entered, the more mountainous-looking one of the pair. Now that he had taken his mask off, I could see that he had been hiding quite the charming face underneath, one that placed his age in his thirties. His skin had been tanned dark by the sun, and his teeth were a bright white.

"Yeah, this place is really beautiful," I replied. "You've got some really big fields! What do you grow here?"

"Vegetables that we eat ourselves, plus tobacco leaves," he said. "We have some mulberry orchards over that way as well, for the silkworms that the women take care of. Tobacco and silk are two of our most important income streams here."

Kinui pointed toward a building that looked like a warehouse. We peeked inside and saw piles of dried leaves that gave off a unique scent. This must have been the tobacco he mentioned. Beyond the building, there was also a wide bamboo grove. Kinui explained that the villagers made excellent products out of the bamboo there.

"We make some really fine stuff here," he said. "Toochika-sama always offers us very good rates for them too."

"He does? How long have you known him?" I asked.

"We go really far back with him, I think," he replied. "He's been doing business with us since my great-grandpa's days."

The people here who had lost the places where they belonged in the human world earned a living by making things in the hidden village and quietly exporting them. Their proxies were spirits who could disguise themselves as humans and mingle with the mortal crowd. Kinui told us that Toochika-san was the first middleman they'd ever had.

"Spirits live much longer than humans, so they don't tend to pass down businesses like humans do. They keep in contact with their clients for much longer too, and they also don't try to rip us off. We once fell into a rotten deal with some pretty bad folks a really long time ago, but after we started doing our business with spirits instead, we haven't had anything like that happen again. Toochika-sama also helps us buy necessities like medicine from the human world. It's been a really big help for us."

I nodded. "It sounds like spirits have become a vital part of your lives here."

"That they have," Kinui said. "Shinonome-sama's also helped us obtain the entertainment of the human world since he started doing business with us. Our lives have improved so much with the help of spirits."

"That's good to hear," I said. There was no trace of unease or hatred on Kinui's face as he spoke so fondly of the spirits, which I found to be an interesting departure from the usual attitude taken by humans.

And I guess Toochika-san's not just any old merchant, huh? I thought. Apparently, there was more to that showy kappa's affairs than I'd assumed.

Plus, it sounds like Shinonome-san's putting a lot of effort into his business too. As I thought about how he'd helped improve the lives of the people here who were cut off from the human world, I felt a warmth stir in my chest.

It didn't last long, though.

"But doesn't anyone ever think of leaving?" Suimei asked.

His question made me freeze in my tracks. "Suimei... You can't ask that!" I gasped.

He frowned. "Why not? I don't think there's anything wrong with wondering about it. Humans aren't like spirits—they thrive when there's change and constant movement. Plus, if they're borrowing books from Shinonome, wouldn't that make them want to leave even more?"

Now that he'd explained, the rest of the party slowly started to agree with his theory. Even Nyaa-san spoke up.

"That's true," she said. "This place is very nice and peaceful, but there's a lot out there that this village doesn't offer. Humans tend to crave what they don't have very strongly, and books can have an extremely powerful hold over people."

"Well, yeah, but..." I tried to argue. I didn't think they were wrong, exactly, but they didn't have to say it so bluntly. An uncomfortable feeling began to gnaw at me. What if the books that Shinonome-san... No, that the *bookstore* brought in were slowly eating away at the village from the inside without anyone knowing?

My heart squeezed with an agonizing pang. I turned to Kinui uneasily, but he didn't seem bothered by Suimei's rude question at all. In fact, he was nodding in affirmation.

"We've actually had quite a few people from the younger crowd leave because they were so captivated by the human world," he explained. "I mean, that's just what humans are like. It's bound to happen."

"So no one tries to stop them or anything?"

"No. And why would we? People are free to make their own decisions. We send them off knowing that once their heart's been taken by the outside, they won't ever come back. If we forced them to stay, it'd only brew trouble. Those who leave are fully aware of what they're getting themselves into. We make them swear that they understand they will never ever be able to come back here," Kinui said. He took out a wooden tag, the same type that Shinonome-san had used.

"We have a system here where you can only come and go if you have a tag whose counterpart is in the village. Once someone leaves, we destroy their counterpart tag. Can't have people just bringing in unscrupulous folks from the human world, now can we? Of course, I'd be sad if any of my relatives left, but I don't really have to worry about that because it's never happened."

"Even though there are young people who leave? But why?" I asked.

Kinui took a slender pipe out of his vest, packed it with leaves, and lit it. He smiled wryly as he exhaled a puff of white smoke.

"Because no one who's been ostracized by the world outside would ever want to go back there."

The village had a mysterious power that only called out to people who would be suited to living there, generally ones who had trouble fitting into society in one way or another. Once they were in the village, they were sent to a new house and welcomed as a member of the community. Those who were single could choose to marry someone from another house and start a new family with the help of everyone else who lived there.

"We've never had a significant dip in population here, except for a few cases of illness. That was unfortunate."

Kinui explained that his ancestors had also never fit into society very well. His people used to drift from mountain to mountain, never settling in one place permanently. They made a living by trading and selling fish they'd caught in the rivers and other bounties foraged in the wild. However, their lives were changed forever when the Meiji government started to crack down on people who didn't possess surnames or proper family registers. To the Meiji government, which was rushing to establish family registers for tax and conscription purposes, vagabonds like Kinui's family were nothing but thorns in their side.

"I hear that some of them were able to settle permanently, but not my ancestors. The government's efforts wore them down more and more, but just as they were driven to the end of their rope, they found this hidden village. I'm only here today because of this place," he grinned cheerfully. He seemed perfectly content with living there and showed no sign of ever wanting to leave.

"The people who live here know the pains of being ostracized all too well. That's why they're all so kind and peaceful. But the outside world is different. There's a lot of folks out there who make life very painful for those who don't fit in. We don't understand the ones who want to leave, because this is our utopia."

"Utopia..."

"That's right! And Toochika-sama and your father have helped us make this utopia what it is. Burdens wear down on our souls, but boredom is what kills the soul. Our village is only able to flourish because of Toochika-sama and Shinonome-sama. So..."

Kinui flashed me a toothy grin.

"...there's no need for you to worry about your dad's work. He hasn't hurt anybody, and he's not going to either."

I gulped. It looked like he'd seen right through my worries. I felt my cheeks grow hot from embarrassment and laughed awkwardly.

Kinui puffed out his chest with pride. "We may be closed off, but we can still recognize the old as the old and the new as the new. The Kunisaki Peninsula is very open-minded about being introduced to new cultures, and we have that mindset in the village too."

I felt that his confident attitude was designed to show me that this mindset, and the influence of Shinonome-san's books, was all part of their culture.

"I guess I was being too much of a worrywart. I'm sorry," I apologized.

"Ah ha ha ha!" Kinui guffawed. "You really love your dad, huh? Don't see that much between adoptive parents and their kids."

"Urk...! Yeah, I do love my dad a lot! And what about it?!" I squawked.

"Not even gonna deny it, huh? I'm impressed," Suimei said. I gulped at his backhanded praise, and a chill ran down my spine. I turned around nervously and saw that he was looking at me with his eyebrow raised, as if to say, *What are you getting embarrassed for, after all this time?*

Ahhh! I feel so attacked! I screamed internally as a wave of embarrassment flooded through me. *I wish I could run away right now!*

At that moment, a group of men emerged from the bamboo grove. Some of them were dressed like classic samurai, complete with suits of armor and helmets. There were also a few young men wearing more modern tracksuits. They were holding rabbits in their hands, which I guessed were today's catch from their traps.

"Hey, Kinui!" one of them called. "Is that Shinonome-sama's daughter?"

"Yeah!" Kinui called back. When he did, the warrior men started to greet us by waving enthusiastically, their armor clanging with every movement.

"Heeeeeey! It's good to meet you!" they shouted. "We're all big fans of Shinonome-san's books! Look forward to the feast tonight, because we're going to cook you all some really good food with what we caught!"

"Sure! I can't wait!" I replied.

The men left, chattering in high spirits. I whispered, "You don't see guys in tracksuits hanging out with fully armored samurai every day, huh?"

"You can say that again!" Kinui laughed. "Whenever I see them, I want to ask if it's hard to move around in all that armor."

"Why *do* they wear armor?" I asked. "I saw some women wearing junihitoe and people wearing other ancient clothes as well. But it's not as if everyone dresses like the old days here, right? There were those guys wearing tracksuits too."

Kinui puffed out his chest proudly again. "They just like to do it for fun."

"For fun?" I repeated without thinking.

Kinui chuckled. "I dunno who started it first, but we've got people from all different time periods here, right? Somewhere along the line, the village decided that each house should keep their own cultures going."

He explained that was the reason why the houses maintained their clothes and ways of living. Not everyone was happy with this, of course, as many said that the older lifestyles were much less convenient and equipped than the modern ones. Those people were free to move to another house if they wished, though.

"That's...a lot easier than I expected!" I said.

"Ah ha ha! Some folks choose to move to the older houses too, you know. Like my ma," Kinui said. "She got hooked on novels set in the Heian era and really wanted to wear a junihitoe, so she moved to a Heian house! She said to me, 'You're a grown man now, you can take care of yourself,' and ran off. She left me in a really tight spot! Now I have to do all the work myself and make my own meals... Though I guess that's just more motivation for me to hurry up and get married."

"Um, I see..." I said, not sure if he was joking. I must have made a strange face, because Kinui laughed, his suntanned face creasing into a smile.

"Shinonome-sama's books also helped us recognize the value in older things. Knowing what something's worth makes a world of difference when it comes to deciding if we should focus on preserving it or not, wouldn't you agree?"

He stroked his pelt vest as he spoke, as if saying that his clothes were part of his effort to pass down the lifestyle of his forebearers.

"The things that have been lost from the human world live on here. We would have never learned of those truths if we hadn't broadened our horizons past our settlement here. We need information to learn about what past generations have valued, and to obtain that information we need records. We have no electricity here, so books are our best source of knowledge. Shinonome-sama and the books he brings for us are such incredible blessings. The old folks here don't just pray to God and Buddha, they pray to Shinonome-sama too."

"That's, um...something," I said. It felt a bit awkward hearing such relentless praise for my adoptive father, but I was relieved to know that his work was so sought after.

Kinui nodded enthusiastically and gave me a huge, carefree grin. "You must be pretty amazing too, since you help out at the bookstore as well."

"Huh?" I blinked, caught off guard by his comment.

Me? Amazing?

I faltered, unable to come up with an answer.

"Oh, that's right!" Kinui said with realization. "Wait here."

Then he took off somewhere.

Silence descended now that the chatty Kinui was gone. I looked around for Nyaa-san and saw her and Kuro in the distance being chased by children.

Fweeeuw. Fweeeuw.

A bird cried from somewhere above me. Feeling lost, I closed my wide-open mouth and looked around. This village really seemed to grow more and more beautiful every time I paused to observe it, like it had been pulled straight from a picture book. It did nothing to quell the gloom swirling inside of me, though. I just couldn't pull myself out of this slump, no matter how hard I tried.

Why do I feel like this? My train of thought was running in a loop, broken only when I heard someone call out to me.

"Kaori?" a voice said. I looked up and saw that Suimei was beside me, looking worried.

"Oh... Sorry, I was just spacing out a bit," I said. I smiled, trying to pretend I was fine and apologize for making him worry. However, Suimei could see right through me. He let out a small sigh and gripped my hand.

"If there's anything on your mind, just tell me," he said. As blunt as he was, his words carried an undeniable kindness.

I grinned and giggled at him. "Thanks, but...it's nothing," I insisted.

Suimei pouted, unconvinced. His silence made it clear that he wanted me to open up.

I winced. "It's just, um...kind of embarrassing, I guess," I tried to explain. But it didn't work, and he continued to stare straight at me.

Looks like there's no getting out of this, I thought as I steeled myself.

"I, um...learned a lot about Shinonome-san's job today. I never knew that he had human customers or anything, and I was really surprised to hear that his book-lending is a big pillar of support for so many people. Before today, I only thought about the spirits that I wanted to share the joy of reading with. I never realized that the scope of our jobs could be so much wider."

I thought about the way Shinonome-san gently held the elderly man's wrinkled hands, his mission to stop any more history from being lost, and the way Kinui gushed about his work...

"I'm really happy to hear about how amazing Shinonome-san is, but it also made me feel kinda...like..."

"Left out?" Suimei prompted. He had hit the bullseye, and my cheeks flushed from embarrassment. I balled myself up and buried my face in my knees.

"He felt like a complete stranger to me. I probably sound really stupid being surprised by this kind of thing, huh?"

"Not at all," Suimei said. He was completely unbothered by my sudden self-deprecation, and he patted my head.

"We all know how much you love Shinonome," he said as he scooted beside me.

"Urgh... Yeah, true, but..." I pouted and pulled a face at Suimei.

"Well, there's nothing wrong with that," he said, smiling at me. "To be honest, I don't really know what it's like to love your own father. I guess that's not surprising considering my whole situation. But even so, I can still tell that you and Shinonome have something special. I really admire it."

I closed my mouth. Things between Suimei and his father, Seigen-san, were extremely complicated. The question of what it meant to be born into an exorcist family and how to carry on its legacy had twisted the two of them. They had long since settled things between each other, but they would probably never be able to have a normal father-son relationship.

"I'm sorry," I said.

Suimei laughed bitterly. "What for? You worry too much, you know." His expression was soft, and looking at him made me feel like I was gazing at a clear autumn sky.

"If you feel left out because you learned all these things you never knew before about someone, then all you have to do is try to find out even more about them," he said.

"Suimei..." I mumbled.

"It's totally normal to want to know more about someone you're fond of," he said, his voice full of kindness.

I gave him a big nod. "You're right."

I looked up from my knees and saw the sun slowly setting beneath the mountains. I tried to cover its brightness with my hand, but its red light still shone through my fingers. The crimson with which it doused the world around me was so vibrant that it made my eyes sting.

"I wonder if I'll ever do anything as amazing as Shinonome-san..." I whispered. My work was still probably nowhere near what he did, and that was most likely why I couldn't respond to Kinui's compliment—I wasn't at a level where I deserved to be called amazing. If I wanted to touch the lives of spirits and humans like my adoptive father did, I had to commit myself even more.

If I work hard, could I catch up with Shinonome-san one day?

"I'll do what I can to help you too," Suimei offered, placing a reassuring hand on my head.

A lump formed in my throat. "...Thanks," I managed. Then a thought popped into my head.

"Suimei, you tell me more about yourself too," I said.

"...What? Why?" he asked, cocking his head in confusion.

I laughed. "Well, it's perfectly normal to want to know more about someone you like, right?"

As if a switch had been flipped, Suimei's face turned the color of a boiled lobster. He awkwardly tried to avert my gaze and muttered, "God, you're too cute," chuckling to himself as he did.

Now it was *my* turn to blush.

"You tell me more about yourself too then, okay?" Suimei said.

I gulped and froze, immediately turning away and mumbling "Yeah" and "I know."

Dammit! I wanted to be the one to tease him!

"What's going on here?" said a voice.

"They look like they're getting along well," said another.

While I was pressing my hand to my warm cheek in an effort to cool it down, Nyaa-san and Kuro returned and were watching us in amusement. I glared at them, and then...

"Heeey! Kaori-sama, come over here! There's something I want to show you!" Kinui called.

"Coming!" I shouted back. I hurried to my feet and bolted toward him, trying to shake off my embarrassment. He was at a single-storied house that appeared to be a weaving workshop.

Skree, skree, ka-lunk. Skree, skree, ka-lunk.

A single woman was weaving in the workshop, the sounds of her loom satisfying to the ear.

"Wow... This is so cool," I blurted out in awe. I couldn't help myself because I'd never really seen anything like it before. She was weaving some white tanmono, a traditional Japanese textile, tinged with a hint of warmth. Its luxurious sheen told me that it was most likely made of a very high-quality silk.

"Hey, is the thing for Shinonome-sama done already?" Kinui asked.

Hearing his question, the woman at the loom stopped working.

"I still need another month," she answered. "It is *the* order of all orders for Shinonome-sama. I have to be extra careful with it."

"Aww, really? I was hoping you'd have something I could show her," Kinui sighed.

"Huh? What are you talking about?" the woman said.

Then we locked eyes. I gave her a small nod, and her eyes almost popped out of her head.

"Um, thank you for always being so nice to Shinonome-san. I'm his daughter, Kaori. Did he place some kind of order with you...?"

The moment the question left my mouth, the woman sprang to her feet.

"What do you think you're doing, you idiot?!" she yelled. Her palm flew toward Kinui's cheek, making contact with a resounding *slap*!

Kinui froze in shock.

"Hey, that hurt! What was that for?!" he protested in a wobbly voice.

"Oh? Yeah, I'm sure it did, you stupid idiot!" she glowered at the man. She turned to me and forced her best smile.

"No, he didn't order anything! Ha! Ha ha ha ha..." she laughed as she guided me out of the workshop with a hand against my back.

She changed the subject as she continued pushing me and my friends out. "Anyway, the banquet should almost be ready! I can smell it from here. I hear the men of our village will put on a good dance performance for you folks, so go and see what it's all about!" The sliding door clattered shut behind us, and Suimei and I looked at each other. We were left wondering what had made the woman so angry as her fury thundered down on Kinui from within the workshop.

"What was that?" Suimei said.

I tilted my head in response, equally confused. The tanmono the woman had been weaving flashed through my mind, and I couldn't help but sigh a little as I recalled its mesmerizing beauty.

The sun had long since hidden itself away, and the world was now drenched in shadow. The village had taken on a new form with its light scarce and darkness deep. Countless stars winked at us from the night sky, and the autumn insects continued their endless symphony as if they were trying to leave a record of their life before passing away in the winter.

The residents had set up our banquet in the center of the village square. Two men with only a single fundoshi covering their well-built bodies were dancing at the very front. Rope made from tree bark was tied across their bodies, bells fastened to their backs chimed with every move, and Shujo Onie masks covered their faces. Both dancers held an axe in one hand and a lit torch in the other, and they slammed their torches into each other as though they were locked in a sword fight.

"Whoaaa...!" I gasped. Every time the flaming sparks flew, the villagers would burst into cheers. The man with his tabi stomped hard enough to make the ground shake. He swung the torch around swiftly and struck it again, dissolving its glowing heat. The space around the dancers would suddenly brighten whenever their torches crossed. Their movements were as smooth as butter, and whenever the blazing sparks scattered, their muscles would emerge from the darkness. The air was freezing, but the men were covered head to toe in sweat, puffing silvery breaths out from under their masks. Steam rose from their skin in crimson wisps whenever it caught the light of the fire.

"They look like real oni," I whispered as my eyes followed the performance from my seat. I had been given a place set aside for guests of honor with Kinui beside me.

He grinned. "They must be doing a good job if you think so, especially since I'm sure you've seen your fair share of oni in the spirit realm! We copied the human world's Shujo Onie dance for this."

"What do you mean?" Suimei asked, pausing his attack on the spicy miso mezamashi-mochi he had been munching on.

Kinui's eyes sparkled as he spoke. "Before they came into contact with spirits, our ancestors had to mingle with the people who lived on the Kunisaki Peninsula. They did what they could to survive on their own, but whatever they couldn't get themselves, they had to buy from others."

Back then, people were a lot more isolated than they were now. It was only natural to be wary of strangers, but the folks from the peninsula were never afraid to do business with Kinui's ancestors. They provided many necessities as well as vital care whenever the need arose. The people of the hidden village developed a sense of gratitude and respect which led them to mimic the festivities held by the people of the Kunisaki Peninsula.

"The oni of the Shujo Onie are kind of like raihojin, don't you think?" Kinui said.

"Raihojin? You mean gods that come from the outside?"

"Yeah, gods that bring blessings from the outside," he nodded. "This village doesn't get gods from the outside, though. What we get instead are guests like you guys and friends who are practically our family."

Kinui grinned, the light of the torches bouncing in his cheerful eyes.

"This dance is meant to welcome those who have sought refuge from the outside in this village. All the people who live here have found their utopia after being driven out of their homes, and we perform this to swear that we will never let this blessing that saved us and allowed us to keep living be extinguished."

"I see..."

The torches sparked again with each new chime of the bell, and as they swirled through the air, they were trailed by glowing tails that faded with the roar of the crowd.

"Hey, did you see that?! That was awesome!"

"Yeah, that fire must be really hot! How are they even doing this?!"

All the villagers smiled with bright innocence, which just made my heart clench even more. The village's population wasn't small by any means, and everyone there must have reached rock bottom before coming to this utopia. Life in the village was the very picture of peace, but the people had to have been persecuted or ostracized in some way before they could reach here. They'd undoubtedly had to leave much of their life behind, and I could imagine that many of them had only the shirts on their backs when they showed up. Their big smiles probably hid an even greater and invisible wound.

Ting!

Another loud chime rang through the air. The torches peppered their glowing ashes as they lit up the surroundings. Suddenly, I caught sight of Shinonome-san a little farther away, surrounded by a horde of villagers.

"Shinonome-sama! I'd love to share some old stories with you that have been passed down through my family for generations!"

"You should hear what my father has to share. He's got a real special one!"

"No, no, we should be first! We need to start with stories that have historical significance!"

Shinonome-san was flustered. He replied, "Now, now, wait a minute! I'm not a saint. I can only hear you out one at a time, so pipe down and get in line!"

He seemed troubled, but he was also clearly enjoying himself and listening very seriously to what the villagers had to say. He opened his ears to narratives passed down from ancestors, stories of past homes, comical anecdotes, and tall tales. Every time he interjected with a disbelieving "Really?" the villagers would whoop with delight. Shinonome-san always remained at the center of the crowd, and he would give his storytellers his most earnest "yep, yep" every sentence or so as he scribbled notes down with a brush and some paper. He was so absorbed that it was almost like there was no banquet happening at all.

"They really love Shinonome, huh?" Suimei whispered as he watched the crowd unleash their stories. "By letting them talk about what they were forced to leave behind, Shinonome's giving them a chance to transform their memories into something more."

I marveled at how succinctly Suimei had described what was happening.

"Yeah... Yeah, I think you're right," I said.

Shinonome-san's job wasn't just to read and let read, it was also to have a vision for the future and make practical preparations for it.

I glanced at my adoptive father again.

"He's amazing," I murmured. I cast my eyes over his figure, hunched and round as he immersed himself in note-taking. Even as he was curled up like this, his back looked so broad and strong. "He's really, truly amazing..."

The dancers' bells continued to jingle with every move, and the torches spat their fiery red sparks. But no matter how strongly they blazed, they still could not hold a candle to the flaming passion that lit Shinonome-san's eyes.

The next day, we bade farewell to the hidden village and all its residents.

"Take care on the way back!" Kinui said, and the rest of the villagers followed. Shinonome-san waved the wooden tag in his hand, and before I could blink, we were back at the bottom of the oni-made stone steps. While I mused about how this teleportation worked, I said to my adoptive father, "Should we go back to the spirit realm, then?"

"Wait. I want you to have this," he said, holding out the travel tag and pressing it into my hand.

I blinked at the weathered piece of wood.

"Why?" I blurted out, tilting my head.

Shinonome-san scratched his head and averted his gaze. "You'll need it soon enough, so just hold on to it."

"So you mean I'm coming to the hidden village next time?" I asked.

"Yeah. I'm thinking of having you take over," he said.

"Is that why you brought me along?"

"That's right. Don't worry, I've already told them about the change."

I frowned. He'd never done anything like this before, so why now?

"But they're your customers, aren't they? So shouldn't you be the one to go?" I said. I tried to return the tag, but he pushed it back to me.

"Nonsense. They can't be just my customers forever. Besides, I'm thinking about retiring from the bookstore to focus on my writing."

I gasped. I could feel my mind going blank from his sudden declaration. "Wait, you're retiring? What do you mean?!"

My voice trembled. I couldn't grasp what was happening. "Why are you...? Tell me what's going on!"

Blood rushed to my head. Shinonome-san was never the type to give away every single detail, but this was too much even for him. He grimaced as I stared daggers at him.

"Calm down. You're an adult now. It's not so strange for me to leave the shop to you, is it?"

"Y-yeah, but..." I mumbled. His logic did make a lot of sense. My anger immediately subsided.

"Shinonome-san..." I whimpered.

He frowned. "C'mon, no sulking now."

"B-but..."

This was all happening so quickly that I struggled to keep up. I tried desperately to stave off the prickling heat welling up in my eyes.

I tried to explain. "I... I don't think I can do your job nearly as well as you, and seeing all those people at the hidden village crowd around you so enthusiastically just hammered that home even more. I know I'm grown now and all, but there's still so much that I want to learn from you. So..."

Please don't say you're retiring.

I couldn't force that last plea out. Shinonome-san gently stroked my cheek, and when I blinked at him, I saw that he was grinning mischievously at me.

"Don't jump the gun, now. It's not like I'm retiring right away. I'll be passing my duties to you slowly over time. Well, if you don't like the people at the hidden village, then that's something we'll have to sort out, but they were a nice bunch, weren't they?"

I sniffed. "No, I don't dislike them or anything..."

He nodded in satisfaction and turned to Suimei.

"Hey, Suimei, once we're back in the spirit realm, come with me for a bit."

The boy raised an eyebrow. "Why? Do you need me for something?"

"I'll tell you later," Shinonome-san said. "I'll tell Noname you'll be with me. Sometimes we men gotta have a heart-to-heart, eh?"

He beckoned to Suimei to follow him and walked off.

The trees around us shivered as a chilly autumn breeze whipped through the air.

What's this about? What's going on?

As I watched Shinonome-san's back grow smaller in the distance, I felt a sense of unease descending upon me.

CHAPTER 2

A Happiness as Brittle as Glass

TWO GOLDFISH LAZED ABOUT with their long red tails billowing behind them on the bulb of thin glass they decorated. They adorned a pipe-shaped glass toy called *biidoro*, after the Portuguese word for glass, *vidro*. These toys were also called *popin* for the silly popping sound they made when you blew into them. They'd been a new product for the summer, but now that time had passed into fall, they had been piled into a basket branded with a sale sign. Now they were nothing more than remnants of a season long gone.

I sagged onto the counter and stared at the basket, my head filled with idle thoughts. *Who would buy these? If no one wants them, will they be tossed?*

"Oh, you're looking pretty free today," a voice spoke.

"Whoa!" I exclaimed, caught unawares by the abrupt comment. I turned, suddenly extremely self-conscious, to find a showy man who looked to be in his thirties.

It was Toochika-san.

"I, um... Sorry for spacing out during my shift!" I quickly bowed my head in apology. I was currently working the register at a general goods store at Kappabashi in Taito City, Tokyo. It was owned by Toochika-san, and he employed me on an informal basis to occasionally run the store. However, this was a weekday afternoon...and not just any weekday but the dreaded hump day, Wednesday. There was not a single customer in the alleyway shop, so with nothing to do, I had let my mind drift off into space.

"That's fine. As long as you properly tend to the customers when they come, you can do whatever. You've been pretty busy learning how to take over the bookstore too, haven't you? How are you holding up?" the kappa asked.

"Fine, physically..." I replied. Mentally, though? I wasn't so sure.

Ever since the visit to the hidden village, my schedule had become more packed. Shinonome-san was completely serious about retiring to focus on his writing, so he'd been introducing me to all of his customers day after day. He valued every single one of them, so I bought a notebook to write about them, and it was already half-full. I'd been carrying it around in hopes of memorizing what I needed to know about them, but I just hadn't had the chance to get around to it. Part of it was because I wasn't sure how I could shoulder the responsibility of all the information packed in my notebook.

The other part was that I was still coming to terms with the true importance of Shinonome-san's work now that I had witnessed it firsthand. Could I really run the bookstore myself after he retired? I felt so immature without a single shred of confidence.

But even so, I couldn't let the bookstore go down after my adoptive father had dedicated his life to it.

My mind kept swinging back and forth without ever settling on an answer. I felt trapped, like I had wandered into an endless maze.

"Toochika-san... Is Shinonome-san really, truly going to retire?" I asked.

"Well, since he's taking the time to introduce you to all his customers and clients...I think so," the kappa replied.

"Yeah, that's true..."

Seeing my adoptive father so nonchalantly prepare for his retirement filled me with anxiety. It was like he was telling me to hurry and grow up, be independent already. I felt as if I was being crushed under the weight of my own immaturity.

Maybe I've been relying on Shinonome-san way more than I thought...

"I wonder why now, though. He's never shown any sign that he wanted to retire," I pondered out loud.

He was never one to reveal his deepest thoughts. He wasn't the type to stay completely silent, but he wasn't in the habit of voicing his feelings directly either, due to his stubbornness and professional pride.

If only he would reveal everything that's on his mind like Noname does... Then he'd be so much easier to understand.

I must have been frowning quite a lot, because Toochika-san stroked his chin and said consolingly, "Well, I'm sure he's got his own reasons."

"But I want to figure out what those reasons are. Do you know anything?" I asked.

"I don't," he said, and all emotion ebbed from his face. A faraway look crept into his eyes. "Not in detail, anyway."

He suddenly flashed me a charming smile that could turn any group of women into a squealing mass and steer the topic at hand into a completely different direction...if it were directed at anyone else, that is. However, having grown up around Toochika-san, I was completely immune to his tricks.

"Fine, don't tell me then," I shrugged, turning my nose up at him.

"Dear, oh dear," he chuckled dryly. "I'm sorry, Kaori-kun. Shinonome did ask me to keep it quiet."

"...That's all right. I knew you'd never talk anyway," I said.

As flippant as Toochika-san could seem, he was always a man of his word. His ironclad sense of honor had earned Shinonome-san's utmost trust, and it was not something I could ever hope to break.

"It's a lot better than getting caught up in the kinds of messes you always seem to find yourself in!" he laughed.

I shuddered as I remembered the messy mermaid meat debacle from a while back. The whole way through, I'd been worried we wouldn't be able to wrap it up properly. However, I'd heard that the two main parties involved, Hakuzosu and Konoha, were able to patch things up and even came out the other end with their father-daughter relationship stronger than ever.

I grumbled. Honestly, I was a bit jealous of them, especially after all the headaches they'd put me through!

As I mulled this over in solitary silence, Toochika-san approached the counter.

"I know how you're feeling, Kaori-kun, I really do. Life events are tough!"

"What life event?"

"You know, when there's a big turning point in your life that will affect your whole future, like starting a new school, getting married, a new job, deaths, illnesses, and whatnot. Not everyone has the same life events, but they're all unavoidable."

"Like what I'm going through right now..." I mumbled.

The kappa nodded. "Exactly. You can't expect to run the store with Shinonome-san forever, can you?"

"Well, I did know I'd have to take over someday..."

I had noticed that Shinonome-san was starting to prioritize his writing over the bookstore. I knew that it would be better in the long run for him to leave the store to me so he'd have more time to write. I understood that in theory, but subconsciously I was still coming to grips with it.

"It's just... Everything happened so quickly," I sighed.

"Ha ha ha! Well, most life events tend to come out of the blue. But let me just say that nothing good will come from running away from them," Toochika-san warned me. He paused for breath before shaking his head softly and continuing.

"It's going to have a profound effect on your life, after all. Well, I can't stop you if you want to run away, but know that you'll end up losing a lot of the trust and goodwill you've built over the years. If you can just get past this hurdle, you'll be able to cruise through the rest of your journey. Just think of this as a test."

Everything he said was very true, and I knew that, but...

"I just still feel so anxious about everything," I said. I felt as if the solid ground where my feet were firmly planted was wavering, and I was too scared to take the steps to safety.

Just do it, Kaori. It's just one step, and you're out of here.

However, the courage I needed never came. While I was occupied with my anxiety, the things around me would keep changing, leaving me behind in my own confusion.

I glanced at the basket with the discounted glass toys. Sometimes they seemed too fragile to touch, like they would shatter if you weren't careful with your own strength. They would be crushed and gone in an instant, and they would lose all their value as toys and objects of art. Their goldfish pattern would be mangled as they turned to nothing more than plain glass scraps.

Maybe my "stability" was actually a lot less secure than I thought, sheltered only by a thin glass bulb that was fragile enough to be crushed with a single squeeze...

"My, you're a lot less confident than I gave you credit for," Toochika-san said, poking my cheek. I jolted with a start and whipped around while the kappa smiled gently.

"I know you can do better," he said as he placed his hat to his chest and flashed me another showy grin. "If you're feeling lost, don't be afraid to ask for help from the people in your life, including me! You don't have to take everything on by yourself like you always try to do. I don't want Shinonome's shop to go under either, you know."

"I feel kind of bad about asking you for help..." I mumbled.

"What, you think I'm the kind of guy to leave my best friend's daughter for dead?" he chuckled.

"N-no!" I stammered. "No, of course not!"

My heart swelled with emotions as the kindness of Toochika-san's words sank in. I felt close to bursting into tears. But he was right—I *could* do better than this.

"And don't forget, I'm not the only one you can turn to for help either," he continued. "You've got Noname, Nyaa, the Tengu twins, and even Suimei. He's quite a dependable guy, isn't he?"

"Yeah..." I wiped away the tears that had leaked out and tried to smile. But my face didn't want to cooperate, and it crumpled itself into something strange. Toochika-san returned a wry grin and gave me a comforting pat on the shoulder.

"Baby steps," he said. "You're going to be okay. Everyone has to go through this at one point or another. In a few years, you'll look back on this and think, 'What was I getting so stressed out for?'"

I sure hope so... I thought. I placed a hand to my heart and noticed that it did at least feel a little lighter. *Yeah... Yeah, I'm not alone.* Just repeating that to myself made me feel safer.

"Ha ha... I really am surrounded by the best people ever," I giggled.

"Took you long enough to notice!" the kappa laughed.

"Sorry," I winced.

He gave me a big nod. "It's nothing to apologize for. We all miss what's right under our noses sometimes."

Fixing his hat on his head, he flashed me a bold grin. "Well, now that you've had that important epiphany, it's time to pull yourself out of the dumps! I can't have my counter girl depressed all day. It's not good for business! I need the usual Kaori-kun back, with her cheery attitude and her love for food and stories. And who's going to put Suimei-kun through the wringer, if not you?"

"H-hey, c'mon! I'm not that bad, am I?!" I grumbled.

"Ah ha ha ha. Whatever you say!"

"You're not going to at least say you were kidding?!"

Toochika-san didn't even look at me...or rather, he couldn't, because his eyes were squeezed shut from the laughter racking his body.

Jeez! I huffed, but my annoyance immediately made way for the smile that broke onto my face. He was right—nothing good would come from me moping all the time. I just needed to believe in myself and keep moving. *Take those steps, Kaori!* Now I was sure that my recent worries would turn into funny memories to think back on in the future.

"Thank you," I said to the kappa. "I feel a lot more ready for this now."

"It's good to see your real smile back," he said. "I like you when you're floppy and listless too, but a cute girl like you looks best with a smile on her face."

"And you really haven't changed one bit," I replied.

We giggled, and then...

Tinkle.

I caught the sound of a bell jingling, and Toochika-san's face darkened. Wondering what the chime was, I turned in its direction and saw a single customer standing in the store. He was young, and his long and loosely tied black hair was topped with a straw hat that would have been more appropriate for summer. He was dressed casually in a white shirt, chinos, and sandals. His tan skin was about as dark as Kinui's. Our gazes met, and as the young man smiled at me, I noticed that his eyes turned green at certain angles.

I frowned. He looked familiar, but I couldn't quite put my finger on where I'd met him before...

"Hey there!" he said.

"Welcome," I said as I dug through my memory to find any trace of him. He gave me a carefree grin and stared straight at me. It was then that a thick and heavy smell of ocean air grazed my nose. The fishy scent seemed to reach deep into the recesses of my mind.

Tinkle.

The bell jingled again, and the memory of what had happened a few months earlier came flooding back to me—the trouble with the fox girl and the man who offered her mermaid meat and promises of eternal life...

"You're the mermaid butcher!" I gasped in fright and backed away, hitting the register with a deafening crash. I winced at the noise, but all the mermaid butcher did was pick up a popin from the basket of unsold toys and smile.

"Long time no see, huh? How've you been?" he asked like he was greeting an intimate friend.

"Uh, fine, I guess?" I answered, unable to hide my bewilderment at his familiar tone.

"Great, great! You know what they say, health is wealth." He blew into the popin, and it made its *pop, po-pop* sound, dissolving the tension in the air, whether we liked it or not. I couldn't drop my guard, though. This was the man whose behavior in hoodwinking a young woman had caused quite a fiasco for everyone involved.

"What do you want?" I asked, still suspicious.

"Hm?" the butcher tilted his head and blew into the popin again. *Po-pop.*

"I just wanted to have a chat with you," he explained. "Would you humor me?"

"Uh, what? Why would you want to talk to me?"

I couldn't see what he was getting at. Was he plotting something again?

"Toochika-san, do something!" I pleaded for help.

I was just a regular human. He, on the other hand, was one of the foremost veterans of Kappabashi. Surely he could show the mermaid butcher a thing or two!

He simply grinned and tilted his head to the side. "Hmm, but why? All he wants is to talk to you."

"Wha... How could you say that?!"

All traces of his earlier reliable uncle vibes had evaporated. I continued to hound him, but he rebuffed me with a casual shrug.

"It'll be fine. He may be pushy and reckless with his mermaid meat, but other than that, he's a completely harmless spirit. Even mermaid meat is harmless as long as you know exactly what you're getting into," he said.

"Yeah, but...!" I pushed back. "The last thing I want to do is talk to *him*."

I still hadn't forgiven the mermaid butcher for what he'd done to my friends Konoha and Tsukiko, and of course to Tamaki-san as well.

Toochika-san chuckled dryly at my stubbornness and turned to the butcher. "Goodness gracious, you seem to be quite hated. What did you do to our poor Kaori-kun?"

"Whaaat?" the young man gasped. "I didn't do anything to her! She doesn't seem like she needs eternal life anyway!"

"You...!" I seethed. "Don't tell me you've already forgotten what you did to Tamaki-san!"

My shoulders were square with anger, and I was breathing hard out of my nose. The mermaid butcher winced awkwardly, and Toochika-san tried to calm me down.

"Deep breaths now, Kaori-kun," he soothed. "And I haven't forgotten about what happened, either. Tamaki was my best friend too, you know."

"Then why...?"

"That was then and this is now," he said with a cheeky wink. "Since you're currently going through a life event, you need to have an open mind. It'll be good for you to talk to someone you've never chatted with before. If you don't like where the conversation is going, then just shut it down. Besides, he's not so ill-mannered that he'd just attack without reason."

He shot a glance at the mermaid butcher and flashed a daring grin. "Isn't that right, young man?"

The butcher nodded and gave an undecipherable smile. "Of course. I didn't come here to hurt anyone."

"Well, you heard the guy!" Toochika-san said. "You can talk to him without any worries, then. And if anything does go wrong, I promise I'll chase him to the ends of the earth, and I won't rest until he's six feet under!"

"H-hey, c'mon, why so violent?! Please be nice to me!" the butcher cried as he turned pale and pleaded with the kappa.

In any case, it seemed like Toochika-san thought it was necessary for me to talk to the mermaid butcher. I found him to be nothing but a nuisance with his insistence on peddling eternal life, but perhaps he could provide me with something I was missing. If that were true, then maybe it really would benefit me to keep an open mind and indulge him...

However, I hit the brakes on my train of thought and shook my head. No, I really couldn't bring myself to trust the person who'd given Tamaki-san and my friends so much grief.

"I'm sorry, but I don't have time for this," I dismissed him and turned away.

"Aww, no way!" he sighed, crestfallen.

"Oops, looks like it's a no. Too bad!" Toochika-san shrugged.

"But... But... Hmm, what to do..." the butcher's shoulders slumped.

Toochika-san frowned in sympathy and suddenly stuck out his hand, plastering on his best customer service smile. "Anyway, sir, that will be 800 yen for the popin."

The young man stared blankly. "Huh?"

"Well, you did touch it with your mouth. That means you're going to buy it, right?" the kappa said.

The mermaid butcher furrowed his brows and dug around in his pockets with the popin still in his mouth. After searching for a moment, all he managed to produce was some lint and a pack of tissues that had been handed out on the side of the road.

"Um, put it on my tab," he said.

"I'm sorry, sir, but we do not offer tabs here," Toochika-san said.

The mermaid butcher groaned and heaved a sigh while the popin popped and crackled with his despondence.

After my shift, I made my way to another part of the city. My destination was Jinbocho, the famous hub of used bookstores. It was where I planned to pick up new stock for our store.

Beneath the clear autumn sky, the town was filled with hustle and bustle. Bookstores lined every street, and if you were to go around to the south side of Yasukuni-dori, you would find even more bookstores with unique shopfronts to feast your eyes on. I alighted in Jinbocho in high spirits and decided to fill my stomach before I headed for battle. Going into a bookstore was like entering a time warp, and since it was so easy to lose your whole sense of time in there, I knew I would need a good pre-shopping nutrient fix.

My first stop was a famous taiyaki shop in Jinbocho well known for their squared edges, which was not so common for these pastries. They were also fairly affordable, which I appreciated because my wallet would only get lighter from here on out. When I placed my order, I was fortunate enough to be given a freshly cooked one, and I could feel its comforting warmth through the paper bag warding off the cold in my fingertips. Today was another cold, dry, and windy day in Tokyo, and combined with the post-shift fatigue, my body was screaming at me to take a bite of the taiyaki already. I stopped by the side of the road and loosened my jaw for a big bite, but I paused as I felt a piercing gaze directed my way.

The mermaid butcher was staring intently at me. He had followed me and was now fixated on the taiyaki, his mouth hanging open and about to drool.

"Can you stop staring at me already?" I glowered, hiding my precious pastry. "If you want one of these, then go and buy it yourself."

He looked troubled by my icy words. Now that I thought about it, he didn't even have the money to buy a popin; Toochika-san had ended up footing the bill. For some reason, the kappa treated him quite nicely. He also spoke of the butcher like he was very familiar with him. Well, Toochika-san was a well-connected and knowledgeable man, so maybe they had met somewhere before...

No, that was impossible. He knew that Tamaki-san had been searching for the mermaid butcher, and there was no way he would leave a friend in need high and dry. Then perhaps they had met after the business with Konoha and the other foxes and tanukis...?

Either way, the kappa had apparently decided that the butcher was harmless, despite all the trouble he had caused. I couldn't understand why.

I decided to ignore him and eat my taiyaki. Suddenly, a great rumble resounded from the butcher's stomach. I glared at the young man, whose cheeks were tinted a rosy shade from embarrassment.

"Ugh, fine!" I groaned. I couldn't enjoy my treat like this! I resigned myself and bought another one, thrusting the warm snack toward the mermaid butcher, whose eyes lit up like fireflies.

"Wooow, thank you!" he cried with genuine happiness. I mumbled something that vaguely resembled "you're welcome" and sighed, leaning against the guardrail that bordered the road. I watched the people in front of me walk around as I stuffed the taiyaki into my mouth. Its crispy edges and spongy body packed to the brim with red bean filling made every bite satisfying. A sweet treat like this really was the best remedy for a fatigued soul.

As I was letting my guard down, the mermaid butcher suddenly said to me, "It's such a blessing to be able to munch on something so tasty by the side of the road like this, don't you think?"

My cheek twitched.

"Yeah, I guess," I replied with a non-committal smile.

He beamed at me, the edges of his mouth smeared with red bean paste. "Eternal life really is the best! I wouldn't have been able to eat something so delicious if I hadn't lived for so long."

He'd already finished his taiyaki and stuffed its paper bag into his pocket. He took out the popin that Toochika-san had bought him.

"I even got my hands on this super cool toy. Praise be eternity! It brings us so many chances to meet new people. And look at this thing! The glass is so incredibly thin! Modern technology sure is amazing."

His shimmery green eyes wrinkled with happiness, and he held his popin up to the sky. The soft daylight of fall splashed the colors of the glass across his cheeks.

He's totally convinced that eternal life is a blessing...

He was like an innocent child who believed wholeheartedly that having no limit to his days was a good thing. I felt conflicted seeing him like this because I believed that his actions had brought nothing but misfortune to a significant number of people. Reminders of how much Tamaki-san had suffered because of his never-ending life continued to linger in my mind. I didn't have it in me to forgive the mermaid butcher for all the suffering he had caused my loved ones.

"It's not even modern technology," I snapped back. "Popins have been a thing since way, way back. Haven't you ever heard of a print called *Young Woman Blowing a Glass Pipe* by Edo period artist Kitagawa Utamaro? You just think it's cool and fresh because you don't know anything about the world around you."

As the final sentence left my mouth, I became filled with regret. *That was a bit harsh. Why did I let my pettiness get the better of me? Ugh, I really need to stay in my own lane.*

"Oh, really? I didn't know these have been around for so long," the mermaid butcher murmured while I was wincing at myself. I watched him blow into the popin, making that loud *po-pop* noise.

A subtle sadness washed over his face.

"I guess living forever isn't all sunshine and rainbows. Maybe having a limited time on this earth is precisely what lets us appreciate things during the moments where they shine the brightest," he said.

I was shocked by his sudden gloomy musing. Only a minute ago, he'd been bouncing full of praises for eternal life, so what was this all about? Had something made him change his mind?

"So, can you please share your opinions with me?" he asked.

"Um... Why do you want to talk to me so badly?" I asked, holding out a tissue to him. As annoyed as I was at him, I didn't really want to let a grown man like him walk around with red bean paste on his face.

"Hm?" he frowned, wiping his mouth so hard that he was practically scrubbing it.

He turned to me. "Well, I've been in a bit of a pickle recently. People keep turning down my offers of eternal life!"

"What's that got to do with me?" I said.

"It's got plenty to do with you!" he declared, pointing at me. My eyes widened in surprise, and he continued with gleaming eyes.

"You know, when you started going on about how bad eternal life is, I was really surprised. I found it very strange, because how can anyone hate it? It's the best! You have a different perspective from mine, even though I've lived for such a long time, and that really interests me. So that's why I wanted to talk to you."

"But what for?" I asked.

"I want to do a little reconnaissance and gather information to develop a plan of attack. Something like that," he answered.

"What is this, a spy mission?"

"Giving out eternal life and making everyone happy *is* my mission! I need to do *something* about my mermaid meat being rejected again and again!" the butcher gushed enthusiastically.

I watched him with a pool of complicated feelings swirling in my mind. I couldn't find any trace of malice or ulterior motive in his words. His heart was clear as crystal in its insistence on selling mermaid meat. He did it because he truly believed it was a wonderful thing, nothing more and nothing less. He wasn't in this for personal gain.

If he weren't so obsessed with eternal life, maybe he would be...a good spirit?

I shook away the thought. So many of my friends had suffered because of him, and I couldn't let myself forget that. Besides, I couldn't have him hanging around me forever. *How did it come to this, anyway? It's not like I'm some expert on eternal life or anything.*

"...Fine, I'll talk to you," I sighed.

The mermaid butcher shot up straight. "Really?!"

"Don't expect anything life-changing, though," I said with a shake of my head. But the man took no notice and continued to beam at me like this was the most wonderful thing ever to happen to him. I couldn't make heads or tails of it, and the confusion gnawed at me.

"All right, let's get this over and done with. I don't think I'll need to get into anything too complicated, anyway," I said. I began to power walk over to the row of used bookstores lining the street and entered one nearby. The faded and browned books that stuffed the shelves greeted us silently.

I took a deep breath. *Ahh, the smell of books is so calming.*

I stopped before one of the shelves and gestured around the shop. "Take a look at all the signs of eternity around us!"

"What do you mean...?" the mermaid butcher stared blankly, uncertain.

"I'm saying that humans don't hate the concept of eternity or anything. This is the result of a lot of hard work and effort devoted to reaching eternity."

"Wait, what?!" he gasped. "So everyone already has their own share of mermaid meat?"

"Um... No, that's not it," I giggled at how he couldn't see something so simple. Taking a volume of classical literature from the shelf, I ran my eyes over its old-fashioned font, felt its slightly thicker paper between my fingers, and checked its publication date. It was printed more than 50 years ago and its pages had long since turned yellow, but the words still read perfectly fine. Its last owner had taken very good care of it. I caught sight of a small note they had written and chuckled.

"I think printing is proof that humans pursued eternity," I said.

"Printing?" the mermaid butcher echoed.

"Printing in Japan goes back to the Nara period in the 8th century. Did you know that in Japan, we have the oldest surviving printed text with its publication date intact?" I said.

"Um, no," the young man said. "When is it from?"

"The whole thing was printed between the years 764 and 770, more than 1,200 years ago. It's called the *Hyakumanto Darani*, or the *One Million Pagodas and Dharani Prayers*, and it's a collection of Buddhist spells. Word is that after the Fujiwara no Nakamaro rebellion, Empress Shotoku wanted a way to mourn the people who died, and so she commissioned these to be printed and had them stored away in little wooden pagoda containers," I explained, lightly touching the spine of the book I was holding.

"Of course, it was printed with politics in mind too, but these dharani were ultimately created for the purpose of mourning the dead. Even after all this time, more than forty thousand pagodas still remain. Isn't that amazing?"

The mermaid butcher gulped. "People were printing more than 1,200 years ago? And the things they printed still survive to this day?" he jabbered with purehearted enthusiasm.

"I think the *One Million Pagodas and Dharani Prayers* could be called a successful example of harnessing eternity," I admitted.

"Wait, what do you mean?" he gasped.

"These dharani have great historical value, and that's why they were able to survive for so long," I explained. "For something man-made to be passed down through eternity, all it needs is to have its innate value recognized. I think that's one facet of printing. If you print something *en masse*, then it's much less likely to be lost completely. Plus, it has a better chance of reaching people who will recognize its value. Therefore, printing is one way for humans to connect with eternity. That's why people spent so much time and effort perfecting printing technology."

From one of the greatest inventions of the Renaissance, the Gutenberg movable-type printing press, much trial and error was conducted to refine the methods of printing. When the mermaid butcher asked what exactly was being refined, I suggested two things: beauty that would impart more value on printed materials and technology for mass production.

"But why? I don't get it," he sighed.

I paused to think, making sure to pick my words carefully.

"Because humans wanted eternity," I said. "They wanted to leave records of knowledge, stories, historical events, significant achievements, and even their own names and ideologies which wouldn't get buried by the rest of history."

I held the volume in my hand out to the young man. "This here's a special edition of a book by a really famous author from the beginning of the Meiji era, and even newer editions have been printed. It's even got an ebook, and I think it's been adapted into a movie and stage production as well."

"...Is this another example of success?"

I nodded. "In a way, yeah. I don't know if it's going to last as long as the *One Million Pagodas and Dharani Prayers* have. But it's been a really long time since the author passed away, and yet the fact remains that this story is still ingrained deeply in our society."

As long as a body of work has had its value recognized, the information it records or the story it tells will be adapted into different media and continue to last, even if the original is lost, all the way until humanity itself perishes.

"But you said the person who wrote it is already dead, right?" the mermaid butcher said aggressively. "What's the point of leaving your works behind if you yourself are dead?"

His protest sounded almost like a wail, and I gave him a dry laugh. "Well, things might be different if every single person were given a chance to eat mermaid meat."

Humans experimented in different ways precisely because eternal life was so impossible to obtain, and the results varied from person to person. Printing technologies were the authors' tools to dabble in eternity and fulfill their common wish of having their stories last as long as possible and be read by as many people as they could reach.

As I turned around and looked over the store, emotions stirred inside of me. The books that filled its shelves were all entries in the never-ending challenge for eternity, and among them were victors which had been deemed valuable as well as losers which hadn't gained that sort of validation. The bookstore was both the front line and the graveyard of this battle for eternity. I was fascinated by the way the fates of each and every one of these books were decided by their readers.

"That sounds like such a pain. Why not just skip all that and accept immortality?" pouted the unconvinced mermaid butcher.

Well, it's true that there used to be people who pursued eternal life. Heck, there are probably people still trying to obtain immortality now, somewhere out there, but they would no doubt be the minority. Although humans don't exactly hate immortality, that doesn't necessarily mean that everyone would want it.

"Because humans only have so much time on Earth, they have no choice but to be realistic in their thinking. That's why fanciful dreams like immortality tend to be shunned. Humans generally have a negative impression of eternal life, and stories about it often have the loneliness that comes with it as a major theme."

A figure flitted through my mind. *He used terms like "major theme" a lot too, huh...*

"Even Tamaki-san tried to make his name famous in a similar way, back when he was an artist for the shogunate. You could call that his attempt to connect with eternity."

The spirit gulped and his face stiffened upon hearing the name of the story-seller who had recently passed away. Tamaki-san had had immortality forced upon him by a fanatical admirer and got caught in a web of misery because of it. His desire to rid himself of it was so intense that he spent many years of his life traveling far and wide to find a solution.

"He didn't feel any joy from the prospect of continuing his artwork forever. Instead, it filled him with despair. He even went so far as to say it was pointless. Some things just have to be done in a limited life span. A lot of people probably wouldn't even know what to do with unlimited time if you gave it to them. I think that's most likely why a lot of people said no to your offer of immortality," I said.

I peeked at the mermaid butcher and gulped. At some point, his eyes had filled with tears, and he was trembling.

"Y-yeah, I suppose," he said with a wobble, "but I still think that living forever is a good thing."

His shoulders slumped, and the tears began to fall.

"I know I did a bad thing by not asking beforehand if he really wanted immortality. It's not like I want to make everyone immortal willy-nilly..."

As the transparent drops slipped from his eyes, the spot where they hit the floor started to darken. *Plip, plip, plip.* As his sadness grew, so did the spots on the ground.

"I still believe that eternity is bliss. I know it. But why doesn't anyone else get it?" he choked, his voice fraught with dejection.

Oh no...

"W-well, this is all just my opinion! I'm sure there are other people out there who would love to live forever," I said and hurriedly offered him a handkerchief.

"Really?!" he gasped, and his eyes sparkled.

I groaned at myself. Why did I say that? I resisted the urge to plant my head in my hands as I internally kicked myself. He'd just looked so sad worrying that I couldn't help it... Seeing him so despondent reminded me of the way I would act if I offered someone a book I liked and the other person wouldn't read it.

I felt a mix of complicated emotions as I watched the mermaid butcher sobbing to himself. Why was he so fixated on immortality? If he weren't so obsessed, we probably could have gotten along a lot better.

"So do I really have no choice but to just...wait until I bump into a person or spirit who needs eternal life?" he said.

"Everyone has their own thoughts about this. If you truly believe that living forever is a good thing, then you have to make a real effort to convince people of your stance," I replied.

"I see..." he nodded. "After all, it's a very important decision that will affect the rest of their life, huh?"

He sighed. "Phooey, I'm not very good at persuading people. I wish I were as good at arguing my points as you are! Maybe then I'd be able to save even more people with the gift of immortality..."

His face suddenly lit up. "Wait, I know!" he declared as if he'd had an epiphany. Beaming brightly, he nimbly darted toward the door and flashed his pearly teeth at me.

"I think I've got it now! Kaori-kun, isn't it? Thank you so much!"

He gave me a big, energetic wave and dashed outside. As I watched him get farther and farther away, I heaved a sigh.

"What was that about?" I frowned. I had a very bad feeling about this.

"Ahem!"

I jumped, sensing the shopkeeper's cold gaze directed straight at my hand. It was so intense that I could practically feel it stabbing at my fingers. That conversation had gone on for a lot longer than I'd realized, and I could sense that he was silently telling me to get out if I wasn't going to buy the book.

I gave him a forced laugh and slid the book back into its gap before leaving the store. A gust of cold wind whipped at my cheeks as I stepped outside, and the fatigue of talking to a stranger for so long hit me like a cannonball. I had no strength left to visit any more shops.

"Ugh, this just isn't my day," I grumbled as my shoulders drooped. I decided to give up on buying new stock and trudged my way back to the spirit realm.

A few days after my encounter with the mermaid butcher, I was clearing out the mountains of books in our shop to prepare for the bookworm prevention tasks that we usually carried out every autumn. When I turned around after setting down a few books, I saw Shinonome-san, Suimei, and Kuro standing behind me.

"What's going on, guys?" I asked as I wiped my sweat away with a towel. Nyaa-san, who had been napping in a corner of the store, stretched and hopped out the window. Kuro, who was by Suimei's feet, cried "Wait!" and bounded after her in a hurry.

Once the cat and dog were gone, Shinonome-san glanced at Suimei and spoke:

"Sorry to be a pain, but could you pay Karaito Gozen a visit and pick something up from her?"

"Karaito Gozen?" I asked.

"Yeah. She's also asked for some books to be delivered, so bring Suimei with you."

"Oh!" I gasped, my eyes widening. "Wait, did she finish fixing your main body?!"

My adoptive father nodded firmly. "She did. I've got my hands full right now, though, so could you get it for me?"

Karaito Gozen was a princess who'd originally lived in the Kamakura period, and after her passing, she became a spirit for reasons unknown. Now she spent her days as a conservator for Tsukumogami, repairing broken main bodies. Shinonome-san was a hanging scroll Tsukumogami, and Karaito Gozen had offered to fix his main body after it sustained some damage during a certain incident. She'd originally said that the repairs would be finished at the beginning of spring, but various troubles kept delaying them until now.

"Finally! That's great!" I exclaimed. "Now we can all rest a little easier."

The lives of Tsukumogami would be threatened if anything happened to their main bodies, so they were generally unable to leave them. Even though the hanging scroll had to be separated from Shinonome-san for repairs, we were still very uneasy to have it so far away from him. When I gave him a relaxed smile, he scratched at his neck with a fidgety hand.

"Yeah, that's true," he said with a weak smile, closing his eyes slowly. His eyes darted to me, then to the ground, and then back at me.

"Sorry for making you run around so much. You don't have to go now; you can finish up with the books first if you want," he said.

"Oh, okay," I said. "Hey, that reminds me..."

I glanced at the sky outside the window.

"Karaito Gozen was one of your clients too, wasn't she...?"

Back during the incident with Kurokami in Aomori, I had recommended Gozen a few books I'd handpicked for her. I was confident she would love them, but she never put in another request for books after that. I'd figured that she was just busy with her Tsukumogami repairs and simply didn't have the time, but I still couldn't help but feel that I had failed.

This could be my chance to redeem myself, though. I needed to put my best foot forward and challenge myself so I could gain precious experience and take over the bookstore smoothly.

"So you just need me to pop over to Aomori and then come back right away? I'll go now," I said, whisking off my apron. If I got this done quickly, I might even be able to make it back within the day.

"I'll go and get ready now. Suimei, you good to go?" I asked.

He nodded. "Yeah, I'm fine."

"Cool," I replied. "You're bringing Kuro, right? Where'd they go?"

I opened the front door with a clatter and peeked outside.

"Nyaa-san!" I yelled. I heard a familiar "meow" from above.

Kuro was waiting under the eaves and looking up at the roof with a lost expression. Nyaa-san probably would never stop messing with him, would she?

I called to them that we were going out, then returned inside to put away the books that were laid out.

"Kaori, it's really no rush," Shinonome-san said with an awkward expression.

I waved a hand and laughed. "It's fine! This is all part of taking over the store, right? I'm used to going on errands for you anyway. Plus, I'd love to take a good look at your scroll for the first time ever."

I'd seen it once, but it had been mercilessly torn apart that time. From what I remembered, though, the scroll depicted a dragon flying through the sky, and it was beautiful and grand even in its ripped state. It was drawn in ink, but its brushwork and gradients were so exquisite that they brought color to the monotone artwork. Just looking at it was a special experience, and I would have loved nothing more than to be able to appreciate it properly, even more so because it was my adoptive father's main body.

"Going to Aomori is nothing if it means I get to see the hanging scroll of good fortune," I joked.

Shinonome-san chuckled.

"All right," he said, patting me gently on the shoulder. "I'll leave it to you, then. Be careful out there."

"Of course!" I nodded, beaming. "You can throw any and all errands my way. I'm going to do my best to take over the store!"

Shinonome-san smiled softly when he saw how motivated I was. I noticed that Suimei was looking sullen, though.

"Suimei?" I probed.

"Wait here," my adoptive father said and returned to his own room. Maybe he was fetching the books that he'd said we needed to deliver. Once he was gone, I approached Suimei. He was still silent, so I stood next to him...and blew into his ear.

"WHOOOAAA!" he yelped, covering his ear as he flushed a bright red. "What was that for?!"

I grinned. "You looked half-asleep, so I thought I'd wake you up."

He shifted his eyes away and stared off into space, refusing to look at me. "I-I'm fine. I've just been busy with the shop lately since everyone's getting ready for the winter, so I'm a bit tired. Gotta save whatever's left of my energy since we're going up north to Aomori and all, right?"

I *had* heard that business was booming at the apothecary. That was probably why I hadn't seen Noname around much, either.

"Oh my, you sound like you've been through a lot. Don't push yourself to come if you can't. I've got Nyaa-san with me, anyway, so I'll be fine," I said.

"No, I'm going. You always get into some sort of trouble when you're by yourself. I can't leave you alone even for a second," he muttered. He sounded more like a parent than a boyfriend with his fussing, and I couldn't help but let out a laugh.

I nodded at the grumpy Suimei. "All right, all right. I'd love to have you come with me. Please make sure I don't do anything weird!"

"...Jeez, what am I gonna do with you?" he grumbled. But even as he turned away, I could tell that he was blushing. I giggled at how bad he was at hiding his feelings and sighed a little inside. It had only been a little over a year since we met, but it hadn't taken too long to figure out that he was an extremely bad liar. He had the habit of not making eye contact when he was fibbing, after all. Which was ironic, since at all other times he was so watchful that his eyes would practically bore holes into me.

Recently, Suimei and Shinonome-san had been spending time together a lot more often. There had to be some business going on between the two of them.

Well, I supposed there was nothing much I could do but wait for them to approach me first. If I tried to force them to talk to me, it might make them dig in their heels. I didn't enjoy being left in the dark, but I trusted that whatever they were up to wouldn't hurt my feelings, so I was fine with waiting for the right time to come. There was no need for me to rush them.

I pushed away the unease in my heart and smiled.

"Let's get some good food once we're in Aomori!" I suggested. "Hmm, I wonder if they'd have any apples yet... Seems like it's a bit early in the year for them, but maybe we could get a bunch of apple pies at Hirosaki and see which one's the best? Or we could get some white bean paste oyaki from Dotemachi. I heard there's a place that has a really good kind. Oh, we should also visit Kurokami and say hi!"

As I rattled off on the detours like I usually did, Suimei creased his brows.

"We don't have the time for all that. Did you already forget why we're going there?" he cautioned me.

"Aw, c'mon! Please?" I begged.

"You sure like your food, huh?" Kuro muttered.

"That's just what she's always like," Nyaa-san replied.

"Hey, since when are the two of you such good friends?!" I huffed.

As I tried to weather their brutal onslaught by myself, a cheery voice chimed in.

"Ooh, ooh, are you going to Aomori? Can I come?"

It was the mermaid butcher.

"Wh... What are you doing here?!" I gasped.

Suimei, upon seeing the young man with whom he'd only recently been locked in a life-or-death struggle, immediately crouched into a battle stance. The mermaid butcher entered the shop all smiles, as if he hadn't even noticed the former exorcist.

"Um, can I help you with anything?" I asked.

Don't tell me he's come for revenge because he didn't like what I said to him at Jinbocho?!

I prepared myself for the worst, but the mermaid butcher simply pressed a paper bag into my hands. It was soft with steam, and warm, and...there was a sweet scent wafting from it.

"Wait, is this...?"

I gulped and peeked inside the bag, spotting something I was all too familiar with.

"T-taiyaki...?"

"The one you got me the other day was so delicious! I just

wanted to repay the favor," he said, grinning with the brightness of a thousand suns. It was so dazzling that I couldn't help but squint a little.

Wow, he went out of his way to buy me fresh taiyaki. I'm so ha—wait, wait, wait! No!

"What are you up to?" I asked. "Don't tell me you poisoned this."

"I'm not up to anything!" insisted the aghast butcher. "How could you accuse me of that? I'm just trying to be nice!"

"But you're broke," I pointed out.

"That's okay. I'm immortal, so all that'll happen if I don't eat is that I'll starve and suffer. It's not like I'll die or anything!"

"That's *not* okay!" I interrupted without thinking, and he chuckled merrily.

I didn't feel too good about taking the taiyaki when he had so little money to his name. As I fretted over whether or not to accept it, a hand plonked onto my shoulder.

"...Kaori?"

I turned awkwardly and saw Suimei staring straight at me with a smile that was almost too perfect.

"Since when are you so buddy-buddy with him? Explain yourself. Now."

"Um..." I stammered. "I mean...we're not *that* buddy-buddy..."

"Yeah!" the butcher nodded. "All we've done is go on one date in Jinbocho!"

"That is *not* what happened! Don't say it like that!" I cried, glaring at him but receiving only a cheeky grin in return.

He clearly thought that everything was fine and dandy between us and figured it would be fine to mess around like this.

"Now what's all this fuss?" Shinonome-san said as he peeked around the corner, curious about the clamor. He surveyed us with a stern eye and caught sight of the mermaid butcher.

"You again..." he scowled. "You just don't know how to give up, do you?"

"Hello, Shinonome!" the butcher said as he pointed at me. "Hey, hey, can I go to Aomori with her?"

Shinonome-san's eyebrow perked up in a suspicious arch.

"What for?" he growled in a rumbly voice, narrowing his eyes into a piercing stare. Those two syllables were enough to strike fear into anyone, but the young man took no notice.

"The other day, um... Kaori-kun taught me a very valuable lesson about immortality," he replied, carefree as ever. "Well, I still believe that a life with no end is really the best way to live, but anyway..."

He smiled, and his eyes arched. The green hue of his irises seemed to become even more vibrant.

"I've just...got some thoughts, you know? Anyway, I promise I won't get in her way, so it's fine, right?"

Shinonome-san continued to glower in silence. In the end, he shrugged and said, "Do whatever you want."

"Yay!" the butcher whooped.

"Hold on a minute!" I protested. "Why did you say yes? And since when are you guys friends?!"

Shinonome-san heaved an annoyed sigh and dragged his

slipper-clad feet down to the store. He pressed the book in his hands into mine and clicked his tongue.

"I've only seen him around a couple of times. He does nothing but bother me and get in the way of my work. If he wants to go to Aomori, then just bring him. I don't see the problem with it," he said.

"Wh-what?!" My eyelids batted in disbelief.

"Hang on, I don't agree with this," Suimei cut in, only to be rebuffed immediately. Shinonome-san made direct eye contact and said, "If I say it's fine, then it's fine."

I flicked a glance at the mermaid butcher and saw that he was rubbing his nose with a grin of satisfaction.

"Wait, so...you're seriously coming with us?" I asked gingerly.

He nodded vigorously and answered with an enthusiastic, pearly white "yeah!"

"I'll leave it to you, then," Shinonome-san said as he retreated to his room.

I apparently had no choice but to take the mermaid butcher with us. So much for my first official job after setting my heart on taking over the bookstore... I couldn't believe that I had to spend it with the butcher. I could already think of so many things that could go wrong with it.

I crumpled my face into a grimace and glanced absently at the book Shinonome-san had handed me. It was *The Records of Tango Province* in an old-fashioned, traditional Japanese binding.

"Huh? *This* is for Karaito Gozen?" I tilted my head, puzzled.

I frantically scrambled toward my adoptive father. "Sh-Shinonome-san! Why did you pick this book?!"

The unexpected title had thrown me for a complete loop. I couldn't figure out why this particular book had been picked for our client, but I knew that if I wanted to complete this job and any future ones successfully, I had to understand the reason.

Shinonome-san turned a relaxed head back toward me. His mouth opened and closed a few times before he muttered an answer: "Why? Because she asked for it."

He hadn't answered my question at all. It was so typical of him and his way with words, or rather his lack thereof. I waited silently for him to continue. Shinonome-san's eyes wandered about as he grasped for a follow-up, until he began to list off other books on each finger.

"The previous titles that she borrowed include *Reflections on Ancient Matters, The Water Mirror, Manyoshu,* and *The Chronicles of Japan.* Oh, and *Otogi Bunko,* from the Edo period. You understand why now, right? If anyone can figure it out, it's you."

I gulped. I dove desperately into my mind to find a common thread.

"I...think I know," I murmured, a little uncertain.

Shinonome-san's face lit up. He seemed happy as he said, "Excellent. And good luck, huh? You're going to be a great successor."

He disappeared into his room. My palms were slick with sweat. I'd been holding my breath even though it wasn't a long conversation.

"All right!" I exclaimed as I rolled up my sleeves, heading for the shelves. I scanned them quickly and began taking out a few volumes.

"What are you doing? I thought we were leaving soon?" Suimei asked in confusion.

"Sorry, I'll only be a minute. I just want to make sure I have the info that I need," I answered without looking up from the book I was holding. I fell silent and began flipping through the pages rapidly.

I can't find it... I swear it was around here somewhere...

"Huh? Aren't we going yet? So I have to wait?... Hey. Heeeeeey!" the mermaid butcher whined. However, I was completely immersed in the swirl of words and took no notice of him. Once I spotted what I was looking for, I returned to the shelves and took out even more books.

I have to make sure the store is in good hands with me. Every job I take has to be perfect!

After a while, I had finally gone through all the books I had a good feeling about. I stuffed the ones I thought I'd need into my bag and called out to the mermaid butcher, who had been playing with Nyaa-san and Kuro to pass the time.

"I'm ready now! Let's go!"

And so we headed for Aomori.

Standing in the town of Ajigasawa in the western part of Aomori Prefecture, we could see white things being dried along the coastline, waving about in the wind. They were squids that had been butterflied, a common sight in a part of town called Yakiika-dori, otherwise known as Grilled Squid Street. As the name would imply, it was host to a number of shops that sold grilled squid, bustling with customers who would stop by on their leisurely drives to browse and purchase seafood.

"Chomp! Chomp chomp chomp! Whoo, I loooooove squid! It's so chewy and... Mmm, that little bit of saltiness is just right. I could eat these all day!" Kuro yelped and howled as he savored the fishy sea breeze. In front of him was a brown paper bag that held a piece of grilled squid, and he had stuck his snout directly into it to enjoy his meal, his tail wagging furiously to and fro.

"Hey, doggo, make sure you eat the beak too! It's a real delicacy," the mermaid butcher suggested as he took a bite of his own squid, all smiles. "You like squid, doggo? I personally prefer sea urchin. Hey, have you ever had a freshly caught urchin?"

"Nope!" Kuro yapped back, and the butcher started describing its taste in thorough detail. He was exactly like a good-natured older brother.

"They are just amazing when they're caught fresh," he said. "Did you know that there's a place here in Aomori called Hachinohe that's supposed to have really great canned urchin and abalone? Actually, Aomori is famous in general for how delicious its seafood is!"

"Whoa!" Kuro's eyes sparkled. "Canned urchin and abalone? That's fancy! What do they taste like?"

The mermaid butcher faltered. "Um, sorry, but I've actually never eaten them before... They're way out of my price range. Ah ha! Ah ha ha ha ha!"

Addendum: He was exactly like a good-natured older brother who was flat broke.

How does he even get money when he doesn't seem to have a job? As I pondered this question, I flipped through the book in my hand. Nyaa-san let out a big yawn as she sat atop the breakwater. There was no sign of anyone coming to pick us up, even though it was well past the time we'd agreed upon.

I was reading a book entitled *The Records of Tango Province*, though I'd already more or less gone through the entire thing. I let out a sigh. As long as I had this one part down pat, it should allow me to carry on a good conversation about the book's contents. But I still felt like I was missing something, and it was gnawing away at me.

Am I going to be okay? Will I be able to do this job properly?

This wasn't my first rodeo, though, and it wasn't anything out of the ordinary. I knew I had what it took, and I had fully embraced my destiny of taking over the store from Shinonome-san.

So why did I still feel like I was floundering?

"Kaori?" Suimei called to me. I snapped out of my thoughts and saw that he was studying me with his light brown eyes, filled with concern.

"Are you all right?" he asked, squeezing my hand. I blinked a few times and let out a breath I had been unconsciously holding. I gave him a nervous giggle, and his eyes relaxed.

"What, were you feeling nervous?"

I shrank back. The mermaid butcher then came up beside me.

"You okay? Want me to go catch some sea urchin for you?" he offered.

Although his words sounded kind, I couldn't help but grimace and reject them. Why was he being so nice to me? And why did he even want to come to Aomori with us in the first place? I was convinced that he had some ulterior motive in mind.

And why did he seem to think that everything could be smoothed over with good food? *I mean, I did end up scarfing down the taiyaki he gave me on the way here, but that's beside the point! He's dead wrong if he thinks he can curry favor with me like this!*

"Who even offers urchin as a pick-me-up?" I said.

"What? Is that weird?" the mermaid butcher asked.

"Well, I can't say anyone's ever offered me something so fishy to cheer me up," I said. "Anyway, you can't just go around catching urchins wherever you like. That's called poaching, you know. You can be charged for theft if you fish in waters protected by fishing associations without their permission."

The color drained from his face. "But I thought the sea was supposed to be for everyone! Wait, don't tell me I've been stealing someone else's urchins without knowing?!"

"You gotta keep with the times," I sighed. "Let this be a lesson to you."

The mermaid butcher's face and shoulders crashed so dramatically that I could practically see manga sound effects flying from him.

"No way! How can I be a hero who saves people this way?!" he cried.

"A hero?" I frowned.

"Y-yeah, I'm a hero who gives mermaid meat to people in need!"

Seeing him panicking over the potential crime he had committed, a light bulb went off in my head.

Oh, I get it now!

He believed wholeheartedly that his actions were righteous and heroic. He was willing to do anything, no matter how drastic, to carry out his mission of justice, and he equated that with being a hero.

"Now, help me help you!"

The words that he had once said to my friend flashed through my mind. To him, "saving" troubled people by giving them eternal life was a prerequisite to being a hero.

I'm sure that he *had* saved people this way in the past, but... I had mixed emotions about this.

However, now I felt like I understood why Toochika-san had decided the mermaid butcher was harmless. As long as he continued to think of himself as a hero on the side of justice, he would probably keep trying to do good for the people around him.

"Well, just be careful next ti... Hey!"

As I started to offer the mermaid butcher some consolation, I was suddenly jerked to the side. I stumbled, trying to find my footing, and whipped my head around to see who had pulled my hand.

It was Suimei, and he didn't look very happy.

"I can get you sea urchins if you want, and I won't even have to poach them," he grumbled.

"What are you getting competitive with that guy for?!" I said.

"Oh, shut up," he muttered and pulled me closer to him. "Anyway, stay away from him. And don't get so chummy with him either."

I gawked at Suimei. The aura surrounding him was positively dangerous now, and yet I couldn't help but sputter with laughter.

He furrowed his brows. "Hey, what's so funny? I meant every word of what I said!"

"Sorry, sorry!" I giggled. "Well, I guess I'd end up with a fishy gift either way."

"*He's* the one who suggested sea urchin in the first place!" Suimei argued.

"That's true," I said with a nod and grin. "All right, don't disappoint me now!"

His eyes widened. "Wait, you're actually serious about the urchin?!"

"Heh heh heh. Well, you did offer," I said. "Mmm, I can't wait. I want enough urchin to eat with an entire bowl of rice. A glowing, golden heap!" I said gleefully as I prodded Suimei, who was now clenching his fists and trembling.

The mermaid butcher shrugged as he watched us. "You two sure get along well. Are you married?"

"No!" Suimei and I cried at the same time. I shot a glance at Suimei and saw that he was looking at me too. Our eyes locked, but we immediately looked away in embarrassment. We both turned the color of tomatoes, and the mermaid butcher cackled.

"Oh, you two are just precious. So you've just started dating, huh?" he said, bobbing his head. "Ah, reminds me of when I first met my wife."

That jolted me. "Wait, you're married?!"

"Yeah. I haven't seen her in a while, though," the mermaid butcher said.

I blinked. I was *not* expecting that, but now this raised a question: What kind of woman would wed an immortal man?

As I sank into my own reverie, a voice called out to me: "Hey, Kaori! How long are you going to stand around and talk for? Come over here!"

I turned around frantically and saw a man clad in black standing in front of the breakwater.

"You are such a bully. I'm not into neglect play, you know. Don't you think she's a bully, Nyaa?" he asked.

"You were the one standing around watching them and going 'ahh, youth,'" the cat returned.

The man in black was Nurarihyon, the supreme commander of all spirits. He held Nyaa-san in his arms while his beard, long enough to graze the concrete below, fluttered in the sea breeze.

"Long time no see," I greeted him. "Um, where is Karaito Gozen?"

I glanced around my surroundings but saw no trace of the beautiful woman with the graceful smile anywhere. Nurarihyon cut my confusion short with a sharp "shh!" as he put a finger to his lip.

"Things have been...messy around here in recent years, so I thought I should volunteer to come pick you up. It's nothing you have to worry about," he whispered, shooting a sharp look at the mermaid butcher.

So Nurarihyon was here as our chaperone of sorts. As this registered in my mind, I noticed a large shadow looming over me.

"Huh?"

When I looked up, I was met with a gigantic, floating jelly-fish big enough to blot out the sky. It was one of Nurarihyon's spirits. When its tentacles drifted toward me, I shrank back with a shudder.

"Um, I appreciate you coming out here to meet us, but can I ask where my client is?" I asked cautiously.

Nurarihyon flashed me a bold grin. "You know how fussy she can be. She's cooped up in a special place right now because she said she can't concentrate on her job above ground."

"What special place? Just give it to me straight," I said.

I had a bad feeling about this. Nurarihyon loved pranks and would often act in the most unpredictable ways. For starters, why did he have his giant jellyfish on standby here? What was he up to?

"Can you just tell me where she is? I don't like it when people try to take me to weird places," I huffed.

"Hrm, it's not weird or anything," the spirit said. "It's a place that you said you wanted to visit when you were little. Do you remember? You were always talking about how you'd love to go to the Dragon Palace."

"The Dragon Palace?" I gasped. It was the underwater castle that Urashima Taro was invited to in the tale of the same title. However, I couldn't remember ever saying I was interested in visiting it as a child. I cocked my head in thought.

"You don't remember?" Nurarihyon laughed heartily. "But you used to read the picture book with such intense sparkles in your eyes!"

"I do remember liking the Urashima Taro story," I said. "But it's not like the Dragon Palace actually exists, right?"

"Nonsense! It exists in Aomori, all right! You've never heard of the ruins of ancient civilizations in the waters of Ajigasawa? It's been quite the hot topic, even in the human world," Nurarihyon insisted.

I blinked in surprise. Ancient civilizations in Aomori? I couldn't say I was familiar with them.

"There's been some...interesting writings on the matter, from ancient scripts to *Tsugaru Soto-Sangunshi*. You'll find mentions of a civilization called Arahabaki if you look into the ancient history of the Tsugaru region here in Aomori. It used to be quite prosperous, but it was wiped out overnight by a tsunami. And now, at the bottom of the ocean in Ajigasawa, there lie remains that look awfully man-made. Doesn't that sound like it could be the Dragon Palace?" the spirit said.

"Interesting" ancient writings and man-made remains? It all sounded dubious. So incredibly dubious.

I reflexively pulled my face into a grimace, and Nurarihyon puffed his cheeks out.

"You don't believe me, do you? How sad," he pouted. "Is it really so weird when you consider all the other mysterious things in Aomori? We've got Jesus Christ's resting place, pyramids, the Sannai-Maruyama site which is said to be the largest Jumon settlement in Japan, and you can even meet itakos on Mount Osore! Having one or two ancient civilizations on top of that is nothing."

"All right, all right, I get it," I said.

The Dragon Palace, huh...?

I clutched my hand against my bag. Was it just a coincidence for the Dragon Palace to come up on the day I was delivering *The Records of Tango Province*? Did it really exist?

No, that was impossible.

"So you're saying that Karaito Gozen is in this Dragon Palace or whatever?" I asked.

"See? You don't believe me. I'm going to be really upset unless you change your mind, you know," Nurarihyon whined and puffed his cheeks again like a child.

I giggled. "Okay, I believe you. Please take us to the Dragon Palace so I can pick up Shinonome-san's main body and finish the bookstore's job."

"...All right," the supreme commander said, smiling gently at me. He gave my shoulder a light squeeze.

"Do your best," he encouraged me, ruffling my hair.

I felt like he was being kinder to me than usual. Maybe he was making a point of being nicer since he'd heard I was going to take over the bookstore? As I pondered this question, the giant jellyfish suddenly grew even bigger and enveloped me.

I panicked and held my breath. I felt its soft, gelatinous body cling to every inch of my skin before it began to float. I spun around in a hurry, trying to check on everyone else. Except for Nurarihyon, they were all trapped in individual jellyfish like I was, and they looked like they were about to drown. Their faces were sickly and pale, and they were all kicking about and struggling for air.

But the jellyfish were completely unbothered, and they continued to float upward until they began moving out to the sea.

"Have a safe trip!" Nurarihyon called and waved to us, his feet planted firmly on the ground.

Wait, wait, wait! I shot out a hand, terrified for my life. *I can't... I can't breathe!*

I didn't know how long this was going to last, but I felt like I was going to suffocate at any moment.

I'd heard that the elusive Nurarihyon usually lived under the sea, so after a lifetime of being surrounded by gilled creatures, maybe he just didn't have the same frame of mind for breathing as humans did. Maybe he'd even forgotten that we couldn't breathe underwater with our lungs...

No, no way! That's a little too ridiculous.

I shivered and curled myself up. *How long can humans hold their breath for, again?*

I wiggled and kicked, trying to free myself from the jellyfish somehow, but it continued its journey without one iota of care. I hadn't noticed before, but now I realized that we were above the waves. The jellyfish began to descend as if it had hit a checkpoint, entering the water with an enormous splash. It pulled me away from the surface and into the depths in a matter of seconds, sinking my entire field of vision into a watery world of intense azure. We were surrounded by the ocean as far as the eye could see. It was a paradise for the fish that lived here, but of course there was no air for us land dwellers to breathe.

I coughed, trying not to choke. A few bubbles leaked from the corner of my mouth. I couldn't hold on for much longer.

I can't do this anymore! I'm going to drown!

I wriggled, the tightness in my lungs unbearable. As I writhed around trying to find a way out, I opened my eyes wide and saw an unusual number of straight stones lined up on the ocean floor. There were also a few round ones that looked like they could be part of a statue.

But what stood out more than anything was the single gigantic bubble sitting in the middle of those stones. Within it sat an extravagant castle with vermilion walls, its surroundings adorned with coral and circled by fish that swam with such energy that they looked like they were dancing.

Wait... Wait! No way, no way!

The jellyfish were like Urashima Taro's sea turtle, bringing us to this underwater paradise.

I can't believe the Dragon Palace actually exists! I thought.

I blinked in disbelief and touched a hand to my bag. However, as the excitement bubbled within me, my vision also started fading to black.

If only the Dragon Palace also had air for us to breathe...

Those were the last words that ran through my head as I sank into unconsciousness.

When I opened my eyes, I was met with an incredible sight. Silk drapes billowed around me as I rose from the soft bedding I had been laid upon, and a small blue fish tickled my nose as it swam past. In fact, there were fish swimming everywhere I looked. I blinked in amazement, and the fish shot away in a panic. I turned my head to survey the room I'd been carried to while I was unconscious.

"Is this the Dragon Palace?" I wondered out loud.

"Oh, I'm so glad to see you've regained consciousness," a voice said. A court lady stood before me, her eyes bright and her cheeks round. Her skin was smooth and flawless, and her hair was tied in a high ponytail and embellished with ornaments made of gold, silver, jade, and shell. Her coral comb swayed with her hair, and her legs and waist were wrapped in a magnificent long skirt. She was so stunning that I couldn't help but stare.

"How are you feeling? You were rescued from the jellyfish right before you would have suffocated," she said.

"I-I feel fine," I answered. "Where's everyone else?"

The court lady beamed and offered to take me to see them if I felt well enough to walk. I nodded and asked her to lead me.

The Dragon Palace was a fascinating place. Not a single spot anywhere was unlit, and you could see the shadows of the waves dancing gently on the sea floor as the sunlight streamed through the surface above. The floor was also covered with sea grass and colorful rocks. Bubbles rose with every step I took. The windows had no glass inside their borders, allowing fish to swim freely through them. The castle grounds were dotted with coral, and between them sprouted various seaweeds and flora. The interior was equally beautiful with its luxurious furnishings of gold, silver, and countless jewels. A single fork had been hung up on the wall, and the sight of it filled me with joy.

This was exactly what I'd imagined the Dragon Palace would be like. I felt as if I had wandered straight into a storybook, and I bounced with extra pep in my step.

The court lady led me into a room, and someone immediately cried, "Kaori!"

It was Suimei. He seemed to have woken up earlier than me.

"Are you okay?" I asked. "Where's Kuro and Nyaa-san?"

"I'm fine, yeah. And they've been awake for a while now. They're off exploring the palace," he said.

"Are they now? I'm glad they're okay," I said, letting out a sigh of relief.

Next to the bed that Suimei had vacated was another one in which the mermaid butcher was laying sound asleep.

"The doctor said he should wake soon," a voice sighed, and in stepped Karaito Gozen. "That absolute dullard! How can he call himself the supreme commander of all spirits if he can't even pick up a few guests properly?!"

She was wearing kochigi robes paired with a dazzling red hakama. As angry as she was, she still looked as graceful as ever.

"Long time no see, Karaito Gozen," I smiled. "Well, we arrived safely in the end, so all's well that ends well, huh?"

"All is *not* well!" she exclaimed. "Whatever would I do if something happened to you?"

Storming toward me, she began to restlessly pat me down and look over every inch of me.

"Are you hurt anywhere? Are you feeling all right? Please do feel free to rest more if you need to," she fussed.

"I-I'm fine, really, but thank you!" I stammered in bewilderment. Karaito Gozen heaved another sigh.

"You have absolutely no sense of urgency," she griped, turning away as she realized her eyes were growing wet with tears. "You humans are a lot more easily hurt than us spirits, so tell me immediately if you feel off, all right?"

She seemed to be quite worried about us. I was thankful for her care.

"There's no need to worry now. Why not celebrate our safe arrival instead?" I suggested.

The moment I finished speaking, a strikingly beautiful woman entered the room. She carried with her a few Chinese lidded teacups and a small teapot, all placed on a style of tray I seldom saw in Japan. I stared, eyes fixed on her as she set the ensemble on the table. When she noticed my gaze, a smile bloomed on her face like a flower.

I felt my heart jolt as it became ensnared by her stunning charm. Her large, elegant eyes were like two black pearls. She had a small, dainty nose, and her lips were lightly colored like delicate petals. On her forehead was a small painted flower that I recognized as a traditional Chinese style of makeup called *huadian*. She had on a long skirt made of layers upon layers of silk, and the pearls she wore swayed with every move. Her air of elegance was tenfold that of any other court lady.

I silently tried to calm my raucous heart. I wasn't used to being so taken with another woman! However, as I was caught up in my own mental jumble, she suddenly spoke to me.

"Are you Shinonome-sama's daughter?" the woman asked.

"O-oh, yes. I'm Kaori," I replied. "What's your name?"

"Well...I suppose you can call me Roshi," she replied.

I tilted my head at her evasive answer.

Roshi finished pouring the tea and said, "In any case, why not have a cup? You must be feeling tired."

She held a cup out to me, then to Suimei and the others present. It came with a lid, and I found a bed of sunken tea leaves when I looked at the bottom. I wasn't quite sure how I was supposed to drink it.

Roshi must have sensed my uncertainty because she told me, "Use the lid to hold the leaves back." I nodded and gave it a try. It was a bit awkward for me, but the tea itself exuded a wonderful fragrance and a mellow sweetness that spread across my taste buds. My lips tugged into a smile from how exquisite it tasted.

"This is delicious!" I exclaimed.

"Indeed," Karaito Gozen agreed. "I can feel my irritation fade by the second."

"It's great. Thanks," Suimei said.

I felt its warmth spread from my mouth to the tips of my fingers and toes. We all nodded to each other in agreement and gratitude toward Roshi.

"I'm glad to hear that. Tea is balm for the soul, even more so when the drinker delights in its taste," Roshi said. "Oh, I wish *he* would tell me it's delicious too..."

I cocked my head again. Who was she talking about?

Her long eyelashes seemed to dust her cheeks as she blinked her beautiful eyes, and she fidgeted as she fell deep into thought. I looked in the direction of her gaze, and...

"Huaaahhh! Wow, what a great nap!"

The mermaid butcher, who had been lying fast asleep, suddenly shot up from his bed. He didn't seem fully awake as he scratched his head absently. He turned and flashed a grin when he spotted me.

"What's up, Kaori-kun? You having tea? Ooh, nice. I want some too!" he chattered.

He wriggled out of his bed, bursting with energy, and plopped himself down on a spare round chair. A little stunned, I asked him how he was feeling.

"I feel fine, like always!" he answered, casually cracking his neck as if he hadn't just been brought to an underwater palace. "Wait, did something happen?"

"We almost drowned in Nurarihyon's jellyfish," I told him.

"Uh..." he paused. "Ohh, riiight! I remember now! Ha ha ha. Sorry, I forgot. Wow, that was bad, huh? It's been a while since I got knocked out like that!"

"How can you laugh about it?!" I gasped. "You could have died!"

"Yeah, but I mean, I'm immortal. I can't really die," he said with an innocent smile.

I groaned. I really couldn't deal with him.

"Well, if you don't care about going unconscious, who will? Not me, when you get swallowed by some giant sea creature."

"Hey, that actually happened to me once!" he piped up. "I got eaten by a giant whale and I ended up swimming around in its stomach acid."

"What."

I really hadn't expected him to have any answer to what I'd meant as a joke. I stopped, unable to think past my shock and come up with a response.

The mermaid butcher laughed without a care in the world and continued. "And there was an old man who lived on a boat inside of the whale. I actually stayed with him for a while. He'd been accidentally swallowed when he was out looking for his son. He was an interesting guy!"

"Wait, that's what happened in *Pinocchio*," I gasped. I pitched myself forward, hoping to get more details on this storybook incident.

The wafting fragrance of a well-brewed cup of tea stopped me in my tracks.

"Now, now, Kaori-san. Let him get settled first. He only just woke up," Roshi chided me as she gave the mermaid butcher his share of tea.

Oops, she told me off... I winced.

"I'll tell you more some other time," the mermaid butcher said, stretching a lazy arm out to take the teacup. He tilted the lid and held it against the vessel, blocking the tea leaves as he drank from it. It seemed like he had enjoyed tea this way a million times before.

"Mmm!" His eyes sparkled as the hot liquid touched his tongue. "Wow, this is amazing. Hey, you make a wicked cup!"

He smiled happily, and Roshi's cheeks flushed.

"O-oh, I'm glad," she said.

"I'd be a happy man if I could drink tea like this every day," he said.

"Oh!" she gasped. "Really? Thank you!"

Her ears, peeking out from underneath her black hair, were a cherry blossom pink. She batted her eyes and brushed her bangs to the side even though they didn't need fixing.

I raised an eyebrow as I watched her sudden change in behavior, and then it hit me.

Wait, is there a love-at-first-sight thing going on here?!

I'd been reading a whole heap of romance novels and shojo manga that Fuguruma-youbi had recommended, so now my eye was honed for this kind of thing. But the bittersweet air that hung in the room was too much for me to handle, because I knew something that would upset Roshi greatly: The mermaid butcher was already married.

Suddenly, he chuckled. "Well, you're good, but not as good as my wife. She's a real pro when it comes to tea!"

The light immediately vanished from Roshi's eyes.

"Oh. I...see," she muttered. She stood up on unsteady legs and collected the teacups in an abrupt motion.

"I'll be taking my leave now. Do excuse me," she said, bowing palm over fist. I watched her leave the room and scrunched my face into a disapproving grimace.

"Oh my God, you can't just say that! That was so heartless of you," I said.

"Hey, how dare you! I may be immortal, but I've still got my humanity!" he grumbled.

"I mean, how could you lead her on and then crush her heart like that? How could you do that to such a pretty woman?" I shot back.

"I mean, she was okay..." he said.

Had his immensely long life warped his taste? I sighed, and the mermaid butcher continued to look at me, dumbfounded. He then turned his attention to our surroundings.

"Actually, where are we?" he asked as he glanced around, cocking his head curiously. "There's a lot of fish here. Are we underwater?"

"That sure took a while," I said, raising an eyebrow. "Oh well. Anyway, we're in the Dragon Palace."

"What?" the mermaid butcher gulped. "*The* Dragon Palace? Like the one Urashima Taro went to?"

"Bingo."

A rosy pink color bloomed on his cheeks. "So this is what it looks like. Wow..." he whispered.

As I strained my ears to hear what he was mumbling about, he started rifling through his pockets and very delicately removed something from their depths—it was the popin from Toochika-san's shop.

"Have you just been walking around with that the whole time?" I asked.

"Yeah! 'Cause I want to be able to show it to my wife. I know she'd love this," he told me as he held it in front of his face. Compared to the colorful tropical fish swimming around the Dragon Palace, the goldfish on the popin seemed almost dull. However, the mermaid butcher spoke so fondly of them that he made them sound like the most beautiful fish in the whole palace.

"Oh, it looks even prettier under the sea! I'm so glad I brought it with me."

What a weird guy, I thought. Even if you ignored his immortality, he was still pretty out there.

My mind began to wander until Karaito Gozen got my attention.

"Oh, Kaori-san? There's something I must tell you about Shinonome's main body," she said.

"Y-yes, what is it?!" I squawked.

I had completely forgotten about why we'd come here in the first place!

I straightened myself in a panic and turned to face Karaito Gozen, who frowned slightly at my lack of organization.

"I'm afraid that I will need a little more time to repair it. My deepest apologies," she said. "Because a Tsukumogami's main body is so delicate, it must be packaged appropriately to prevent it from breaking. I would usually have prepared something in advance, but when I heard what happened to you, I rushed over here in great haste."

"I'm really sorry about that..." I said.

"No, please. It is not your fault," she said with a shake of her head. "I do appreciate the thought, but rest assured I will make sure to have a stern word with the true culprit when I return to the surface."

She exhaled sharply in annoyance and turned to the side. I couldn't help but let out a wry chuckle when I imagined the hell that Nurarihyon had waiting for him.

Suddenly, I remembered my other duty. It was now time for my job for the bookstore.

"Oh, by the way, I have a book from Shinonome-san for you," I said. I produced *The Records of Tango Province* from my bag and examined the cover, checking that it was in good condition. I mentally ran through the script I'd prepared and took a deep breath.

You can do it, me! You got this! I thought, trying to muster up some courage. It was time to pull up my bootstraps and get to work!

"Oh, that book isn't for me. I didn't order it," Karaito Gozen said.

"What?" I blurted as I felt my jaw drop. The wind had been taken completely out of my sails, and I must have looked so foolish.

The woman covered her lips with her fan and smiled. "You see, there is someone here who is dying to read a book from the surface, so I took it upon myself to request it for them. I apologize for the misunderstanding. I shall tell them to come and collect it."

"O-oh, okay," I mumbled, my shoulders sagging as my enthusiasm was shattered.

Sensing my obvious disappointment, Karaito Gozen let out an exasperated sigh. "Come on, no sulking. Now, how about a nice walk around the Dragon Palace while you still have some time?"

She pointed at Suimei. "And you too!"

"Me?!" The boy jumped at the unexpected attention.

"Don't tell me you are the type of man to leave a woman to fend for herself in an unfamiliar place," Karaito Gozen said accusingly.

"No, I..."

"There are a lot of fine gentlemen here in the Dragon Palace, you know," she warned him. "They're also very interested in women from the surface. If you're not careful, you might find the one you hold dear whisked away."

"Wh...?!" Suimei choked, his eyes zipping about.

Karaito Gozen grinned at us and hid behind her cypress fan. "Don't worry, you won't have to wait too long to finish your job. However, do feel free to take in the sights of our lovely utopia here in the meantime."

It didn't seem like she was going to take no for an answer, so we set off to explore what the Dragon Palace had to offer.

We exited the resplendent building and found ourselves in a tidy, Chinese-style garden in the courtyard, complete with a bridge and a pond even though we were underwater. A dense cluster of seaweed was growing on the side, and it tickled our arms as we walked past.

I exhaled a sigh that rattled in my throat. In any other situation, I would be ecstatic to walk through the Dragon Palace, but now my heart just wasn't in it. I crouched down and ran my hand along the seaweed. *What a fabulous specimen of kelp.* No doubt it would be delicious dried or turned into a soup, or even shredded and stewed with some meat and vegetables. Did the denizens of the Dragon Palace eat this every day? If they did, they'd probably never have to deal with constipation.

"You're thinking about something weird again, aren't you?" Suimei said.

"Ack!" I winced, looking up at the amused voice coming from above me. Suimei seemed a little troubled as he offered his hand to me. I took it, and he pulled me up.

"Sorry, I was just...thinking about stuff," I said.

"Well, I don't think anyone would blame you. No one likes having to hit the brakes after spending so much time getting ready for something," he comforted me.

How was it that he always seemed to know me better than I knew myself?

"I got excited because it was my chance to represent

Shinonome-san, you know?" I sighed. "I put a lot of thought into researching what to say, especially because the book was so deeply linked to this place."

Just my luck that the one who ordered the book was someone else! I felt like a bucket of icy water had been poured over me while the engine was running and I was about to hit the gas. Anyone's mood would crash from that, right?

Suimei furrowed his brows. "How is it linked? Did they write about the Dragon Palace in that book or something?"

"Well, not exactly," I replied. "It wasn't *the* Dragon Palace, but it wasn't *not* the Dragon Palace either."

"Wait, what? What's going on?" the mermaid butcher cried as he suddenly slid into the conversation. He'd apparently gone exploring by himself, but now he was back with shells and starfish in his arms.

I raised an eyebrow at him. "Uh, what are you going to do with all that? Don't tell me you're taking them with you."

"I am! They're souvenirs for my wife!"

"At least leave the living creatures alone. I feel so bad for that starfish," I sighed.

"Aww..." the butcher puffed his cheeks out in a pout and reluctantly let the starfish go. It made its way to the waving kelp, where its bright red body seemed to splash on like a splotch of paint.

The butcher turned back to us. "Oh, well, there it goes. Anyway, let me know more about what you said just now! It sounds really interesting. Hey, have you read *The Records of Tango Province* before? Tell me more about it!"

"Uh..." I muttered.

"C'mon, I'll give you a shell," he offered. "Here, I've got an abalone! Did you know that their colors change on the inside?"

"I'll pass," I declined.

I glanced at Suimei, trying to distract myself from the childish mermaid butcher. Suimei was massaging his temples with a stormy look on his face, but he made no move to stop the conversation.

Oh well. What's the harm?

I decided to share what I knew. We still had time to kill before Karaito Gozen was ready, anyway.

"All right. Story time then, I guess. Ahem!" I cleared my throat before continuing. "There are a few variations, but *The Records of Tango Province* contained the original story that *Urashima Taro* was based on."

"Wait, it was based on something else?"

I nodded. "Yeah, *Urashima Taro* was transformed through the ages into what it is now. The version that we know of today, where he saves a turtle and is taken to the Dragon Palace, is actually a relatively recent one. *The Records of Tango Province*, *The Chronicles of Japan*, and *Manyoshu* all contained earlier versions of *Urashima Taro*. Although the original copy of *Tango Province* was lost long ago, it still exists in other literature that referenced it."

As I lifted the book out of my bag, a small school of fish gathered above its cover as if they, too, were curious. This volume had been compiled by gathering the bits of writing that still existed in other texts.

"The general story of a young man being invited somewhere

only to find out that hundreds of years had passed upon his return is the same, but the name 'Urashima Taro' only started being used during the 15th century. Before that, the protagonist was one Ura-no-Shimako. And *The Records of Tango Province* also included a Ura-no-Shimako of Mizunoe, who supposedly lived in Tsutsukawamura and was the ancestor of Kusakabe-no-Obito."

"Ancestor?" Suimei tilted his head. "You make him sound like he was real."

I nodded enthusiastically. "Well, that's exactly it! *The Records of Tango Province* did treat Ura-no-Shimako like a real person. *The Chronicles of Japan* and *Manyoshu* did as well. The 'Records' in the title isn't just for show; this book really did record the history of the Tango Province. It wasn't a book for made-up stories. And, you know, *The Chronicles of Japan* was a history book too."

"Isn't that a bit much, though?" Suimei said. "I mean, can you imagine living there and then someone who lived hundreds of years ago suddenly turning up? That's ridiculous."

"You're not wrong there," I said. "However, in China, there used to be a time period where stories of the weird and wonderful called *zhiguai* were classified as historical texts. The story of Urashima Taro might seem like fantasy to us, but that might not have been the case for people back in the day. Perhaps that was why this story was written down as a record of history. Isn't it fascinating how different people will have different interpretations of reality?"

During the modern age, if anyone tried to claim that they had lived three hundred years in the past, they would most certainly be laughed at. While technology and science have granted us precious knowledge, perhaps we could also say that a good number of us have become overly reliant on them to answer all of our questions and that many of us have been robbed of our imaginations in the process.

A dark shadow passed over us, and I looked up to see a sea turtle flying up above. There was no sign of Urashima Taro on top of its shell no matter how hard I looked, but even so, the Dragon Palace that he visited was real. So would it really be strange that he, too, had existed once upon a time?

However, I digress.

"Anyway, back to our main topic. So, Urashima Taro was actually someone called Ura-no-Shimako. Rather than helping a turtle, he caught it on his fishing line. The place he visited wasn't the Dragon Palace but Mount Horai. The princess he met was Kamehime rather than Otohime, and she gave him not a treasure box but a jeweled comb box. And when he opened it, he didn't turn into an old man or a crane. Anyway, that's how the original went. Later texts then introduced different variations that featured Urashima Taro instead of Ura-no-Shimako."

This was what I found so fascinating about *Urashima Taro*. It had been shaped and molded by the influences of Taoism, societal changes, and the medium it was published in. There were various theories surrounding its origins, but its appearance in a historical record that did not allow fanciful fiction was what made it all the more curious.

"Do you remember the titles of the books Shinonome-san mentioned before we left?" I asked.

The mermaid butcher cried out "Ahh!" as he struck his palm with a fist.

"He said he lent out *The Chronicles of Japan* and *Manyoshu* too, right? There were a bunch of others that I can't remember, but wait...did they all have something to do with *Urashima Taro*?"

"Correct!" I said. "The others were *Reflections on Ancient Matters, The Water Mirror,* and *Otogi Bunko.* Although they were published in different times, they all included *Urashima Taro.* I figured whoever borrowed them must have loved this story, so I studied up on it a lot."

Since the client loved the story enough to read all the books related to it, I knew that I'd need to equip myself with the right knowledge if I wanted to serve them properly. The flames of motivation had been lit within me, and I also looked forward to getting into a friendly argument about it. It would've been such fun! I'd been ecstatic to take on such a rewarding job, but fate had other plans for me.

"I guess this is where it ends, though," I sighed. "I couldn't even give the book to the client like I wanted to."

My shoulders dropped. I'd never ever had a job where I couldn't even meet the client.

"Ugh! I guess this is what I deserve for getting my hopes up and thinking I could meet Otohime-sama. Serves me right," I groaned.

The mermaid butcher cocked his head. "Hmm. Otohime-sama, huh? I looked all over the place, but I couldn't find her at all."

His words took me off guard. I blinked at him in amazement.

"You actually went and looked for her? Why?" I asked.

"'Cause I wanted to see her, duh. Otohime's the Kamehime in *The Records of Tango Province*, isn't she?" the butcher replied.

"Wait, you've read that book?" I gasped. I hadn't expected this, either.

The butcher gave me a casual nod. "Yeah, of course! I mean, it *is* about me. I'm Ura-no-Shimako."

"Uh..."

My mouth opened and closed like it belonged to a fish as my brain struggled to find the words.

"You're WHAAAAAAT?!" I screeched. I must have sounded completely off my rocker.

The mermaid butcher frowned. "Jeez, was that really necessary? You even said yourself that Ura-no-Shimako was a real person, didn't you?"

"Y-y-y-yeah, but...but...I didn't expect him to *actually* be here right in front of me!" I stammered. "Oh my God. You're serious? You're really Ura-no-Shimako of Mizunoe from Tsutsukawamura?"

I swooped behind Suimei, using him as a shield to hide myself. As I cowered, the mermaid butcher's face was blocked from my view.

"What are you doing? Why are you hiding?" Suimei sighed.

"Because... Because the main character of the story I was just talking about is *right here*!" I cried. "I'm nervous, okay?!"

The boy only stared dumbfoundedly at my behavior, but could you blame me? Getting to meet someone from a story I loved was like running into a celebrity in the middle of town. Of course I wasn't going to have it completely together!

The butcher shrugged. "I stopped calling myself Ura-no-Shimako when I found out that none of my loved ones were left in my hometown, though. As I wandered around the human world, I was really shocked to find out how much my story had changed. I've always thought it was super interesting!"

Despite his cheerful words, his face became overcast with darkness.

"Kaori-kun? Since you've read *The Records of Tango Province*, you know that the place I went to with Kamehime wasn't the Dragon Palace, right?"

"Y-yeah," I responded. "It was Mount Horai."

According to legend, Mount Horai was a divine realm where immortal transcendent beings lived. It was said to be found on the back of a gigantic turtle called the Reiki, or spirit turtle, that swam in the Bohai Sea.

The mermaid butcher continued. "This Dragon Palace isn't the place I was brought to, but they're both in the middle of the sea and related to the Urashima Taro legend, so I thought I might have a chance at finding her here."

"You mean your wife? I'm guessing she's Kamehime," I said.

"Yeah," he nodded. "She's the most beautiful woman ever to have lived in this world, and I'm proud to call her my wife. I've been searching for her all this time."

He looked down at the souvenirs that he was cradling in his arms with kind, gentle eyes.

"Before I left Mount Horai, I was told that I might never see her again, but I was just so desperate to return home. I was such a fool. I should have prioritized my darling wife who was right beside me over the parents and homeland I had gone so far away from. And I just had to go and open that jeweled comb box... My relationship with Kamehime might not have been torn apart if I hadn't done that. But that's all right, because I have all the time in the world to find her. I know that I'll see her again someday, and I'm sure she's waiting for me too!"

"Is that why you think eternal life is a good thing?" I asked.

"Yeah! It gives me a chance to redo my mistake," he said.

The biggest mistake made by Ura-no-Shimako would have to be his opening of the jeweled comb box, or treasure box in Urashima Taro's version. In *The Records of Tango Province*, he didn't turn into an old man or a crane but was instead sent somewhere far away. The story ends with him and his wife never meeting again.

He rummaged through his pocket and produced the popin again.

"People often say 'you only live once' and 'there are no do-overs in life,' right? Well, that's certainly true for most people, but I can redo things as many times as I want. I truly believe that immortality will lead me to my happiness, so I'm going to keep at it! As long as I have eternity on my side, I know that I will be able to find my wife."

He blew into the glass toy, and it made that goofy *pop po-pop* sound again.

"Heh heh, I can't wait to see her. I just know that she's going to think this sound is the most hilarious thing ever!" he giggled.

Now I finally got why he was so obsessed with immortality. It was because the happiness he sought and the most precious person to him in the world were both tied to it. He was so insistent on sharing it with everyone else because it had such a powerful influence over his own life.

Although he could go overboard with his approach, he was still a kind soul at heart.

"I hope you can see Kamehime again," I said.

"Yeah! Thanks!" he grinned, pure as a child.

I switched the topic back to *The Records of Tango Province* to hide the mixed feelings brewing inside of me.

"I really love the poems at the end of the book. The first time I read them, I got goosebumps from the beautiful choice of words! Even though they're so melancholic, you can still tell that they're filled with love. I thought it was the perfect way to finish the story."

"Um, what are you talking about?" the mermaid butcher cocked his head.

Did I say something weird? I thought as I flipped to the back of the book and opened to the five poems at the end of the story. The butcher stared intently at them and knitted his brows.

"So when I came back from Mount Horai, they asked me a whole bunch of things, and the story that ended up in *The Records of Tango Province* was based on my answers. I didn't mention any poems, though. Kamehime and I did write some to each other, but I don't remember any of this."

I blinked, stunned, as the mermaid butcher chattered fondly about what a fantastic poet Kamehime was.

"But... But what about the poems in the book...?" I babbled.

I looked down at the volume again. Come to think of it, I had heard somewhere that the poems at the end were a later addition. It would make sense for the mermaid butcher not to know about them, then. However, the feelings expressed by the poems just seemed so genuine and raw. There had to be a bigger story lurking behind the curtain.

Who added the poems, then? I wondered while I watched the immortal man play with the popin. As I released a sigh and spun around absentmindedly, I spotted a woman standing on the bridge that arched across the pond.

It seemed to be Roshi. When our eyes met, she turned and ran.

"Oh, wait!" I cried. I chased after her, driven by some indescribable impulse.

"Kaori!" Suimei shouted after me.

"Huh? Where are you going?" the mermaid butcher yelled.

As worried as they sounded, and as much as I would've loved to give them an explanation, I couldn't stop my legs now that they were moving...especially because it looked like Roshi was crying.

I just ran and ran and ran, fueled by a growing hunch.

"Roshi!"

By the time I caught up to the woman, we found ourselves in a drafty hallway in the Dragon Palace. Fish of emerald green, red, yellow, and a plethora of other colors swam between the crimson rounded beams standing around us.

"Are you all right?" I asked.

Hearing my question, Roshi sniffed.

"I wish you would save your energy and leave me alone," she said.

"I'm... I'm sorry. I just felt like I couldn't leave you alone," I apologized, flustered. Now that I was thinking more clearly, I could see that it was pretty rude of me to chase after Roshi, especially since we were practically strangers.

Ugh, I messed up, I thought.

But despite my regret, Roshi was smiling slightly to herself.

"Don't say that, now. I feel so guilty for making you feel that way," she said as she turned to face me. Her eyes were red and puffy, a clear sign that she had indeed been crying.

"Did something upset you?" I asked, offering a handkerchief.

That kind of question is okay for breaking the ice, right?

Roshi accepted the handkerchief and shook her head.

"I've been feeling upset for the last thousand years or so," she admitted.

"You seemed to be enjoying yourself when you were talking with the mermaid butcher, though," I pointed out.

She giggled. "I suppose I was. But you are the same, are you not?"

"Me?" I asked. "What do you mean?"

"Don't you also find yourself smiling when you're talking to someone you love from the bottom of your heart, especially if it has been so many years since you last saw them?"

I knew it!

I took a deep breath as I realized with utter certainty who Roshi really was. I was fairly sure she was also the one who'd been borrowing books through Karaito Gozen.

I tried to steady my racing heart as best as I could.

It was time for me to get to work as an employee of the spirit realm's only bookstore.

I dug around in my bag and produced the book Shinonome-san had given to me.

"Thank you for your patronage. Could you please confirm that this is the book you requested?"

Roshi's lips relaxed as she traced a finger along the cover of *The Records of Tango Province.*

"It is, thank you. I've been wanting to read this for a very, very long time," she said.

She held it close to her chest, displaying the same affection she would embrace a loved one with. Her expression was so tender that I wanted to look away and give her some privacy. As I let my eyes wander around the scenery, I gulped and decided to ask the question that was on my mind.

"Why did you want to borrow this book? I mean, you're in it... right, Kamehime?"

Roshi's expression stiffened, and a troubled look appeared in her eyes. She squeezed the book tighter and furrowed her brows as her face gave way to pain.

"Why do you think that I am Kamehime?" she asked.

"Simple," I began. "From the very beginning, I noticed that you had an unusual interest in the mermaid butcher. Your emotions sprung to life with his every word; when you were happy you were really happy, and when you were sad you were really sad. You acted like a young maiden in love around him. But what stood out to me the most was when you made tea for him."

The kind of tea Roshi had prepared was not a type the average Japanese person would know how to drink. Until she explained it to me, I couldn't even imagine how to go about it. However, the mermaid butcher showed no sign of hesitation. Even though he was too poor to even afford a single popin, he was somehow extremely familiar with this Chinese style of drinking tea.

"Which led me to think that he was used to drinking the tea you made. If he'd been able to drink it frequently, then you two might have been fairly close."

Roshi blinked a few times when I finished telling her my theory.

"A popin..." she whispered and let out a chuckle. Then she gazed directly at me and nodded. "Jeez, he hasn't changed a single bit! You are correct; I am Kamehime."

She apologized for giving me a fake name and explained that she had borrowed it from a classic work of Chinese literature in which the Roshi character was a dragon girl. When I laughed and said I wasn't bothered at all, she seemed visibly relieved. Now that she was more relaxed, I thought this might be a good opportunity to ask her a few more questions.

"Um, can I ask you something?"

"What is it?" she replied.

"If the story of you and the mermaid butcher is like it's described in *The Records of Tango Province*, you must have been on good terms, right? So why did you both pretend to not know each other when you met again?" I asked. "He even went so far as to say that Kamehime wasn't here. I think that was a bit mean."

Kamehime hung her head sadly. "I don't really wish to speak about this, but... How can I explain..."

She took a deep breath and raised her head as if she had steeled herself for what was to come.

"He doesn't recognize me," she said.

"Huh? What do you mean?"

"The jeweled comb box prevents the person who opens it from being able to recognize the one they love the most," she explained.

"Wait, but you two were just talking, so..."

She nodded. "Yes. I suspect that he thought I was merely one of the many court ladies here."

I stared with stunned, wide eyes. So he couldn't recognize the woman he loved the most, even if she were right in front of him?

"That can't be true," I gasped in denial. "He's been searching for you for so long."

"I am aware of that."

"He even gathered all these souvenirs that he wanted to give you. He's devoted himself to spreading the justice he believes in so he could become a husband for you to be proud of..." I babbled.

"Yes...I know," Kamehime said.

"He's always going on about how immortality is his lifeline and how it's given him a second chance."

The woman fell silent.

"And yet...you two really can't see each other again? Ever?"

Kamehime's face crumpled, and large, pearly drops began to fall from her eyes. She made no move to wipe them away.

"This eternity is a punishment," she whispered, her lip trembling.

"And not a lifeline like the mermaid butcher says?"

"No! Far from it!" Kamehime gasped. "It is like a chain wrapped tightly around him. His love is deeper than the ocean, so I know that he will continue to search for me endlessly with his unlimited life span as his crutch."

Which meant that the mermaid butcher would search for someone he'd never even be able to see, forever and ever...

That was just too cruel!

I felt like my heart had been ripped to shreds. The more devoted and earnest he was, the tighter he would be bound by these chains, and he wouldn't even realize how stuck he was. In fact, he was even thankful for being caught in this web!

He thought immortality had given him a chance to redo his mistake, but this situation was more like dangling food in front of a starving man and never letting him eat. It was so heartbreaking.

Rage bubbled within me as the mermaid butcher's smile flashed across my mind. His perseverance had already driven him to search for Kamehime for more than a millennium. He had the option of calling it quits and starting a new life with a new love, but it was precisely because he was immortal that he never gave up—he thought that he had a silver lining to look forward to.

"Did you try telling him who you were?" I asked.

"Of course I did!" she cried. "But he just got mad because he thought I was trying to pose as his wife."

"Um, maybe you could get someone else to help convince him?"

Kamehime shook her head wordlessly.

"That's awful..." I mumbled.

As I did, Kamehime whispered self-deprecatingly, "This is just a consequence of making the wrong decision."

The mistake of the mermaid butcher—or Ura-no-Shimako—was that he broke his promise to never open the jeweled comb box.

But then what was Kamehime's?

"An immortal like me should never have brought a mortal into my world," she said.

What?

My blood ran cold, and my heart began to beat faster. The heat drained from my fingers, and my body grew chilly. Had the space around me suddenly gotten colder?

No, that wasn't it.

"As denizens of different worlds, we should have never gotten involved with each other," Kamehime sighed. "We shouldn't have stayed together or opened our hearts to each other or loved each other. I've only known suffering since I met him. Our love was wrong from the very beginning."

Her words had sapped all the warmth from my body and my heart. Shinonome-san's face emerged in my mind's eye. My adoptive father had found me and raised me since I was a tiny little girl. Did he ever regret it like Kamehime regretted her love for the mermaid butcher?

I shook my head. This was a ridiculous comparison to make. He wasn't like Kamehime.

"There is nothing left for me but regret," the woman said, closing her eyes in anguish.

I felt sorry for her. It was so a sad, painful, and lonely to have to regret meeting someone. It wasn't normal, but the fact that Kamehime was feeling all these emotions showed just how much her soul had been worn down.

"I actually have something in mind that would let me meet him and have him recognize me," she admitted.

I jolted forward at the unexpected revelation.

"Really?!" I exclaimed.

"Of course. I would not lie about such a thing," she said, her pretty smile hanging beneath a faraway and unfocused look.

"The person he is unable to recognize is not me exactly but the one he loves the most. So all I have to do is make sure he falls in love with someone else."

I was lost for words. Kamehime's love for the mermaid butcher had endured for so many centuries; if this ever happened, reality would surely turn into a living hell for her.

"There's really no way for you two to be happy?" I blurted out impulsively.

The woman scoffed. "If there is, I would certainly like to know it."

A look of defeat settled in her features, like she had given up. Seeing her like this sent a pang through my heart.

"This is all way too harsh, don't you think? I mean, all Ura-no-Shimako did was fumble on a promise and open a box," I muttered without much thought, again.

Kamehime shook her head. "It might seem that way on the surface, but it was a choice that he should have avoided at all costs. Every lifetime comes with its own decisions, and he made the wrong one. That's why he received this punishment. Nothing more, nothing less."

She stroked the cover of the book again. There was an undeniable fatigue clinging to her graceful visage. She hugged it to her chest once more and turned her back to me.

"Thank you again for bringing this to me. I will definitely order more books. If you have any recommendations of modern works, I would be glad to see what they are."

"Oh...sure," was all I could manage.

"Make the right choices, Kaori. There is nothing more soul-crushing than a life of regret," she warned as she slowly began to put distance between us.

"Can I just ask you one more thing?" I called. "When you're reading stories about Urashima Taro, how do they make you feel?"

She stopped and said without turning, "These books are filled with the happy days I spent with him, and they will stay in these pages...for eternity."

Like a storm rushing in, a school of countless fish swooped between Kamehime and me. They flashed emerald, red, yellow, and purple like a violent flood. By the time they were gone, the woman had vanished.

My gaze fell to the ground as I recalled a verse from *The Records of Tango Province*.

"The lady divine, with her sweet voice, sends her sorrows to the air..."

> *Gales from Yamato*
> *Chase through the clouds in the sky*
> *Even as they part*
> *As you once did from my side*
> *I hope you never forget me*

It's a verse that means, "Even if we become separated like the clouds that become scattered by the winds blowing from Japan, please always keep me in your heart."

This poem was not written by the author but added on later by someone else. However, their identity remained unknown.

I frowned and rubbed my arms, trying to alleviate the cold. But no matter how quickly or forcefully I rubbed, not a speck of warmth returned.

I started to make my way back to the guest room, walking lightheadedly through the corridor leading to it. Before I reached the room, I ran into Suimei, who had been looking for me. When he spotted me, his eyes looked like they were about to pop out of his head. I must have looked dreadful.

"Where'd you run off to?!" he cried. "What happened? You look ill."

He whipped off his coat and threw it over my shoulders. I let out the breath I'd been holding as the remnants of his warmth wrapped around me.

"I'm fine. I was just doing my bookstore job," I told him.

"So you met the client?" he asked.

"Yeah. I gave them the book with my own two hands," I said, trying to force a smile.

Suimei frowned. "I see," he nodded.

Even as I was talking to him, my mind couldn't stop playing back my conversation with Kamehime. I could feel her pain like it was my own. I didn't know how I would face the mermaid butcher either, now that I had found out the truth about his situation. How would I even be able to look him in the eye? Just thinking about it made me feel hopeless.

I gripped Suimei's hand, trying to feel less alone. Finding my silence strange, Suimei widened his eyes and allowed his gaze to drift over me.

Finally, he whispered, "I'll always be here for you."

"Huh?"

"You'll always have me. Don't ever forget that, no matter what happens," he said.

There was something off about his reassurance. Sure, I'd been acting quiet and dejected since my return, but did it warrant such a drastic declaration?

"I should be asking you what happened," I said. "Are you okay?"

He flicked his light brown eyes away. I could tell that behind them, he was thinking about something else.

"Nothing," was all he said.

He made eye contact again. "I'm just...worried about you."

Did he just lie to me?

Suimei's tell was that he'd avoid eye contact whenever he lied. I squeezed his hand, trying to suppress the anxiety bubbling within me like a spring.

Why is everyone so worried about me? I wondered.

Now that I thought about it, a lot of people seemed to be paying more care than usual to me. Toochika-san tried to be encouraging while I was working at his store, Nurarihyon was being a lot nicer, and Karaito Gozen had acted like an overprotective mother. It was all very strange. I was no child, but they had all insisted on telling me to do my best and not give up. They were doing everything they could to support me and say everything was going to be okay.

"You know, when there's a big turning point in your life that will affect your whole future, like starting a new school, getting married,

a new job, deaths, illnesses, and whatnot. Not everyone has the same life events, but they're all unavoidable."

Toochika-san's mention of life events, the hurdles that everyone would have to overcome at different points in their lives, popped into my head.

I'd originally thought everyone was just worried about me having to take over the bookstore, but what if that wasn't the real reason?

Suddenly, an argument broke the silence.

"Enough, I said! You are getting in the way of my work!"

"Awww, c'mon! Throw me a bone here!"

"I do not have the time to concern myself with you when I have to deliver this!"

The shouting came from the room where I'd found Suimei and the mermaid butcher, and it sounded like Karaito Gozen and the immortal man. Karaito Gozen appeared to be finished with her preparations too.

Suimei and I exchanged glances and moved to enter the room until I heard "Hey, c'mon, tell me how much time Shinonome has left."

I froze in my tracks, shocked.

Suimei tightened a fist. Karaito Gozen seemed to have missed our presence as she waved her arms at the mermaid butcher, trying to shoo him away like a bug.

"Stop pestering me! I do not, and cannot, know a specific time frame! It's nothing out of the ordinary for a broken Tsukumogami to weaken over time like a deflated balloon. Do not ask me how much time he has left! I am not a human doc—"

"How much time he has left? What?" I whispered as my world spun into a sickening vertigo.

I let go of Suimei's hand and swayed toward the woman with shaky steps. Finally realizing that I was here, she picked up a long, slender box made of paulownia wood. While I was in my dazed state, she faced me and opened her mouth like she had overcome a difficult decision.

"Um, Kaori-san..."

"What's this about the time he has left?" I said with a flat poise that surprised even myself. Everything around me was trembling. Maybe an earthquake had struck? But everyone looked so calm. Why? Why did they look so calm?

Karaito Gozen's eyes wandered, not knowing where to look. She then decided to place the box on the table and open it to show me the scroll lying within.

"Take a look," she said as she unfurled it.

I saw an ink painting of a dragon flying through the sky. It had been torn in half and burned in a previous incident, but now it had been repaired beautifully...that is, the decorative parts such as the fabric and the border around it, anyway. The drawing itself remained so heavily burned that no viewer could tell what had been depicted in the bottom half.

"I thought...you said you finished fixing it," I mumbled and turned to her stiffly, staring at her with an unbroken gaze.

Karaito Gozen closed her eyes like she had been struck. "I've done everything I can. Please return this to Shinonome."

"But... But this..." I reached a quivering hand out toward her and wrapped it around her skinny wrist, shaking it. This scroll was far from fixed. It wasn't meant to be like this. Shinonome-san's main body was supposed to be a much more beautiful thing.

"Please fix it again," I begged, words forming a stinging lump in my throat. My thoughts felt like they had been thrown into a blender. "Fix Shinonome-san."

In that moment, I caught a glance of Karaito Gozen's hand. It was tiny, much smaller than mine, but it was covered in marks and toughened skin. It had a distinct, bony definition to it, and her nails were also darkened by ink. It was the hand of a true artisan, one that could only be shaped through long, countless hours of work.

A single "Oh..." dropped from my mouth as despair started to take hold. The strength evaporated from my body, and I fell into a sitting position. Whatever had been in my head was now replaced by a static white, and I was unable to even think of the next step.

"Look at the poor girl! I knew she wouldn't take the news very well. That's why I offered to tell her instead!"

The mermaid butcher placed his arm around my shoulders and looked intently at me, with a grin.

"So now do you know why I wanted to come to Aomori with you? It's because I needed your help with some persuading!"

"Per...suading...?" I muttered.

"Yeah!" he exclaimed. "I'm not a good talker, so I couldn't persuade Shinonome. I figured if I had his daughter's help, I might be able to present a good case for him to eat mermaid meat, since he is sort of reaching the end of his life and all."

His green eyes glinted with a bewitching flash, a poisonous green that made me think of a bottomless swamp that you could never escape after you stepped into it.

"It'd be so, so much of a tragedy for him to leave behind his most beloved and adorable little daughter!" the mermaid butcher cried. "He wouldn't have to worry about it if he became immortal, and you wouldn't have to think about saying goodbye to him either. You'd be able to stay with your wonderful adoptive father forever! Everyone's happy this way, right?"

"Stop it!" Suimei shouted.

"Whoa!" the mermaid butcher cried as the boy shoved him away. Suimei pulled me into his arms and glared at the man.

"Leave Shinonome and Kaori alone. It's their business, not yours," he spat.

"What's your problem?!" the butcher whined. "I don't see anything wrong with it. Besides, Shinonome wouldn't even have listened to me in the first place if he weren't at least a little bit interested in the idea!"

His face suddenly bunched up as if he had realized something, and he slowly reached into his pocket. He pulled out what was left of the popin, now reduced to scraps of glass.

"Aw, man! It broke!" he sighed. "This thing is so brittle."

I continued to shiver in Suimei's arms. I felt like I was freezing while my brain scrabbled desperately to make sense of what I had heard. Shinonome-san knew the mermaid butcher because

he'd been approached and offered the chance to become immortal. The butcher only showed himself to spirits who were
desperate—so desperate that their problems could only be fixed
with immortality.

Which meant that Shinonome-san knew that he didn't have
much time left. What kind of emotions were running through his
head as he spoke about retiring?

"Suimei," I mumbled, looking up into his light brown eyes.
Come to think of it, he'd been spending an awful lot of time with
Shinonome-san lately. He most likely knew what was going on.
Toochika-san probably also knew about the mermaid butcher
through Shinonome-san, who most likely would have told his
best friend about the situation for business purposes at the very
least. Even Nurarihyon, the supreme commander of all spirits.
Everyone... *Everyone* knew that Shinonome-san's clock was
ticking.

"Suimei..."

Everyone except me. His daughter. I was the only one who'd
been left in the dark.

"Sui...mei..."

All of their kindness stung like thorns.

I couldn't breathe. The world blurred into a haze. My eyes
were seared by hot tears threatening to overflow like magma.
I shook my head, trying to clear this suffocating feeling away, and
caught sight of the mermaid butcher. Seeing the popin as it lay
broken in his hands made my chest squeeze painfully. One of the
two goldfish that had been swimming on its surface had been

crushed into bits, and like the rest of the popin, it could never be returned to its former glory.

This toy of thin glass, along with all the love that it harbored, had been destroyed.

"Kaori," Suimei murmured as he swept me into a tight hug.

"It's going to be okay. I'll always be here for you," he whispered over and over. "No matter what happens, you'll have me. Please, please don't forget that I'm here. Please always remember that, no matter what."

❧✦❧

When I returned to the bookstore, my mind was still dazed. It was already deep into the hours of the night, and the entire town in the spirit realm was deathly quiet, save for the occasional haunting bird cry that pierced through the silence. But the bookstore was lit, its windows glowing with a soft, warm-toned light.

I found my adoptive father writing in his room. He didn't seem to have realized that I'd come in.

"Shinonome-san," I said and knelt down, resting my forehead against his broad back.

His brush paused.

"You're back," he said.

It was rare for him to react to me while he wrote. He laid his brush down and asked, "What's wrong?"

He tried to turn around but stopped when I threw my arms around him. I didn't want him to look at me right now, even

though he was my adoptive father, because my face was an absolute mess.

"Are you really going to die?" I moaned.

"Ah..." Shinonome-san sighed. He scratched his head and faltered for a moment before saying in his usual tone, "Yeah, I guess."

I squeezed him even tighter. I wanted him to say no. I wanted
this all to be some sick joke that everyone was in on. I could feel
my heart sinking faster and faster with every second.

"Are you going to eat the mermaid meat?" I asked, unable to
stop my voice from trembling.

Consciously, I knew that mermaid meat was like the for-
bidden fruit, something we should never allow ourselves to eat.
However, there was also another side of me trying to find a way
for my beloved adoptive father to be the exception.

"No," Shinonome-san said. Unlike my indecisive thoughts, his
answer was loud and clear. "If this is how my life plays out, I don't
see any reason to struggle against it. Things break eventually, you
know?"

His logic made sense, but I was not in a state to accept logic.

"No..." I whimpered.

Shinonome-san's shoulders shook as he laughed.

"Silly girl," he chuckled. He seemed to have already resigned
himself to his fate.

I felt the heat tingling in my eyes again and squeezed them
shut tightly as my vision began to shake once more.

Shinonome-san was going to die. The man who took me in
and raised me was going to take his last breath soon.

I heard something snap in my head, like the world was cracking apart. I couldn't even begin to imagine what it would be like without my adoptive father around.

A Question of Authenticity

IN THE SPIRIT REALM, the town always sprang to life when autumn arrived. All the spirits would come out and shop for the coming winter, and the streets would become lined with stalls and carts. There was a young oni looking pleased with itself, licking away at a lollipop during this rare trip into town, and a pensive mother worrying over whether she had bought everything she needed. The other spirits that milled about all looked pleased, having satisfied their shopping urges.

This kind of hustle and bustle, where the spirits were living to their fullest, could only be seen in the short window of time before the harsh winter hit, the same as it was hundreds of years ago.

Their cheer could be heard all the way inside the bookstore, but unlike the outside, the interior was silent and still. At the front of a shop hung a notice of temporary closure, and its door showed no sign of opening.

This was the first time in the bookstore's entire history that it had ever been forced to close for multiple days in a row. Kaori had shut herself inside her room ever since she returned from the Dragon Palace, and Shinonome's declining health and life span meant that he was in no state to serve any customers, even with the medication he was taking.

"Jeez, no wonder Kaori just wants to lie around in her room," a voice grumbled.

It was Noname, who was coming down the stairs from the second floor. At first glance, she looked like a beautiful woman, a far cry from the man she used to be—the auspicious beast from China called Hakutaku. As Kaori's mother figure, she had tried to ask her daughter to leave her room again today, but to no avail. Noname had left in disappointment and was now giving a grumpy frown to Shinonome, who was smoking his pipe beside the brazier.

"You should have just told her the truth straight-out! Why did you leave it so long that she found out from someone else?" Noname complained.

The Tsukumogami rubbed his head and pouted, "I couldn't think of a good way to tell her."

Noname's eyebrow shot up. "You're good for everything until you turn into a coward like this! You couldn't spare any of your usual pompousness for this? Look at what poor Kaori's been reduced to. You're stupid, stupid, stupid!"

"Stop calling me stupid so much. You're going to make me even sadder," Shinonome protested with a weary groan.

"You deserve it," Noname huffed and turned the other way. "When did you realize that things were going south, anyway?"

Shinonome had told Noname how little time he had left even later than Kaori, and she seemed to resent him for it.

"A little while before the mess with Hakuzosu, I think," he said. "I could feel that I was getting weaker. Just when I was thinking that something was up, Karaito Gozen told me she might not be able to fix my main body."

"Why didn't you tell us about it then?!" Noname cried.

"Karaito Gozen promised me that she wasn't going to give up without a fight, so I still had a little bit of hope left," the Tsukumogami pointed out. "Well, I guess it didn't end up working out, though."

She'd only recently been given the final word on his condition. The only ones who knew from the very start were Tamaki and Toochika; aside from them, Shinonome had been very selective with whom he'd told about his situation.

He scratched his head as Noname glowered at him with watery eyes. She had shared a lot of blood, sweat, and tears raising Kaori together with him, so she'd arguably spent even more time with him than his two best friends. No one could blame her if she felt betrayed—that was how deep Noname and Shinonome's connection was.

"I'm sorry for not telling you sooner," Shinonome apologized, "but you're not the best at keeping secrets. Knowing how much time you spend with Kaori, she would've been sure to see through you right away."

He'd wanted to avoid shocking Kaori at all costs.

"Maybe so, but I wish you would've told me anyway. I thought you trusted me," Noname said, her head drooping. Tears started to fall, drop by drop.

Shinonome sighed. *Dammit, I didn't mean it like that,* he thought. Of course, keeping this secret from Kaori had been a huge consideration, but more than that, he'd delayed telling Noname the truth because he had faith that she would accept the news no matter how it was revealed to her.

He opened his mouth but closed it immediately. He wanted to give Noname a full explanation, but he suddenly felt embarrassed at praising her like this. Besides, he didn't trust himself to find the right words to convey how he truly felt.

So, in the end, he remained silent, inarticulate as always.

Meanwhile, Noname continued to cry and sniffle. Shinonome was at a loss, unable to stop the situation from worsening. He tapped the ash from his pipe into the brazier, trying to distract from the frustration in the air. As he reached for his tobacco pouch, he came face-to-face with a pair of red eyes, like two giant pomegranate seeds.

"Shi...Shinonomeee..."

It was Kuro. His little legs pitter-pattered, and he settled in the Tsukumogami's lap, whining as he looked up with his big, shiny eyes.

"Are you sick? Maybe I can give you some of my partner's medicine. I'm sure that'll help!" he offered.

Shinonome smiled at the dog and ruffled his head.

"No, it's all right," he said. "I wish I could solve this with medicine, but I can't."

Kuro whimpered. "So are you really gonna die?"

"I will eventually, but it's not like I'm going to kick the bucket right this minute," the man said. "Save your tears for later, okay?"

"B-but..." the dog paused before he whispered, "That's what Midori...Suimei's mom also said."

His ears flopped downward, and Shinonome gave him a bitter smile.

"Oh," he said gently. "I'm sorry if that brought back some bad memories."

Kuro's tailed wagged around in reply. Then, someone came and placed a cup containing a medicinal brew on the small table Shinonome was sitting at. A sour, bitter scent drifted from the vessel, and Shinonome flinched with a small groan. It helped with the pain, but he couldn't stand the taste of it.

"It might not help you live longer, but make sure you drink it," said the white-haired boy who'd brought it. "None of us can handle you moaning in pain."

He then shot a stern look at Noname.

"I know you're feeling anxious, but there's no point in taking it out on Shinonome. Kaori's suffering more than anyone here," he said.

"Suimei..." Noname whispered, looking back at him in surprise. The boy placed another teacup in front of her, this one filled with green tea.

"The black cat will take care of Kaori. Instead of making things more awkward by worrying too much, let's find something more helpful to do. You're usually a lot more levelheaded than this, Noname."

The boy took his seat beside Shinonome and continued to look intently at the crying spirit.

"Even if you're not connected to Kaori by blood, you're still her mother, right? And as a mother, you should be thinking about your daughter's future, not picking fights. What good will come from blaming Shinonome for something that can't be changed? What do you hope to achieve by making him apologize? That would only help you, not the situation at hand."

Noname's face flushed. Suimei's firm words had struck a nerve. She wiped her tears with a handkerchief and took a sip of her green tea.

"It's delicious," she smiled gently. The storm that had been clouding her face had vanished in an instant.

"You're right. We need to focus our energies on what's to come. Sorry, I wasn't thinking very clearly," she apologized.

Shinonome blinked, stunned at how quickly Suimei had managed to calm Noname down. As he fixed his gaze on the young man, it dawned on him: He'd grown so much.

Suimei was seventeen years old when he arrived in the spirit realm. He was found lying unconscious in the drizzling rain, surrounded by glimmerflies. Back then, he had closed himself off from the world around him and cursed the unfair life he'd been handed.

But people change, and he had transformed into someone Noname could fully trust, someone whom the customers of the apothecary would specifically ask for. And getting settled in the spirit realm couldn't have been easy for the former exorcist, who used to earn a living by slaying the realm's own denizens.

Shinonome believed Suimei was a capable young man whom he, too, could trust, which was why he'd told Suimei about the dimming of his life's fire earlier than Kaori. He knew the young man could support Kaori and be the help and salvation she needed.

Suimei had proven himself a man to Shinonome.

Two months earlier, a while after the Hakuzosu incident was settled, Suimei came to the bookstore alone. Kaori was out, and when Shinonome asked him what he was there for, he gave a shocking response.

"Kaori has feelings for me."

Shinonome's mind went blank, and he made a strangled croak like a frog that had been stepped on. He balled his fist, ready to punch the boy, but then Suimei folded his legs under himself and sat with his hands on his knees.

While the Tsukumogami was still stunned, Suimei said, "And I like Kaori too, but I'm very aware that I am an exorcist, albeit a former one. My hands are stained with the blood of countless spirits, so I don't expect you to accept me."

He moved his hands to the floor and bowed deeply. "But I feel like I can truly be myself when I'm with Kaori, and that's one thing I will never compromise on. So, I've come here to ask for your forgiveness."

He sounded strained, like he was doing everything he could to fight against his trained, emotionless state and convey what he felt.

Shinonome mulled over Suimei's words, until he finally said, "Just one hit."

He threw his best punch into Suimei's stomach, but it only made him feel worse. There was a part of him that deeply admired Suimei, and he had complicated feelings about the fact that he was hearing this from the young man rather than Kaori herself. But he knew that there was no way she would tell him—she was more than aware of her adoptive father's overprotective streak and knew the potential trouble that would ensue.

Suimei, however, took the risk of seeing Shinonome himself because he wanted to do things the proper way. He had the guts to own up to his personal history and consider how Shinonome would feel, all while defending his desire to stay with Kaori. It must have been harrowing to plan too, and required a lot of courage. How could Shinonome be anything but impressed? He even tried to scare Suimei a little by warning him in a threatening voice to take full responsibility, but the young man shot back "I'm ready for that" without a moment's hesitation.

Cocky little brat, Shinonome laughed to himself.

"You sure I can trust you with Kaori?" he mumbled.

"Of course," Suimei answered with a serious nod.

That night, the Tsukumogami went into town. He had stopped drinking when he noticed that his body wasn't working the way it should, but he just had to have a drink or two after the young man's visit. He needed liquid courage before he could prepare himself to give away a precious...no, *the* most precious thing in his life.

He would remember how the drink tasted on his tongue that night for the rest of his life.

After Karaito Gozen told him that his main body would be impossible to fix, Shinonome decided that he would leave everything—the relationships that he had fostered over the centuries as well as his business—to Suimei and Kaori. He knew that the two had what it took to succeed him. When he settled on this decision, he started asking Suimei to tag along with him whenever the opportunity arose, including the trip to the hidden village. It was partly because he wanted the young man to understand the work, but there was also another reason: Shinonome wanted to show that he was a great father and a committed man. Plus, he secretly wanted to intimidate Suimei and make sure he knew exactly what he was getting himself into.

And because of that, Suimei's conduct had changed. He stood taller when he listened to Shinonome talk. His sense of dedication drove him to ask about anything and everything. Shinonome could only chuckle dryly to himself as he witnessed how eager and capable Suimei was, coming face-to-face with the mixed sentiments stirring inside of him as he watched the boy mature.

As Shinonome let his respect for Suimei sink in, the young man asked, "So, do you really not want eternal life?"

The Tsukumogami laughed, surprised at the young man's no-nonsense approach. He had told Suimei about his remaining time only a short while ago, and this was the exorcist's first question to him. He was smart, so he must have realized this option was on the table the moment the mermaid butcher walked into the picture. He'd probably stayed quiet, though, to give Shinonome the time and space to decide what he wanted for himself.

Suimei stared straight at Shinonome during the silence that followed, emotionless as always when he talked to the spirit. How ironic, considering the boy would go through the whole gamut of emotions when Kaori was present.

He's even more awkward than me. It would've been more interesting if he hadn't realized mermaid meat was an option, Shinonome thought as he stroked his stubble.

Then he declared, "No matter what happens, I will never eat mermaid meat."

A shade of perplexity came over Noname's face as she interjected, "Not even if Kaori wants you to?"

"No," Shinonome shook his head without hesitation.

Suimei's expression grew dark. He let his eyes wander for a few seconds before making eye contact with the Tsukumogami again.

"I'm not completely against immortality like Kaori is," he said. "I believe you should take advantage of what's available to you. There's not much to think about except how important she is to you. If she is precious to you, then you wouldn't want to make her sad, right? Wouldn't you be willing to choose eternal life to keep her happy?"

Shinonome found this surprising, considering that Suimei's own father had obtained immortality by eating mermaid meat. It almost sounded like the young man approved of his father's actions.

Maybe they've made up, at least a little bit, he thought. *Interesting.*

"Kaori is very important to me, yes," the spirit answered. "She's why I wake up every morning. She's my everything. But even so, I have my own way of life. I want to reach my final destination the way I planned it, and let me tell you, it'll be almost impossible to convince me to take another path."

"Final destination?" Suimei repeated, frowning.

Shinonome laughed. "Besides, Kaori's always been afraid of dying first and leaving the rest of us behind. Even if I were perfectly healthy, she'd probably still be scared of death, no matter who it happens to."

Kaori never said it out loud, but she didn't have to. Shinonome was very aware of what bothered his daughter. Even though humans and spirits had some things in common, they were still completely different species. The more they loved each other, the harsher the consequences would be. There was no escaping this inevitable cycle.

Suimei shook his head, his voice becoming tinged with urgency. "Maybe so, but losing your father while you still have so many years ahead of you is worse..."

"But that's normal, you know?" Shinonome interrupted.

Suimei blinked, not knowing what to say, and Shinonome gave him a crooked smile.

"It's normal for parents to die before their children. Kaori and I happened to be outliers, but I guess the current circumstances have brought us back onto that track, huh?" he said.

Suimei frowned. "But..." he started, not wanting to back down.

"Here, I'll help you understand a bit better. Come with me. I figured I'd have to tell you sooner or later anyway," Shinonome beckoned to Suimei and moved from the loungeroom to the store, stopping at the furthest bookshelf.

"Shinonome, are you really going to...?" Noname asked with a troubled look on her face. The Tsukumogami grinned in reply and pulled a single book forward. A dull thud sounded through the room and the bookshelf slid to the side, revealing a staircase that extended underground.

"Isn't this where you keep your main body?" Suimei asked.

Shinonome nodded. "Yeah, at the back of the underground room."

He made a move to step into the pitch blackness of the space, but he suddenly remembered that Suimei was only human and did not have the ability to see through the darkness.

"Noname, I need a..."

As if she had anticipated this, Noname held a glimmerfly lantern out to him.

"Jeez, where would you be without me?" she frowned.

Shinonome's face lit up as he clapped the other spirit on the back. "You always know what I need, my dear old wife!"

"Who are you calling your wife?!" Noname protested. "And stop it, that hurts!"

They continued to squabble as they descended. They headed for a bookshelf that looked particularly important, its shelves packed with volumes that sported the same titles on their spines.

"How many of these do you have?" Suimei gasped as he stood

still, taking in the sight. Anyone would be surprised at the sheer number of them: The work was called *Nanso Satomi Hakkenden*, and it spanned 98 chapters over 106 books.

Shinonome took one of them in his hands and smiled with fond nostalgia.

"These were left here by the founder of this bookstore," he explained.

"What do you mean?" Suimei asked, his light brown eyes glowing in the faint light of the glimmerflies.

Shinonome gave a firm nod and began to reminisce.

"I'll tell you all about how the bookstore and I came to be," he said, "and all the things that made me realize what kind of ending I wanted for myself."

He turned to Suimei, his eyes filled with nothing but serenity.

Shinonome was the Tsukumogami of a hanging scroll that was drawn sometime in the middle of the Edo period, and the artist who created him was said to be Maruyama Okyo.

Maruyama Okyo, beloved by the wealthy, drew heavily from nature and possessed an artistic style that was likable and pleasing to the eyes. His animals were so stunning that they could almost trick the viewer into thinking they were alive. Each one of his strokes was painstakingly laid, and they all came together to build beautiful scenes of creatures living and breathing in classical Japanese scenery.

The dragon depicted in Shinonome's scroll was also breath-taking enough to make any viewer fall in love with it, but it harbored a secret within itself.

Shinonome was created in a dilapidated house in an unknown corner of Edo. On the day he was born, there were two men in the house. One of them, whose thin eyes slanted upward like those of a fox, looked like any other townsperson. But if you examined him more closely, you could see tattoos peeking out from under his sleeves. He tricked people for a living—yes, he was a con artist and clearly not a regular civilian.

The con artist was inspecting two scrolls that had been laid out on the floor. They looked like they could have been clones—the composition, the figure and expression of the dragon, and the gradients in the ink were all identical.

He nodded in satisfaction. "Lookin' great. Anyone would be convinced that it was real!"

Hearing this, the other man, who was sitting on his knees in the room, bowed deeply. Dressed in rags, he had a thin frame and an unkempt beard. The top of his head had been shaved, as was typical of the men in that era, but his hair had begun to grow back roughly, a sign of his neglect in maintenance.

"Oh, thank you!" he gasped. "Um, about the payment..."

"Here. I'll be back again, *sir*!"

Once the man had packed the scrolls away, he threw a pouch filled with coins to the floor, letting the shrill jangling of the currency inside ring out. Kicking aside the brushes that were scattered on the floor, the con artist left. Once the door was closed, the remaining man let out a sigh. He picked the pouch up from the floor and plopped down on a straw mat, knocking back a bottle of alcohol and gulping it down.

This man, who had once studied under Ishida Yutei with Maruyama Okyo as a fellow pupil, was Shinonome's father. His skill as an artist was genuine, and the light of his future had shone brightly until he lost himself to the drink. He drifted and meandered through life until he began resorting to drawing forgeries to cobble together food for the table.

That's right—Shinonome was a forgery, a fake made in imitation of Maruyama Okyo's style.

Things that are treasured and used over a long period of time can change into something that goes beyond their origins. Tsukumogamis, spirits born from old tools or artworks that were imbued with life, are one example. Shinonome's scroll was expertly illustrated with a solid foundation, and it could fool any amateur art appreciator into thinking that it was nothing short of a magnum opus. However, the trained eye of someone like an appraiser could tell that it was not the genuine article, and that was exactly what happened. The scroll remained unsold, gathering dust, and usually a story like this would end with it fading into obscurity. No one would ever keep it as their treasure, and no Tsukumogami would be born.

Shinonome was nothing more than a fake, after all.

But everything changed ten years after the dragon was illustrated.

"This isn't a forgery, it's a scroll that brings forth good fortune," said a con artist trying to give Shinonome a bit of value and get it out of his stock. There was absolutely no proof to this claim, but truth proved stranger than fiction when family after family that welcomed Shinonome into its doors was indeed blessed with good fortune. Wives would find themselves with child after years of infertility, and households would launch their names into distinction, among other joyous happenings.

Of course, this could have all been a chain of coincidences, but no one could say for sure. The only thing that was certain is that Shinonome's value skyrocketed.

Then, the con artists who tried to sell this scroll would begin to claim that past appraisals were wrong and that it had been drawn by Maruyama Okyo's own hand. At the time, his works were all the rage, with the Maruyama school outstripping the Kano school. Everybody wanted Maruyama's work on their walls, and the con artists were eager to squeeze as much money as they could out of Shinonome's scroll.

Shinonome was undeniably a forgery, but that was not what the bribed appraisers said. And, to add to his fortune, the real painting was said to be long lost. But more than that, this streak of good fortune was what solidified his status as a genuine article.

Thus, he had been transformed from fake to real.

The con artists found themselves rolling in money, and the scroll, once doomed to wither away unappreciated, was now treated with even more care than genuine pieces of art. Years and years—about a hundred of them—passed before Shinonome started to gain an inkling of a consciousness.

"Ha! Hah ha ha ha ha! It's finally mine! Now I will be blessed too!" cried a blood-smeared ronin.

At that moment, Shinonome's mind began to crawl into existence.

As the man pulled the artwork to his chest and into his slightly soiled clothes, Shinonome suddenly became aware that he was in a large feudal estate. He had been brought there as a gift for the shogun, but now this man had resorted to stealing the scroll after reaching the ends of both his fortune and his wits.

Shinonome floated about in the air and frowned at the dire sight before him. The tatami was drenched in red. There was a man who appeared to be a servant huddled on the ground and a housemaid bound in rope and trembling.

How could this man have done all this just to steal me? Shinonome fumed. He felt nausea rise within him as he caught the putrid stench of blood in the air. Having just been born, he did not yet have the power for a physical body, so he could only let his consciousness drift about like a ghost. His existence was similar to that of a soul, but he could not establish any mutual communication with anyone. The most he could do was fly around the area near his main body, unable to stray too far.

He was forced to look at what the man had done, whether he liked it or not.

"You did a good job bringing me here. Here, I'll free you in return."

Shinonome had to watch the woman struggle for her life before she was mercilessly slain by the ronin. He also witnessed the man being apprehended, leaving behind his young children. He remembered the empty look in the children's eyes as they clutched their empty stomachs, staring dazed at their thieving father being led away. He saw it all, clear as day.

Some scroll of good fortune I am! he sneered.

It upset him to see people destroy their lives for something so selfish. He was only a fake, but the people around him had branded him a real artwork with divine powers for their own purposes.

I'm a forgery! Stop banking on me to grant your wishes!

Even after the ronin, countless people still sought Shinonome for his luck. Blood would flow and politics would be involved. That was how much people were willing to pay for this scroll of good fortune.

All these people have holes where their eyes should be, Shinonome thought with disdain. *I wasn't drawn by Maruyama Okyo. I'm not even real. I was done by some drunken forger in a house that was falling apart!*

But no matter how much he wanted to scream those words, they would never reach any of the humans who continued to treat him as genuine.

"O scroll, please, please bring glory and wealth to my family!" they continued to beg endlessly. The Tsukumogami's heart grew colder and colder every time he had to witness the pathetic wretches clinging so desperately to this false hope.

These humans can all go to hell. They're all fakes with corrupt eyes. You must be joking if you think I'd want to give you even a speck of good luck! No way!

As a result of these thoughts, fortune began to evade those around Shinonome. Interest in him faded like smoke, and when he realized that he was simply a fad, he felt like throwing up.

If there's someone out there who's sincere and not shallow like the rest of the riffraff, I wonder how they would look at me, he began to think.

He was sure that they would shine very brightly, even at his first glance. At the very least, a genuine person would not try to hinge their wishes on a fake like Shinonome.

I wish I could meet them just once, he hoped. Every day after that, he began to wish harder and harder for this sincere person.

Suimei, Noname, and Shinonome emerged from underground and returned to the loungeroom, placing volumes of *Nanso Satomi Hakkenden* on the coffee table. They were all Shinonome's favorite volumes. He turned them over in his hands as he finished telling the story of how he became a Tsukumogami and noticed that Suimei was making a strange expression.

"You're a forgery?" the young man asked.

"Oh, are you surprised?" Shinonome returned.

"It's just that I heard that a Tsukumogami's strength was based on how valuable and significant its vessel was."

A forgery would naturally be priced lower than the genuine article. As Suimei mumbled and muttered, Shinonome gave him a wry grin.

"So, you're wondering why I'm stronger than the average spirit? Well, when you think about it, whether something is real or not is dependent on the whim of man."

"You mean to say that if someone important says it's real, the general public would agree?" Suimei said.

"Exactly," Shinonome nodded. "Plus, I had quite the reputation for being a scroll of good fortune, and that also helped raise my value. I'm an outlier of a Tsukumogami, I really am."

He mumbled and drained his cup of medicinal brew in one go. He scrunched his face at its acrid taste, and Suimei picked up the conversation again.

"So, how did a forgery like you become the head of a bookstore?" he asked.

"That's what I'd like to know too," the older man scoffed. "I find it all so strange."

Far from being interested in stories, Shinonome harbored a lot of bitterness toward the humans who tried to impose on him their idea of what was valuable.

"There's really nothing strange about it," Noname chuckled. "Spirits change when the right people walk into their lives. Just like how I was saved by Tamaki and Oyuki-san, your life was changed when you met that man. Life is so unpredictable, huh?"

"What's this, what's this?" Kuro yelped with excitement, cocking his head. "Who'd Shinonome meet? Was he cool?"

"He was," Shinonome nodded as he continued his story.

"My life had a few significant turning points. The first was when I was branded a scroll of good fortune and became a

Tsukumogami. The second was when I ended up in the possession of a certain grumpy old man."

Crackle. A spark flew from the fire in the brazier.

It was a day when the freezing cold blanketed the entire town, just like it did today...

The chilly wind whipped through the trees under a clear autumn sky. Around this time, Shinonome's scroll was being passed around from merchant to merchant. It had once been lauded as a scroll that brought its owner good luck, but now that its effect seemed to have disappeared, the word "allegedly" had been tacked on to every description of its reputation. Despite that, it *was* still a fantastic piece by Maruyama Okyo (or so everyone thought, anyway), so it remained quite desirable among art collectors. During its journey of being bought and sold, it landed in the hands of a certain man.

He was Takizawa Bakin, also known as Kyokutei Bakin, an author who was active during the latter half of the Edo period. He penned *Nanso Satomi Hakkenden* and was known as the first writer in Japan to earn a living from manuscript fees.

Shinonome had been brought to Bakin by his friend, a merchant called Ozu Keiso. Ozu had acquired it through another middleman and given it to Bakin as a way of sharing the wealth he reaped. At this time, Bakin was plagued by bad luck. The adoptee he brought into his home would keep running away for four or five years, and around fifty ryo that he had saved for the opening and running of a rental bookstore ended up being squandered.

Oof. He's really *down on his luck,* Shinonome thought.

The Tsukumogami grimaced as he listened to Ozu talk about him. Staring at Bakin, he noticed how plain the author looked. He was in no way well off, which was very unlike his previous owners. All of them, including Ozu, had been dressed very well, but Bakin was a classic example of an old man who lived a frugal and bare-bones life.

The merchant unfurled Shinonome's scroll at the entrance of his friend's home.

"Look at how amazing this dragon is!" he chirped. "For many years, this scroll was said to bring good luck."

The Tsukumogami froze and braced himself. The narrative usually went the same, with the person then gushing about how this had been painted with Maruyama Okyo's very own brush, and this part of the spiel was the one that pained Shinonome the most.

However, what happened next surprised him.

Bakin glared at it contemptuously and huffed before turning his back to it.

Huh? What gives? Shinonome thought, stunned. This was the first time he had ever been faced with such apathy.

"Oh my," Ozu laughed. "I chose a bad day to visit, eh?"

Being familiar with Bakin's odd temper, Ozu took no offense at his attitude and simply left the scroll with him. His wife Ohyaku brought it into the house.

"Well, it's a nice gift," Ohyaku said. "Shall we hang it in your study?"

Bakin answered her suggestion with silence.

The scroll was hung up, and thus began the old author and the scroll's (plus Tsukumogami's) curious cohabitation.

Shinonome's first impression of Bakin was that he was a weird and stubborn old man. He also noted that the author had an almost scary devotion to routine. His morning began when he rose at six, and he would wash his face, pray at the family shrine, and do some peculiar exercises in the yard until eight o'clock.

He would groan as he looked to the sky, massaging his face and tugging at his ears. He would then rub his arms, chest, and hips before planting his hands on his lower back and bending, moving his head back so that he would look at the empty sky once more. Then he would stop and hold that position for a moment.

He's being weird again, Shinonome thought as he watched Bakin's standing figure from within the room where he was hung.

It was, apparently, the daily exercise regimen favored by the feudal lord who ruled the Mito domain.

A gust of wind, so cold that it pricked at the skin, rushed through the air, and the dried leaves rustled with the sudden movement. It was the kind of weather that would make anyone want to bundle up at home. Yet, this withered stick of an old man was standing out in the yard in light dress, completely unbothered.

You know, you're going to hurt your hip doing that, Shinonome thought.

While he watched and quietly fussed over the man, a voice called out that breakfast was ready. Bakin returned to the house through the veranda and spoke in a flat, unemotive voice.

"Ohyaku, do we have the right amount of dried radishes this year?"

"Yes, we received what we usually get," she answered.

"Hm..."

If Shinonome had a face, it would be in disbelief right now. He had overheard the context of this remark a few days ago when a maid was talking about it.

Last year, the farmer who usually came around to collect the night soil happened to be unavailable one day. Another farmer came in his place, but he left fewer eggplants in return for the soil than what Bakin's family was used to. When the author asked his daughter-in-law to find out why, the farmer insisted that they were not missing any eggplants.

It turned out that their usual farmer had been leaving them vegetables for both adults and children. The replacement farmer, on the other hand, left only enough for the adults. This was the usual way things were done, which meant that the original farmer had been giving them extra vegetables for free.

Bakin was furious at the replacement farmer and turned down his eggplants. They usually treated their farmer to lunch before he went on his way, but this time Bakin chased off the replacement farmer without any further argument. After this fierce quarrel, the family returned to using their old farmer.

That was last year! Why do you have to keep checking that

you got the right number of vegetables?! Learn to let things go! Shinonome thought incredulously and scoffed to himself as he imagined the old man eating his meal quietly.

Bakin was also quite picky, to the extent that if he decided he liked a certain seller for daily condiments and spices, he would insist on purchasing from them forever, no matter how far they had to travel. He couldn't rest unless his accounts were settled before the new year began, and he hated having guests over. If he could help it, he would never let any outsiders enter the house. He refused to meet anyone new without a letter of introduction, even if they were a friend of a friend. He also wasn't the best at talking face-to-face with people, which was why he had his daughter-in-law settle the incident with the farmer instead of dealing with it himself.

He's quite awkward when it comes to social matters, isn't he? It feels like even his family can't really handle him, Shinonome noted.

Honestly, the Tsukumogami was stunned. But as incomprehensible as he found Bakin to be, he couldn't take his eyes off the author.

Although Bakin was stubborn and quite idiosyncratic, he would change completely when the time came for him to work.

After finishing a simple breakfast, he would retreat to the guest room and sit beside the sliding door, where he would enjoy a cup of tea. He would finish it right around the time the cleaning was done, and then he would move to his study and write a diary entry for the previous day.

"...All right."

Now it was time to get to work. He straightened his posture and took a deep breath.

Breathe in. Breathe out.

Then, as if the air had been let out of him, his entire body would relax. His eyes narrowed, and his gaze softened.

He focused his gaze on his draft and fell deep into thought as he ground his inkstone. Taking his brush into his hand in one fluid motion, he dipped its tip into the fresh ink and began to write.

The thick smell of ink wafted throughout the study. The only sounds that came from within the room were the soft shuffling of Bakin's kimono and the sparking of the brazier that his wife had prepared, quietly going *pop, crackle*. The merry voices of children playing and women gossiping as they did their laundry could be heard outside, yet the study's stillness made it feel like a world of its own. The air was tense as Bakin's story flowed fervently from his brush with the occasional pause. Sometimes he would crush a piece of the manuscript that he felt was no good and toss it away, then continue writing until he finally halted altogether and sank back into thought.

Hmm... Shinonome pondered as he floated around the study.

The Tsukumogami stared intently at the old man's back. Sure, there was nothing better for him to do, but in any case he found himself strangely drawn to the author. Perhaps it was because his curved back would straighten whenever he sat at his writing desk, and he would seem so much more dignified and poised. Or perhaps it was the passion that would burn in his eyes whenever they became fixed on his draft. Maybe it was even because he never asked the scroll for good fortune, not even once.

Either way, Shinonome was starting to think that maybe humans weren't all insincere scum, contrary to what he had believed for so long.

Bakin was so engrossed in his writing that he sometimes even forgot to breathe, and as Shinonome watched him, a thought began to dawn on him. Being a newly born Tsukumogami, he'd never known the feeling of being completely and utterly immersed in anything before. Wondering what Bakin found so interesting in his work, Shinonome peeked at his writing.

He frowned.

Dammit, I can't read! he cursed.

But of course he couldn't. He'd never been taught, after all. He clicked his tongue and turned away.

Time passed in a flash, and the sun had set before he knew it. Bakin wrapped up his work, finished his dinner, and hurried back to his bedroom. Shinonome stared vacantly at the room from his spot in the study, with nothing to do but listen to the loud, exuberant chorus of insects in the autumn night.

The bedroom's sliding door was aglow with the light from within. Bakin had once again plunged straight into reading. That was another one of his habits, one that he seemed especially fond of. Despite his usual stinginess, books were one thing that could make him dramatically loosen his purse strings, something that Ohyaku often complained about. As a young man, Bakin often read late into the night, but after it started to cause problems for his health, he would cut himself off at ten o'clock. If he didn't stop reading then, he probably never would.

He's so weird, Shinonome thought.

As he contemplated what he'd seen that day, he sighed.

Morning routine aside, Bakin's day revolved so strongly around stories. Day after day, it was stories, stories, stories. Did it ever get boring at any point for him? And surely writing wasn't an easy process. Did he ever find it unpleasant?

He peeked at the writing desk. The manuscript still lay there, its letters indecipherable as ever. He glared at it, grumbling. These letters were an uncanny thing to Shinonome. They twisted and wriggled like worms at times, yet at others they appeared like pictures. Although the scrawls made no sense to him, it was clear that humans could read them and derive some sort of enjoyment from them.

What did those inky words reveal? A white-knuckled adventure? An emotional tearjerker to be read with watery eyes? Or even a spine-chilling tale of terror?

Who cares? Shinonome began to scoff, but the smile faded from his face when the shadow of Bakin's back reappeared in his mind.

His mere presence made you realize how serious and committed he was. His eyes were always filled with determination as they followed the words he wrote down. Back when Shinonome had hung on the wall of a certain merchant, he had seen someone similarly dedicated and passionate about their work.

Then, another figure flashed through his mind—one who neglected to shave regularly, with a scraggly beard and shabby outfit, who poured his dedication into each painting with unblinking focus...

Tch.

Shinonome furrowed his brows and clicked his tongue loudly. He shook his head, trying to scrub his mind's eye.

In any case, he had no doubt that Bakin was someone quite special. He might even have the sincerity that Shinonome had been yearning to see all these years.

Things are getting interesting, he thought.

Just as well, because he was beginning to grow tired of simply floating around the room he was hung up in. He chuckled and looked out the window into the night sky. The moon really was especially beautiful during the fall. He let himself soak in the moonlight, his heart as full as it was bright.

He would soon bear witness to the steely resolve that makes a person genuine and sincere, and just how fearsome that resolve could be.

A few years had passed since Shinonome entered the Takizawa home, and within that time he realized just how shockingly fast life in the human world could change.

The Takizawas were met with misfortune after misfortune. Bakin's right eye was the first to show signs of abnormality, then the left. His vision weakened bit by bit, and as an author, this was a matter of life and death for him. While he sought out every possible method of treatment, his son Sohaku, who had always been of weak disposition, passed away.

Bakin had originally been born to a samurai family, but life had led them to abandon the sword and become merchants instead. He'd wished to return to his warrior roots one day, but now he was without an heir. This was a far more pressing issue than his eyes, and he was so distressed that he couldn't bring himself to eat or, for a short time, even write.

Bakin wasn't the only one who was affected by the death of Sohaku, either. Ohyaku already didn't have the best of temperaments, but the passing of her son only served to worsen her mental state. The entire household had been upturned with no time for rest.

However, the misfortunes didn't stop there. One day in the year of 1839, the biggest fear for Bakin—or any author, for that matter—finally knocked on his door.

His eyesight had diminished so much that he was practically blind.

"Father, won't you consider giving up writing?" Omichi, Sohaku's widow, asked.

But he did not have the energy to respond. He just wanted to keep writing, as if he had been nailed to his desk. His sitting posture had also changed. No longer was his back straight and poised, but curved with his nose almost touching the paper. His eyes were bloodshot, his topknot was loose, and his cheeks were hollow and ashen. He was a shell of his former self.

"You can barely see anymore. It's not possible for you to keep writing!" Omichi continued to plead.

Bakin dug his heels in and refused to listen. Thin streaks

of smoke were snaking their way into the study, and the room was choked with the scent of incense. Ohyaku had probably lit some to commemorate the day of the month on which her son had died.

The author snorted and glared at Omichi.

"Who will finish *Nanso Satomi Hakkenden* if not me?" he scowled, his voice hoarse. It was mostly due to his age, of course, but it had also undoubtedly begun to atrophy because he spoke so little. His eyes, although they could barely see anymore, shone with fiery determination. It was hard to believe that someone so old and frail could exude such energy.

Omichi trembled. "But I've heard that you're writing much more slowly than before, and the publishers are quite troubled about it."

"Forget about them. They need to have some patience," Bakin grumbled.

"Mother is also very worried, even if it seems like she's only concerned about how much money we have left..."

"You mind your own business!" Bakin bellowed.

Omichi squeaked in terror. The author put down his brush, realizing he had gone too far.

"Just focus on raising Taro well," he mumbled, not looking at the daughter-in-law who stood beside him.

A redness flooded into Omichi's cheeks. She balled her fists and hung her head. Taro was Omichi and Sohaku's son, and Bakin's last hope for an heir.

"I apologize for my conduct," Omichi said with a bow.

The dejected woman shuffled out of the room. Bakin turned back to his desk and began to write in silence. Time ticked by, and he tossed away failed draft after failed draft. He drummed his fingers against the desk's surface and shot up like an idea had struck him. He sunk his head down again to write. The ink smudged onto his nose, but Bakin paid no mind to it. He was completely lost in the world of his own creation, his hand moving up and down without pause.

He's crazy! Shinonome thought, shivers running all over him.

The old man couldn't possibly see anything with his eyes— Shinonome knew all too well how much he struggled with everyday tasks. However, that didn't lessen any of the time Bakin spent at his desk. In fact, it only seemed to grow longer and longer with every passing day. Not even the sun setting into darkness could get him to stop writing.

It was truly as though he had been possessed by something monstrous. No, he *had* to have been possessed. It was hard to fathom that he would push himself so hard otherwise.

"Hey," Shinonome blurted out to Bakin.

He knew that there was no way the author would hear him. After all, he was nothing more than a ghost, with no mouth or vocal cords to give sound to his thoughts. Even so, he couldn't stop himself from trying to talk to the old man. Every time Shinonome looked at him, the spirit would be filled with a cloudy and inexplicable feeling that couldn't be dispersed. He had to get to the bottom of it, or else he would remain forever scared of being swallowed whole by this mystifying force.

"You're at that age where you should be slowing down and living out the rest of your life peacefully. Haven't you already done enough?"

Bakin, at this time, was already seventy-three years old. Anybody else would have already retired, but this old man chose to grind his inkstone like he was grinding his very soul.

"At least wish upon me for good fortune. It might even come true!" Shinonome shouted.

But no matter how much energy he put into his pleas, they wouldn't fall on anyone's ears, and Bakin never turned around.

It was then that the spirit realized that Bakin was mumbling. His words were usually unintelligible, but today they were clearer somehow. Shinonome had an inkling of what the old man was going to say, but he approached him anyway. He held his breath and leaned in.

Suddenly, he jolted back like he had been struck. Bakin's words were so strange that he sounded like an eerie beast, and Shinonome could make no sense of it.

"Wait for me. It'll be your turn once I've finished writing this," the author said, his dried lips parting ever so slightly as he continued to pour his undivided attention into his manuscript. "Be nice and patient, now. I promise you'll see the light of day soon. Don't even worry about my vision; it's nothing. I'm still going to keep writing, so just wait for me..."

He usually showed almost no emotion, but he looked so kind speaking into the void at that moment. The fever in his voice alone could set a forest ablaze, filled with a passion that one would only reserve for a lover.

"I'm not going to die before I finish you," he swore.

He's...being fueled by his stories! Shinonome realized.

Now, he felt more excited than scared by Bakin's remarkable personality.

Shinonome could only think that the author was the puppet of something that had an intense fixation on creating stories and controlled every muscle of his being. It was what made him eat, sleep, and sit at his desk. Everything it made him do was for the sake of sending stories out into the world. Come rain or shine, the author wouldn't—*couldn't*—put his brush down.

And, annoyingly, there was more than just one thing that possessed him. Every story came into existence separately, and they all beckoned him to write new novels, write more stories, write, write, write...

This was all in Shinonome's head, or at the very least, he couldn't bring himself to believe it was actually true. But if there really could be someone who fit Shinonome's ideal of genuine sincerity, wouldn't it be Bakin?

He gulped.

"Hey, old man. Are you...the real deal?" he asked.

Bakin did not answer.

Shinonome trembled. Suddenly, without a single sound, the author turned away from his desk and looked straight at the spirit.

Shinonome flinched and shrunk back. He snapped back to his senses and shook his head in a hurry. It must have just *seemed* like Bakin was looking at him. After all, it was simply not possible for the old man to visually register the spirit. He wriggled uncomfortably and turned away, trying to escape the author's cloudy gaze.

"You fake..." Bakin said.

"Wait, you..." Shinonome frowned. He almost asked Bakin if he could see him but stopped himself. He noticed that Bakin's gaze was aimed past himself and at the dragon scroll, which meant that he was probably cursing it for not living up to its reputation.

"...Dammit," Shinonome whispered. Whether or not Bakin had been looking at him, those words were still meant for him.

He balled his fists and gritted his teeth. Just as the author said, Shinonome was a fake and a forgery. However, he was not so indifferent that he was going to let that slide.

"I didn't ask to be branded a scroll of good fortune! Those bastard humans did that! I've never once thought of myself as good luck. In fact, I know I can't bring any of that shit!"

He glowered at Bakin, eyes streaked with rage.

"So don't call me a fake! Don't treat me like I'm some sham! I'm...I'm...!"

As he shouted, he could feel the corners of his eyes growing hotter.

"What the... What is this?" Shinonome gasped. He'd never felt anything like this before. While he was caught off guard, the sliding door of the study opened to reveal Omichi. She had returned with her kimono sleeves tied up and her own brush and inkstone in her hands.

"Omichi?" Bakin said in confusion. The woman sat before the author, her legs folded under her, and she turned to him with a newfound determination in her voice.

"I'm a woman of the Takizawa household," she declared with shining resolve. "I can't just stand by and watch my father suffer alone. Please allow me to be your scribe. Even if you cannot see, you can still tell your story to me. I will write everything you say, and this way you will be able to finish *Nanso Satomi Hakkenden*," she implored, bowing her head low.

Bakin was stunned. He could only sit and blink at her until his face suddenly transformed. His eyes began to glitter, and his face lit up with delight.

"Is that so?" he whispered. Shinonome found himself dazed by the timbre of Bakin's voice.

"So you're still gonna write, huh?" the spirit murmured.

He's the real deal, all right. He's the kind of person I've been looking for!

Someone who was completely genuine and sincere would never compromise on their way of life, even if they could no longer see.

Shinonome felt a burning heat rise within him, and his cheeks became colored with red. He felt jittery and giddy.

"He's so cool..." he babbled as he continued to watch Bakin intently. The author's eyes were shining as he spoke with Omichi. To Shinonome, Bakin's indomitable spirit that could overcome all difficulties shined brighter than any star.

He wanted to be as genuine as the author. But, no matter how much he fought against it, the fact remained that he was a fake.

"Dammit," he scowled. But even then, he couldn't take his eyes off Bakin.

Soon after that, Shinonome left the Takizawa home. They sold him off to obtain more money for living expenses, and he didn't hold it against them. A scroll of good fortune that brought no such thing was useless, after all.

He changed hands many times in the following years, but he never met anyone who was nearly as genuine as Bakin. To Shinonome, the average lives that all the other owners led felt extremely shallow. He couldn't help but feel that a truly genuine person would require a passion that consumed their entire soul.

One day, he heard through the grapevine that *Nanso Satomi Hakkenden* had been completed down to the very last volume. Bakin had finished the story by dictating it to Omichi, who then transcribed it for him. It took twenty-eight years for the whole body of work to be published, starting from the first volume. Shinonome was overjoyed and very impressed, but at the same time, uncertainty weighed on him.

What can I do to be as genuine as him? he thought.

Even though he knew full well that he was a fake, Shinonome couldn't stop wondering how he could become someone like Bakin, who created such significant art. He couldn't shake his desire to be something real, and it only grew more intense with time.

What made Bakin so *real*? What were his fundamental building blocks? His stubbornness? His constant fussiness? Or perhaps his habits, or his writing...

Or maybe his drive for creation that raged so fiercely even as his vision completely faded?

The worm-like scrawls that humans called scripts popped into Shinonome's head. When enough of them were gathered, they would create a novel, something that humans were willing to pay money to read. Many of these readers were probably like Bakin, forgetting to sleep and eat once they became engrossed in a story.

Why did humans have such a strong desire to read these stories? Maybe, Shinonome thought, there were other people just as sincere as Bakin, and they, too, would write books just like he did.

If he took up writing himself and published something that everyone loved, maybe he could become real as well!

Oh, if only I could read a book. I really think that I'll strike gold if I could just read one!

This had to be the key to turning himself real!

However, at the end of the day, he was a Tsukumogami. He had no opportunity to even learn how to read single characters, let alone an entire novel.

"Dammit! There must be a way, somehow!" he cursed.

This thought would go on to plague him for countless sleepless nights.

Years passed, and soon Edo gave way to an era of cultural change and enlightenment. At this point in time, Shinonome was being displayed in the mansion of a wealthy merchant. The third turning point in his life happened here—it was the place where he finally obtained a physical body, now that he had evolved as a Tsukumogami.

"Wow," he whispered as he inspected his body in the empty room. He clenched his hand, then released it. Even just standing atop the tatami was new and exciting to him. Delighted, he hopped over to look in the full-length mirror...and his heart froze when he saw his creator's likeness in his own face.

"Tch," he scowled and sighed. He shook his head and quickly took hold of his scroll, rolling it up and holding it close to his chest. Now that he had a body, he could learn how to read and enter the world of fiction. He was getting closer and closer to becoming real...!

A wave of happiness flooded through him. He raced out of the room without a second thought and dashed through the large estate, launching himself over a wall and into the world beyond.

Oh, I'm free!

He began to walk in high spirits.

"Oh no!" came a voice.

Shinonome had been spotted by one of the servants, who noticed that the man he had just seen was carrying something out of the house. He rushed into the room to check what it was and saw that one of the master's favorite scrolls was missing. The house immediately burst to life like a wasp nest had just been dropped inside it, and the manservants all chased after the Tsukumogami.

The spirit in question, however, had no idea that the men

were pursuing him. He was simply enjoying the human world by wandering aimlessly through the diverse city of Edo, happy as a clam and just as clueless.

Books, books, books... Wait, how do I even get one? he thought.

In the crowd, he could see people dressed in familiar, traditional Japanese clothing mingled with others who were wearing Western clothes. Fancy buildings lined the streets, and there was even something called a railroad transporting people across the city. Shinonome, constantly turning his head and gluing his bulging eyes to the building tops, looked to the townspeople exactly like a country bumpkin. But no matter how much they snickered and giggled, he heard none of it. He was too busy absorbing the sights of this new, unfamiliar world.

While he could still tell this was Edo, the changes it had undergone were stark. It had rid itself of the shackles of old tradition and embraced this new age of reform. Everyone in this city was filled with hopes and dreams, and Shinonome felt lighter just by being there. He was convinced that here he would be able to fulfill his dream of becoming real in no time.

"There he is! Get that man!"

A sudden shout interrupted his thoughts, and he snapped his head back in a daze to see who it was. A group of furious men were gunning straight toward him. The frightened Shinonome clutched his scroll even closer and bolted like a terrified rabbit.

"Stop, thief! Bring that scroll back at once!" they shouted.

"I'm not a thief!" Shinonome yelled back at the false accusations. "The scroll is me! I'm the scroll!"

But the men paid no attention, and the Tsukumogami had to keep weaving his way through the crowd. His feet, with their new and tender skin, became grazed and wounded in no time. He winced in pain, but even as he sped through the city, he found himself marveling at the sensation of his heart thumping away. For something so freshly formed, his body could move pretty quickly and gave his pursuers a good run for their money.

But no matter how fast he was, he was still ignorant of the world around him. The men's familiarity with the city had him easily beat, and they were closing in on him.

"Over here! Round him off!" they called.

"Dammit!" Shinonome muttered as he scurried into an alley. His feet were reaching their limit. He could hardly take another step and a cold sweat drenched his skin. Sure, he was glad to have a physical body, but how he wished he had the convenience of floating through the air again!

He collapsed to his knees with a thud, his shoulders rising and falling with each heavy breath. He could still hear the angry shouting in the distance; it was only a matter of time before he was caught.

"What do I do?" he whispered, but no ideas came to him. He gripped his scroll. What would happen to him if it were taken? His head sagged toward the ground, and then he noticed a pair of shoes on the edge of his vision. They were black and polished so meticulously that Shinonome could see his reflection in the leather. His face shot up, and he blinked at the figure in front of him.

"Why, hello! How are we today?" came a lofty voice. It was from a gentleman who was stroking his perfectly coiffed mustache, and he extended a hand to the spirit.

"You look like you're in a tough spot. Would you like my help?" he asked.

Shinonome's first impression was that this man reeked of suspicion. He scrunched his face.

"Who are *you*?" he asked.

He wrapped his arms even tighter around the scroll. The man chuckled; he seemed to find the spirit's wariness amusing.

"Oh my, I seem to have neglected to introduce myself," he said. "Well, perhaps if you had just stayed put and let me come and get you like I'd planned, maybe neither of us would be in this situation right now."

"Get me? What do you mean?" Shinonome frowned, puzzled. However, the next thing he saw stunned him.

The gentleman lifted his hat and revealed a gleaming white dish atop his head.

"I'm Toochika," he introduced. "I'm a kappa spirit. I'm a merchant living in the human world to serve the rest of my kin. You're the scroll of fortune, aren't you? I sensed that you would gain a body soon and planned to take you into my possession before you caused too much of a fuss, but I suppose I was a bit too late."

He's a kappa?!

The Tsukumogami was lost for words as he realized that this was his first meeting with a fellow supernatural being.

Toochika stared into the distance and let out a dry laugh.

"Looks like you kicked up a bit too much of a fuss," he said.

Suddenly, Shinonome heard a crowd of stamping feet drawing closer and closer. His eyes darted about, trying to get a grip on the situation, when the kappa spoke again.

"I could offer you a place to hide if you like," he offered.

Shinonome blinked. He hadn't expected that.

"I'm...I'm a Tsukumogami. I've only got myself. Where could I possibly hide?" he asked nervously.

Toochika gave him a mischievous wink and replied, "I'll take you to a place where you'll fit right in—the spirit realm! It's a wonderful world that all of us fantastical and freaky creatures can call home."

The Tsukumogami felt his jaw drop while the kappa continued to smile at him. In any case, it seemed that his only option was to trust this dubious man.

"Um, sure, I guess," he said.

"You got it!" Toochika exclaimed. He grabbed Shinonome's hand, flashing a grin so charming that it could melt any maiden's heart.

And so a friendship that would last for centuries was born between the scroll Tsukumogami and this kappa dandy.

"...And that was how I came to the spirit realm with Toochika's help," Shinonome said.

Crackle. The charred wood in the brazier sparked again.

At some point during this story, Kuro had flopped over onto his back and fallen asleep. The Inugami sighed a little as Suimei covered him with his jacket.

"Kyokutei Bakin, huh? He had quite the impact on your life," Suimei said.

"He sure did!" Shinonome laughed. "He was an interesting fellow, that one. When I said he was stubborn, I really meant it. He was always grumpy over one thing or another, but he wouldn't say straight out what exactly was annoying him. He'd just make a face like this and try to pressure someone else into noticing."

As he spoke, Shinonome did his best to imitate what Bakin used to look like. The expression he ended up making was quite terrifying, and Suimei couldn't help but laugh.

"Yep, that's how every grumpy old man looks, all right!"

Noname, who had finished refilling everyone's tea, piped up.

"Oh, this takes me back. You look just like Bakin sometimes too, you know."

"No, I don't!" Shinonome retorted. "How can I, anyway? We're not even related."

"Are you sure? Because I've seen that look on both your faces," Noname said. "And over stupid little things like your salmon being too salty or your pickled radishes being too sweet, no less."

She placed a metal mesh over the brazier and dug around in her bag for some rice cracker dough to prepare some snacks for the group. She was still grinning when she picked up a bottle of soy sauce as well, and Suimei tilted his head.

"Noname, did you know Bakin?" he asked. "You sound like you've lived with him before."

Shinonome and Noname both looked at each other and exchanged a small giggle. The Tsukumogami turned to the young man with a mischievous grin.

"Hey, Suimei, do you think an old man who insisted on writing even after losing his vision would give up on his craft so easily, even in death?"

Suimei's expression darkened. "Wait, so..."

Noname chuckled. "Yep, Bakin wanted to keep writing even after he died. His unprecedented fixation and determination turned him into something more than human."

Shinonome glanced around the room, thinking about how this old house felt so similar to the one that Bakin once lived in.

"The one who founded this bookstore was Bakin," he said.

Suimei gulped. His brown eyes remained fixed on the spirit.

"I went from the plain old Tsukumogami of the scroll to Shinonome here in the spirit world," Shinonome smiled as he continued his tale. He began to tell Suimei how the old author, now a supernatural being, met the Tsukumogami with his newly formed body.

One day in the spirit realm, Toochika was sitting silently on the veranda of the bookstore, gleefully watching a rowdy argument unfolding before him.

"Whoaaa! No, please! Jiisan, calm down!"

"You stupid scroll, how dare you scribble graffiti all over my manuscript again! You're not getting away with it this time!"

The whole living room was in an uproar, with bowls and books being flung across it by an oni who had gone red-faced with rage. It was Bakin, who had been transformed by his obsession with writing.

According to Shinonome, he looked a little different from his human form. He was younger than he'd been when Shinonome last saw him, and he had a small horn protruding from his forehead. He could see again but still needed a monocle to aid his vision. The only thing that remained unchanged was his stubbornness.

The oni Bakin stomped over to Shinonome, who broke out in a cold sweat.

"I-I'm sorry," he stammered as he backed away. "I was just trying to learn how to read and write."

"And I've told you before, you can do that somewhere else. Stop getting in the way of my work."

"Come on, we live under the same roof," Shinonome pointed out. "There's no need to be like that."

Bakin huffed. "You vex me. Stay away and don't make a sound. Don't even breathe near me!"

"I'll die if I don't breathe!"

"Good! Maybe then I'll be able to get some work done!" the author yelled.

Now it was the Tsukumogami's turn to go red in the face.

"What's your problem?! This is all because you won't teach me how to read anyway!" he shouted back.

"And why do I have to teach you anything?!" Bakin thundered.

"Why not? It's no skin off your back!"

"It is. It cuts into my time to write. If you want to learn, then go and find a teacher, not me!"

Bakin gave Shinonome a final huff and turned his back, trying to start on his manuscript.

"Dammit! I'm not giving up on this, you hear?! I'm going to learn it so good, and then I'm going to read all the books I want! I swear I will!" yelled the trembling Tsukumogami.

"Do whatever you want. Just leave me out of it," Bakin replied without even turning back around.

Shinonome's eyes creased with anger, and he balled his fists, slamming them into the tatami. The rickety house shook from the force. The air in the room still felt tense, like a single spark could blow everything sky-high.

"Oh dear. Looks like this house is still as noisy as ever," came a voice.

Someone else had been watching over the two with Toochika—Noname. The two of them had been sipping on their own cups of tea, but they only looked at each other now.

"Ah ha ha, so you saw everything?" Toochika laughed. "They're full of energy as always, eh?"

"Easy for you to say," Noname sighed. "I'm the one who has to clean up after their temper tantrums, so some sympathy would be nice."

"Sorry, sorry," the kappa apologized. "I promise I'll make the scroll leave the nest eventually after he's gotten more used to his humanoid body. If I order from your apothecary more, could you please look after him for a little longer?"

He flashed Noname a sweet smile, but she frowned.

"...Oh, fine. But you'd better make good on that promise."

"Of course! I've never broken a promise, have I?"

Noname couldn't help but smile wryly at Toochika's blinding cheeriness.

How had Shinonome come to live in the spirit realm's bookstore? Well, Toochika was the one who pulled the strings there too.

A few weeks earlier, Toochika had rescued Shinonome from the uproar he'd caused and brought him to the spirit world. The first problem to be solved was where the Tsukumogami would live. Tsukumogamis who had only just obtained their bodies were like babies, ignorant of the ways of the world. They would normally be taken care of by a foster guardian until they were independent enough to survive by themselves.

As the kappa mulled over who he could find as a foster guardian, Shinonome suddenly spoke.

"Hey, I wanna read!" he said.

Toochika then decided to take the Tsukumogami to the newly opened bookstore, which was being run by an old man who had recently turned into an oni. He didn't have the most solid grip on day-to-day life, but Noname from the apothecary was lending him her assistance. The kappa *did* consider that he could probably just dump the Tsukumogami on Noname if push came to shove because she was so good at taking care of others, but...

"Whaaaaaat?! Wait, wait. I know this old man. You're Bakin!" Shinonome shouted.

Bakin stayed silent, staring quizzically.

"It's me!" the Tsukumogami continued. "Me, me! Man, it's been so long, huh? You still doing those weird exercises?"

They seemed to (probably) know each other, so Toochika decided to let Shinonome live at the bookstore.

"I can't believe that stubborn old man agreed to do this," Noname said with a raised eyebrow.

"Hm? He didn't," Toochika grinned.

"What do you mean?" Noname asked.

"Do you really think he could have said no, when I was the one who found him at his grave all clueless, looked after him, helped him set up shop, and lent him all the money he needed?" the kappa pointed out.

Toochika made a living selling this and that, but Nurarihyon had also asked him to take care of any spirits that were having trouble in the human world, so naturally he was the one who brought the transformed Bakin to the spirit world as well.

Noname took a second to collect herself after hearing the kappa's bluntness and said, "Wow, you are ruthless. You helped me set up my store too, so I also know that the old man won't be able to say no to you."

"He didn't let me go without glaring at me first, though,"

Toochika said. "I know he's extremely unhappy about it, but it should be smooth sailing right after he gets over the initial bumps."

"What makes you so sure?" Noname asked, tilting her head in confusion. "They've been arguing so loudly every day that the whole neighborhood can hear them."

Toochika grinned, and the two peeked into the author's room. Shinonome was still staring angrily at Bakin's back, but now he was reaching toward the writer's abandoned drafts. He spread out the crinkled balls of paper and began to trace his eyes over the writing, following the words with his finger to practice his reading.

"Those two refused to even talk to each other at the beginning, so I'd actually call their arguing an improvement. Their relationship is getting better by leaps and bounds, wouldn't you say? And I think it's only going to get better, so that's why I know things will turn out fine," Toochika said.

When he saw the draft that Shinonome was practicing with, he allowed himself a chuckle. It was a fairly easy read for its genre, and Bakin had even carefully written the readings next to the more difficult kanji. The author was never one to show his true feelings on the surface, but even he couldn't deny Shinonome's deep yearning to learn and read. He treasured creating stories above all else, including his own life, so how could he refuse?

He did leave a lot to be desired when it came to expressing his kindness, though. He did it in such a roundabout way that Shinonome could detect none of it. Not that Shinonome was any better—he, too, could have just politely asked Bakin to teach him how to read. His aggressive way of talking only served to aggravate Bakin's stubbornness.

"They're both so emotionally inept," Toochika sighed. "I can only imagine the kinds of headaches they'd cause."

"It's the only way they know how to express themselves," Noname grumbled. "I'm already sick of it."

The kappa laughed to himself. He was curious to see how these two would change in the future.

If he were to be completely honest, he'd sometimes set up things for a little bit of entertainment, doing stuff like...well, putting two people who got along terribly together in the same house. He knew that this made him a little twisted, but he couldn't be the nice guy all the time. He was a kappa spirit, after all, and kappas had an infamously mischievous nature.

"Ah ha ha!" he chortled. "I'm excited to see how this legendary author and immature Tsukumogami matchup turns out. Oh, I simply can't wait."

"Don't come crying to me when things go pear-shaped," Noname sighed.

"I'll just let Nurarihyon handle it if things come to that," the kappa shrugged. "The spirit realm is outside of my jurisdiction."

"Hmm," Noname said disapprovingly, leaving it at that. Toochika laughed again merrily, amused by the whole situation.

Suddenly, a chain of loud thumps disrupted them. They both peeked into the room again and saw that Bakin had stopped writing and stood up. He was quickly approaching

Shinonome, who was blinking at him in surprise. A blood vessel bulged with rage on Bakin's temple, and he tugged Shinonome toward him by the chest. His opposite hand was gripping a piece of his manuscript that looked like it had been doodled over by a child.

"You wretched scroll! Does your graffiti know no bounds?!" he roared.

"I-I'm sorry. I didn't mean it," the Tsukumogami stammered.

"Get out back so I can beat some sense into you!"

Now that Bakin was an oni, his temper was also a lot shorter. Toochika and Noname looked at each other without making a single move to break them up, and Noname shook her head in defeat.

"I worry about those two," she lamented. "Anyway, why is Bakin still calling him just 'scroll'?"

As they were born from objects, Tsukumogamis didn't come with names, so their guardians normally gave them one. However, Bakin had never tried to think of a name, nor did it seem like he was going to at any point.

"He'll get a name eventually," Toochika shrugged. "If not, then you can give him one. Try to think of something cool and manly for him!"

"My pleasure!" Noname exclaimed. "Maybe I'll call him something super adorable, like Hanako-chan!"

"Ha ha! Our scroll's got a hard life ahead of him!" the kappa guffawed. "But that sounds fun too. I kind of want to see you call him that now."

Bakin and Shinonome had been thrown together because of Toochika's love of mischief, but this decision had a profound impact on Shinonome's life...and on Bakin's too, as his heart was slowly melted by the Tsukumogami's unfettered hunger for knowledge. Despite their differences, the two unexpectedly turned out to be quite like-minded.

The author and the Tsukumogami were always together, though it may be more accurate to say that Shinonome constantly followed Bakin around like a baby duckling.

When they rose in the morning, they would do Bakin's exercises together in the yard. When they complained about the pickled radish at breakfast, they would both get an earful from Noname. They would also drink their tea and start their literary time together. As Bakin continued to quietly work on his manuscript, Shinonome would sit beside him and dive back into his reading practice. His motivation was boundless, and he made impressive strides in his literacy, especially with Bakin occasionally making corrections for him.

"C'mon, do you have to be that picky?!" Shinonome would sometimes complain about Bakin's red markings on his work.

"Picky? This is the bare minimum," Bakin would reply.

Although they sometimes quarreled over the author's teaching standards, time would fly by when they were together. After all, there was something much more appealing than arguing that dangled over them—books.

Bakin's life in the spirit realm was even more steeped in

books than his existence as a human. He would write all day to his heart's content, run the bookstore until the sun went down, and then close up shop and read until daybreak.

And of course, Shinonome would be reading beside him too.

His constant efforts had paid off, and now he was able to read some simpler works. The previously unexplored world of writing was so much more fascinating than he could have ever imagined. When he was still just a scroll, all he'd been able to do was wait his time out as he hung upon the wall, but now he could go on countless adventures through books. He found himself falling hard for the world of literature and reached for volume after volume. Whenever he didn't understand something, he would ask Bakin about it right away. Strangely enough, Bakin seemed to be unbothered by this.

"Hey, what's so good about this?" Shinonome asked, pointing to the book he was reading. "I don't get it. It's so boring."

"Give it here. The whole point of it is to read it while thinking about the societal context it was written in."

Considering Bakin's circumstances, all the people he was close to would have already passed away. He must have been feeling quite lonely without anyone to discuss books with. Finding friends to talk about the same stories you were reading, or those you'd already read, was not an easy thing to do.

When he had explained the book's background to Shinonome, the Tsukumogami's face lit up.

"Oh, I get it now. That does make it more interesting!"

Bakin watched Shinonome discover the joys of each book

with something like fondness in his heart, and he would quietly slide his next recommendation next to the Tsukumogami's pillow. It was his own unique way of showing that he cared.

This was how the two of them would spend their hours together. It still came with the occasional fight, but Bakin no longer complained about Shinonome like he did at the beginning.

One day, while the two of them were reading before bed as usual, Shinonome suddenly called out to Bakin from beside him.

"Hey, you know what I want to do when I get even better at reading?"

Bakin replied with only silence, but that was his usual reaction. Shinonome continued like it was normal.

"I want to try reading *Nanso Satomi Hakkenden* then."

Silence again.

"It took you twenty-eight years to finish, right? That's so awesome. And you kept writing it even after you lost your vision! That series has got your entire soul put into it. It's the work of a real artist. I can't wait until I can read it! I wonder when that will be."

Bakin shot a glance at Shinonome.

"You..." he began but closed his mouth. Shinonome tilted his head, trying to figure out what the author wanted to say.

Bakin scratched his head awkwardly and turned away.

"It's quite a long series," he muttered. "You really think you can handle it?"

Shinonome flashed him a toothy grin.

"Of course!" he exclaimed proudly. "I promise I'll read it to the very last page. I'll even give you a review of it! Isn't that exciting?"

He flopped onto his futon and stared up at the ceiling.

"Every time I finish a book, I think about how amazing all these writers are," he whispered. "How can they just create these characters and stories out of nothing? They're like gods of their own little worlds. It's so cool. I wish I could be like them. And out of all of them, you're one of the most amazing for writing so many stories that so many people love."

He put his hands up in front of his face and inspected them. There was nothing noteworthy about them, except maybe for the fact that they were big. These were the hands of someone who had never created anything. Meanwhile, Bakin's were calloused and stained with ink. Now *they* were the hands of an experienced writer, of someone who had created countless things.

"You look so cool when you're writing your stories," Shinonome continued. "I hope I can write my own someday and make people feel really excited when they're reading my stuff too. Then maybe I could be real like you."

Bakin said nothing. Shinonome fell silent as well, except for the sound of steady breathing; he had fallen asleep. The author looked up at the scroll that was Shinonome's main body, hanging on the wall. The dragon on it was flying above the clouds as always, but now day was beginning to break, and it suddenly seemed so much more striking than usual in the faint light of the early hours.

Bakin closed his book with a thump and reached toward his lamp. He opened it and released the glimmerflies within, letting darkness flood the room. He crawled under the covers of his futon, but instead of sleeping, he mulled over his thoughts for a while.

On another day when Bakin was running the store, he said, "Hey, scroll. Go to the back."

Shinonome had been practicing his reading in the room and looked up in confusion, but he heard some noise coming from the shop. Bakin probably wanted the Tsukumogami to stay out of his and his customer's way.

"I'm not even gonna do anything," he said, puffing his cheeks out and pouting like a child. He continued with his work as Bakin returned to the store, but eventually his curiosity got the better of him. He really wanted to see what the old man was like when dealing with a customer, and he was getting tired of just doing rote learning anyway, so he put down his brush and crept toward the shop. He opened a tiny gap in the door that connected the store to the loungeroom and watched Bakin and the customer through the sliver.

"Oh, I really can't believe my luck! I'm so honored to meet a great author such as yourself here in the spirit realm!" the new arrival said.

There was something arrogant about the stranger's manner that made the Tsukumogami suspicious.

Wait, is he even a customer? Shinonome thought.

The guest was large and plump, with a flat nose and thin eyes that made Shinonome uncomfortable. Holding a book with fingers that made the Tsukumogami think of caterpillars, the guest was talking to Bakin animatedly.

"I became an oni recently myself, you know. And can I just say that the availability of entertainment here is dire? I was almost going to die of boredom when I heard there was a bookstore on the outskirts of town. I find the idea of borrowing books that have been in other people's grubby hands quite revolting, to be honest, but I had to cure my boredom somehow, right?"

The oni paused, waiting for someone to validate him, and a tall man behind him nodded. He was pale and ashen, and although he was standing, it didn't feel like he was alive. Perhaps he was one of those animated corpses.

"It must be fate for us to meet here!" the oni babbled on, his face red with excitement. Bakin gave the occasional monosyllabic reply to show that he was paying attention, but he said nothing else. Shinonome couldn't see the old man's face from where he was standing, but he was sure that Bakin probably looked like he wished he were dead.

Customer service is a tough gig... Shinonome thought.

While Shinonome was feeling sorry for the author, the customer suddenly said something surprising.

"You know, I think I wouldn't mind becoming your apprentice. All right, that's that!"

Shinonome's eyes nearly popped out of their sockets. He was stunned.

What do you mean you 'wouldn't mind'? Is that how you ask anyone for a favor? Is he all right in the head? the Tsukumogami thought. How could that oni be so confident that his proposal would be accepted? Did the thought of rejection ever cross his mind? Probably not.

"Sorry, but I don't do apprentices," Bakin said.

Duh, Shinonome thought with a snicker.

If the old man hated the simple idea of teaching someone to read, how was he ever going to entertain the thought of taking someone under his wing for even a single second?

"Um, sorry, I must have heard that incorrectly," the customer said. He was clearly shaken by the refusal, and his eyes were wandering all over the store. His face had grown pale, and he was sweating. He tried to regain his composure and kept hounding Bakin.

"You've been graced with the chance to take someone as talented as me as an apprentice! You should think of yourself as lucky! When I get out there and publish my works, you're going to get even more famous too. You don't even have to worry about the fact that we're both oni, because I've got connections in the human publishing industry. Basically, you're getting the chance to publish something extraordinary handed to you on a silver platter!"

"I told you, I don't do apprentices. Don't make me repeat myself," Bakin said, refusing to budge.

The customer's face immediately grew stormy and he threw the book he was holding to the ground.

"You... Who the hell do you think you are?!" he snarled, baring his teeth. Veins began to pop up on his forehead, and his skin turned bluer and bluer with each second. The horns on his head grew longer, and his nails sharper.

He was a blue oni!

Now that he had shown his true form, the customer continued to shout.

"I gracefully give you the chance to take me under your wing and you dare say no?!" he bellowed, spittle flying though the air. "Looks like you're still old and senile, even as an oni!"

He stormed toward Bakin and grabbed him by the collar.

"Ugh, this is why I hate old people. To hell with Kyokutei Bakin! The only impressive thing about what you've done is how you've managed to pump out so much rubbish!"

The author said nothing.

"But Santo Kyoden? Now there's someone worthy of my respect. The worlds he creates are truly wonderful," the blue oni jeered. "Which reminds me...you asked Kyoden to take you as an apprentice, but he refused, didn't he? Ha ha! Did you turn me down because of your grudge? Oh, how despicable!"

Bakin held his ground in the face of the verbal abuse being hurled at him, and the other oni took this as his cue to keep going.

"He said no to you precisely because you have such a rotten personality. Oh, what was that famous series of yours called again? *Nanso Satomi Hakkenden* or something?"

Silence from Bakin again.

Shinonome could feel the blood rushing through his temple as his scowl grew more severe by the second. However, the blue demon took no notice of the Tsukumogami's presence.

Instead, he sneered, "What a load of trifle that was. And so pointlessly long! I've never seen such a redundant and sluggish plot. And did you really think of everything in there by yourself? My friends agree that *Nanso Satomi Hakkenden* seems to have been lifted wholesale from *Water Margin*!"

His face twisted into something ugly, like all the hate and disgust in the world had been distilled into him and it was now overflowing.

He gave Bakin a violent shove and shouted, "I bet you stole ideas from other people for all of your stories, you hack! A fake like you has no right to be my master anyw—Urk!!!"

In a flash, the man flew backward upon being struck by a potent force. It was Shinonome, whose eyes still burned with the rage that made him throw his fist into the oni.

"Who are you calling a fake?!" he roared, lightning crackling around his hands. Scales had emerged from his skin, and his entire body was glowing with an intense blue-white light. The large man who had been silent during the conversation had managed to catch his companion, but the blue oni had sustained a bloody nose.

"Hey, what was that for?!" he protested. "Not even my own father would hit me like that!"

"Shut up, you filthy scum!" Shinonome yelled. He had completely snapped. The lightning now zipped around his body, and he slowly approached the blue oni, who swallowed nervously and ran to hide behind the large man.

"All I did was tell the truth! Don't you dare take another step closer to me!"

"What?" Shinonome growled. The large man glared back at him. The two of them differed quite considerably in size: at a glance, they seemed like adult and child. The air around them was rife with tension, but the Tsukumogami had no intention of backing down.

"What truth? Our jiisan is more awesome than you'll ever know!" he bellowed, and the lightning grew more intense. The blue oni squealed in fright.

Shinonome rambled on, speaking so quickly that it seemed like his words were tripping over his feelings.

"He spends every one of his waking moments thinking about stories. No one would be foolish enough to spend that much time copying other people! He pours all of his blood, sweat, and tears into each one of his sentences, even to the point where he hurts himself. He takes writing more seriously than anyone else! How can you call someone like that a fake?!"

The more intense his emotions grew, the more his lightning sparked and the stronger it became. At this point, he was more like anthropomorphized lightning than a spirit.

"St-stop! I said, stop! Get away from me!" the blue oni screamed. "Hey, help me!" he begged the large man, who remained expressionless as he raised a gigantic fist.

His punch swooped toward Shinonome's cheek with a loud *whoosh*, but the Tsukumogami curled his body and dodged the threat.

"That stubborn old man is more real than anyone!" he shouted. When he twisted back, he launched a powerful kick straight into the large man's solar plexus.

Neither the man nor the blue demon knew what hit them. Screaming, they were propelled backward into the door, knocking it clean out of its frame. As they tumbled out into the street, Shinonome followed, his face still contorted with rage. He thumped the ground lightly and flew to the duo's side in a blink. His fist continued to fizzle with lightning, and as he rose it to hit the two...

"Stop it," said a voice.

Shinonome grunted in confusion as he felt someone pull him back by the collar.

He coughed. "Hey, what gives, Jiisan?!" he protested, teary-eyed.

Bakin, breathing heavily, frowned.

"Jeez, just take a look at what you've done," he said and pointed to the large man.

He had lost consciousness after receiving that huge kick from Shinonome, so there was no point hitting him again.

"And look there too," Bakin continued and pointed to the bookstore.

The Tsukumogami turned to look, and his eyes grew round. The store was covered in black patches burned by the lightning he'd been emanating.

"I'm...I'm sorry," he said, scratching his head awkwardly.

Bakin let out a small sigh and stared at the other man. Shinonome tilted his head, confused. Then the blue oni, who had tumbled next to the large man, groaned.

"Dammit... You won't get away with treating me so poor—ghoof!"

Bakin kicked him before he finished his sentence, and he fell unconscious. The Tsukumogami stared in astonishment, but what he heard next surprised him even further.

"How about Shinonome?" Bakin said.

"Whuh?" the Tsukumogami blurted out.

Bakin scratched his head.

"It's written with the kanji for 'east' and 'clouds,' and refers to the clouds to the east in the morning. It means daybreak," he clarified.

"Uh, yeah, but what about it?" the spirit frowned, puzzled.

Bakin, still looking the other way, whispered so lightly that a single gust of wind could have blown his words away.

"You know, it's not uncommon for masters to think of an alias for their apprentice."

He left Shinonome with that sentence and headed back to the shop, but the spirit was still left dumbfounded.

"Wait, what's that supposed to mean? What apprentice? Am I your apprentice?" he shouted after the author.

Bakin stopped and peeked behind his back.

"You want to start writing stories, don't you? If you're hoping to improve quickly, you'll need someone to teach you," he said and began walking again.

Shinonome stared at the old man, stunned.

"Wh-whaaaaaaaaaat?! I thought you didn't take apprentices!" he cried, dashing straight to Bakin. When he caught up, he started slapping Bakin on the back, saying, "Is this for real, Jiisan?!" between laughs.

The author swatted at the other man, sighing in annoyance.

"We have to fix up the shop first," he reminded him. "And who are you calling a stubborn old man?" he grumbled with a glare.

The rice crackers that had been laid upon the mesh over the charcoal fire had now swelled, their outsides golden and crispy and covered in the soy sauce Noname had been brushing on them. They filled the room with a delicious aroma that would make anyone drool.

"So Bakin was the catalyst for your writing career," Suimei said.

Shinonome rubbed his head bashfully.

"Yeah. He was also the one who gave me my name," he said. "I was really excited back then. I thought I could finally make myself real too, just like Jiisan."

"Did you become real like you wanted?"

The Tsukumogami shook his head in reply.

"I still believe that Bakin was real, and that someone can become real by creating things. But that didn't automatically mean that *I* could do it, right?"

He chuckled bitterly.

"I was so naive back then. I thought that if I just did what Bakin did, I would become real too."

When he finished speaking, he stared into the air.

Noname shrugged. "Your temper really was something back then. Remember how you'd get into a rage when you felt like what you wrote wasn't good enough?"

"Well, what was I to do? I just couldn't write anything proper when I actually sat down and tried it," Shinonome laughed in embarrassment.

Then the faraway look returned to his eyes.

"I just couldn't figure out why I wasn't doing very well. I thought it was just putting down words on a page. How hard could it be?"

Once again, Bakin was the one who told him what he was missing.

"Listen up, Shinonome. Before you can write a story, you need to have experienced something that moved you emotionally," he said thoughtfully, as if he were conjuring this lesson from the depths of his mind.

"It doesn't matter if you felt proud, angry, sad, or excited. Anything that humans do is sure to have emotions entwined with it. People don't do things if they don't feel anything. So to capture emotion, you need to have seeds of experience within you first. You can't grow anything without seeds, can you? Same goes for writing. If you haven't got anything in your head, then you won't be able to imagine anything."

"So you're saying that I lack experience?" Shinonome asked.

"Exactly," Bakin nodded. "You were practically born yesterday, so right now you have as much experience as a baby. People usually build experience starting from their early childhood, but you don't have that either. You're much too fresh, so you're not even close to being able to imagine a new world from scratch."

People were like trees, whose branches grew with each new

experience. And those branches could become anything. They could be cut down and crafted into tools, or become a nesting place for birds, or even grow lots of leaves that would then drop and turn into fertilizer for the earth.

"When you create something, you have to concentrate all your effort into it, or else it won't bear fruit."

Mix experience with a bit of fantasy and the branches will bear your very own unique fruit. They could then drop and sprout their own plants, but not even the creator would know what form they would take. All they know is that their ideas can only come to fruition if they constantly devote their life to their craft.

"To create a story is to make up someone's life. You must be ready to completely commit yourself to it. It's not uncommon for an author to think they're going crazy, because all the sound around us will disappear and leave us alone with our paper. Our thoughts then spill out from our minds through our brushes and turn into inked words that go on to build a story. Then we find ourselves gasping for air and snap back to reality, realizing that we were holding our breath the whole time. So intense is our fervor that we forget to do the very things that keep us alive. We're just that absorbed in turning our fantasies into something real. And to do that, we have to know how to easily draw upon our experiences."

Shinonome was taken aback. Bakin never spoke this much, which just proved how passionate he was about writing and creating.

"Something real..." he whispered, and he felt himself choking back tears.

He wanted more than anything to write, but he still didn't have what it took. He was annoyed at how helpless he was. He hated it, yet he couldn't stop his desire from surging.

Then he had a thought. It wasn't his lack of experience that was stopping him from writing.

"It's because I'm a fake, isn't it?" he muttered.

"Sorry, what was that?" Bakin asked.

Shinonome shook his head, quivering. He looked at the ceiling, not knowing what to do.

"Dammit! When the hell can I start creating stories?!" he moaned.

"You're lucky, because spirits have a very long life span," Bakin said kindly. "There's no need for you to rush. Just take each experience you encounter one at a time."

Although he was kind with his words, Bakin never pulled any punches.

"You've already set your mind to it. Don't give up now."

Whenever Shinonome remembered what Bakin had told him, he couldn't help but laugh. It was these moments that made him feel more grateful than ever for having met the author.

"Bakin was always so patient with me. He'd teach me how to craft stories bit by bit as I tended to the store. There were a few spirits that would make fun of me because they'd never heard of a spirit who hadn't even started out as a human writing stories," Shinonome said.

Many spirits couldn't let go of the belief that creating things was an activity exclusively for humans.

"And you shattered that with *Selected Memoirs from the Spirit Realm*, huh?" Suimei said.

Shinonome and Tamaki had both had a hand in creating the anthology, and there was no doubt in anyone's mind that Shinonome the Tsukumogami had written it.

The older man chuckled dryly. "No, I don't think I'd count that as my story."

"Why not? You published it," Suimei pointed out.

"Well, think about it. An anthology, by definition, is a collection of other people's stories, isn't it?" Shinonome replied.

"...Oh."

The Tsukumogami sighed. "Sure, the project was created with my interpretation in mind, and I did write an introduction for it, but...I still don't quite have the courage needed to write my own original book."

His eyes crinkled with kindness as he smiled. "I'll still give myself the credit for being brave enough to publish an anthology, though. I wasn't sure if my writing was good enough for other people to read. Bakin may have taught me how to write, but he never critiqued any of my stuff. Even so, I still had it in me to publish *Selected Memoirs from the Spirit Realm* because I had friends like Tamaki..."

Suddenly, he glanced toward the stairs.

"...and you, Kaori."

At some point, Kaori had come down from the upper floor. She remained silent as she stared at Shinonome, but she looked like she had something to say. Noname, on the other hand, immediately burst into speech.

"Oh my! You've finally left your room! I knew I was on the right track roasting some rice crackers," she beamed.

"Urk... Did you put them on to bait me?" Kaori winced.

The smell of charred soy sauce wafting through the air was enough to tantalize just about anyone.

"Heh heh," Noname giggled. "This secret trick has worked ever since you were little. Come, sit. They always taste the best when they're fresh!"

"Ugh. Fine, but that doesn't mean you're off the hook," the young woman grumbled as she scrunched her face.

Shinonome broke into a grin, delighted to see his beloved daughter after so long. But at the same time, he felt his heart squeeze with pain as he noticed that she had lost a bit of weight. It was only then that he realized how brutal the aftershock from his death would be, and he kept his mouth shut. He hung his head and stared into the brazier.

Kaori noticed her adoptive father's depressive state and sighed. She walked over and sat beside him with a *thump*, close enough for their arms to graze against each other. It was the kind of proximity a child would seek if they were feeling particularly affectionate toward their parent.

"You know, I would've loved to hear your story from the beginning too," she pouted.

Shinonome laughed heartily. "I was planning on telling you properly when I had the chance."

"It's not fair that you're always telling Suimei things before me," Kaori continued to grumble.

Hearing this, Suimei gulped. Shinonome found it odd that those words had disturbed the young man's calm, but he let it pass as he lifted a hand to ruffle his daughter's hair.

"Sorry, I didn't think that it would matter either way. I apologize," he said.

"Hey! How come she gets an apology when I don't?" Noname protested.

"Oh, quiet now, dear," Shinonome said as he shot the other spirit a glance.

Kaori tugged on her adoptive father's sleeve and looked up at him as she asked, "I never knew that Kyokutei Bakin lived here! I've never even seen him around. Wait, did he...?"

Shinonome chuckled, amused by the way she had jumped to conclusions.

"No, no," he said. "Jiisan's just gone because he said he wanted to travel and write."

"You mean, like, make a chronicle of his journey?"

"Yeah," the Tsukumogami nodded. "He was always big on traveling. He took the first chance he could to dump the bookstore on me and run off. He's been gone for a couple of decades now, so it's no wonder that you never knew about him. There well and truly is nothing but writing in that man's head. That's just how the real artists differ from the rest of us."

Kaori frowned. "Don't you miss him? He did practically raise you."

Shinonome smiled when he realized that Kaori was feeling empathetic for him.

"I do miss him," he said. "He also has this weird knack of popping in for just a little bit every time things seem like they're getting way too much to handle on my own. He's saved me so many times doing that."

Bakin had been traveling in the same sort of outfit since the Edo period. It was composed of a conical straw hat and a striped cape called a shimagappa. He'd have his short kimono sleeves rolled up, shins wrapped in leg covers, and belongings slung over his shoulder in a bundle. Whenever Shinonome was feeling lost and saw that familiar figure, he'd know he was in good hands and realize all over again just how much Bakin had influenced his life.

"Actually, the last time he came back was just after I found you. Wanna hear about it?" Shinonome asked.

Kaori nodded. When the Tsukumogami opened his mouth to speak, she leaned in and a wave of nostalgia flooded over her.

This feels just like when he used to read picture books to me as a kid, she smiled.

Shortly after Shinonome began learning how to write, he became completely stuck. Whenever he sat before some paper, his mind would be just as blank with nary a story coming to him.

All that appeared in his head were boring ideas that he couldn't possibly write about, and so his hand remained unmoving. The most he would do was accidentally get some ink on the paper, throw it away, and rinse and repeat.

Bakin wasn't exactly what anyone would call a good teacher. He taught a few basics and then went traveling, leaving Shinonome to his own devices as a writer while also putting him in charge of the bookstore. The Tsukumogami was at a loss, especially with his new responsibility of running the store. Although he felt angry at first, he couldn't help but laugh about how typical it was of Bakin to do something like this.

Although he hadn't intended to take over the store, he understood that it was a job worth doing. However, while he found great interest in delivering books to places that didn't have any, he would be lying if he said that it didn't bother him, either. Basically, it wasn't what he truly wanted to do—he'd never been able to cast away his dream of becoming something genuine.

When will I turn into something real?

His dream grew stronger by the day, but at the same time, telling himself that the right time would eventually come was slowly chipping away at his will.

Was he the weird one for having a dream like that when everyone else just wanted to lead a peaceful life? After all, it wasn't as if being fake affected his daily life in any way.

Maybe it was impossible for him to become real because he'd been born a fake.

These thoughts of despair crossed his mind often, but he

would shoot them down every time. Plus, he thought there might be other ways of becoming real aside from creating something. But even as he considered other options, nothing caught his interest quite like creation or writing. Over and over again, he would see the image of Bakin facing his desk with utter commitment in his mind. He also recalled the forger who created him, as much as the mere memory of that man irritated him.

When he finally took a closer look at his quarters, he realized he had left everything in a mess that belied the small amount of work he did. His writing desk was covered in scattered instruments, his brush had rolled away with dried ink on its bristles, and a thin layer of dust had started to gather on his inkstone.

"Characters need conflict. Only those who can overcome conflict are strong."

This was around the time that Shinonome met Tamaki. The first thing he noticed was the man's gloom, and he could never figure out what his new acquaintance was thinking at any given time. He also found the occupation of story-seller to be a strange one, not to mention his habit of comparing everything to stories. Tamaki also hated the old and championed the new, and was locked in a struggle to rid himself of his immortality.

For some reason, though, the two got along quite well. Maybe it was because they both had a passion for creating art.

When Shinonome had stopped even taking his brush in his hand, Tamaki said to him, "Everyone gets sick of their passion at one point or another. I think that's what you're feeling right now."

His eyes softened as he peered through his colored glasses at Shinonome, who was drinking with a sour look on his face.

"But if you do truly love creating things from the bottom of your heart..."

He downed his glass in one gulp and glanced at his right hand.

"...you'll return to it eventually, whether you like it or not. For now, just rest."

"Really?" Shinonome asked.

"Yep," Tamaki replied.

His words were just as brutally honest as Bakin's had been, and coming from someone else who had dedicated his entire life to art, they carried weight.

"Let me know when you feel like writing again. I'll give it a good read and critique it to hell and back. If you still feel like you can write after that, then I'll help you put out a whole book," Tamaki said.

"Who do you think you are?" Shinonome laughed.

"Ha ha!" Tamaki laughed back. "I can't help it. All artists are harsh to the newbies."

The time he spent with Tamaki was worth more than gold to the Tsukumogami. The man was his first friend, and he felt at ease with him. Soon after Shinonome befriended Tamaki, Toochika became another close friend.

"What are you guys talking about so seriously?" the kappa chimed in. "You should be giving me first dibs on any hot women you've found, you know."

"Look what the cat dragged in," Shinonome said. "Anyway, I thought you already met someone over in Shinjuku. You were so madly in love that you couldn't shut up about her."

"Shinonome, how could you?!" Toochika gasped. "Shinjuku, huh? I think I did meet someone there, but I don't even remember what she looks like anymore. I always look to the future, never the past!"

"...Would it kill you to settle down with just one woman and love her for the rest of your life?" Tamaki muttered.

"Ooh, what's this?" the kappa perked up. "I didn't think you were the kind to believe in true love. Now you've *got* to tell me more about your love life!"

"Never," Tamaki insisted. "I won't do her dirty like that."

Shinonome enjoyed simply sitting around and chatting with just the three of them. This was his first time experiencing back-and-forths like these. He was beginning to collect more and more experiences within himself, planting seeds of emotions. They were not enough for him to write, though. Whenever he was faced with his blank pieces of paper, he would be gripped by fear. He couldn't help but feel that he had no way of becoming real if he couldn't write.

It was like a pair of hands had closed around his throat.

He buried his head in his arms. He felt trapped. Now that he had a body, he could go anywhere he wanted, but not a single muscle in him wanted to move.

That was eighteen years ago. It was also the time when a little girl entered his life.

"Waaaaaahhh!"

"Hey, Shinonome, can you take care of her?"

The request was from a black cat who had brought with her a human girl around three years old, the age when any child would need a parent. Her chestnut eyes were filled with fear and overflowing with tears as she cried on and on.

The black cat said, "You sell human books, so taking care of a kid is nothing, right?"

Shinonome frowned, not understanding the situation. After all, he'd never raised a child before.

"Hey, you, cat! What do you think you're doing?" he said.

"Oh, you know. I just thought of you and figured I should bring her here," she replied.

"Mama!" the girl whined. "Mamaaa!"

Noname and the black cat had set the girl aside to discuss things between themselves. Shinonome, unable to leave the child wailing by herself any longer, reached out to gently pat her head. He'd seen some father somewhere do the same thing to his child, so he thought he should do it too.

"Don't cry. That won't solve anything," he said, squatting down to look at the girl. He flashed the child a toothy grin, and she stopped crying, blinking at him with her big, damp eyes. They were clear as crystal, and different from the eyes of the people Shinonome had lauded as real.

"Where's my mama?" she asked.

"Your mama's, uh...somewhere," Shinonome said.

He hoisted the girl into his arms, and she peered around.

When she realized that her mother was nowhere to be seen, her face scrunched up, and she threw her arms around the Tsukumogami's neck.

"Mama... Mama..." she bawled.

"I'm not your mama, but, uh, everything's going to be all right. There's no need to be scared," Shinonome soothed her, stroking her head gently.

She squeezed him closer to her, and Shinonome felt a warmth and gentleness that he didn't know how to describe. It was the first time he had experienced anything like it, and it left him a little bewildered.

Noname and the black cat stared at him as he embraced the girl.

"You seem pretty good with children," the woman mused.

"Do you have a kid you haven't told us about?" the cat asked.

"What?! No!" Shinonome sputtered, his face red. "I don't need the two of you ganging up on me."

But his outburst backfired on him as the girl, frightened by the loud noise, began to whimper.

"Whoa, I'm sorry! Don't cry, please!" the Tsukumogami panicked, trying to calm her back down. Once she was quiet again, the spirits began discussing what to do with her. They decided that the black cat would search for Kaori's mother, and those at the bookstore would look after her in the meantime. It was all planned on the fly, but it would be too coldhearted of them to leave a human girl alone when there were so many spirits out there that hungered for human blood and flesh.

It's just for a little while, Shinonome had figured. *It's not like I'm going to be raising her forever.*

And, like always, he was still unable to write, but he tried to convince himself that this was all part of building experience.

Two weeks passed. They'd all thought that finding the girl's mother would be an easy task, but the black cat struggled and turned up nothing in the end. And so they continued to tend to the child, but it proved to be a very tough battle. Perhaps because she felt nervous being separated from her parents, the girl had problems with wetting herself and was constantly on edge, crying from fright when she saw the glimmerflies that followed her.

They'd already lost count of how many times they needed to change her in one day and how often they needed to comfort her and sweep her into their arms. By nightfall, Shinonome would be run utterly ragged, but he'd still need to stay by the girl's side until she fell asleep.

"Mama... Mama... Mama..." she'd mumble as she drifted in and out of consciousness. Not knowing what to do in this situation, Shinonome simply stared into the darkness around him.

So humans can't fall asleep if they're alone? What a troublesome bunch.

He felt a stab of irritation. Usually, he'd be able to spend this time reading a book, but he couldn't even light the room with this child here. He hated that he was barred from partaking in one of his favorite pastimes.

I never thought this would be so tough!

As he wallowed in the hardship of child-rearing, he became tempted to dump all the work on Noname. However, as he cast his eyes down to his sleeve, he saw that Kaori was gripping it with a tiny hand. She seemed to like Shinonome the most out of all the spirits. It wasn't as if she disliked Noname, but even having Shinonome out of sight would upset her.

I need you, her delicate hand seemed to say.

But I don't have time for this, he grumbled internally.

Kaori murmured and turned over, making eye contact with him.

"Shinomeme," she mumbled as she beamed like a blooming flower.

The Tsukumogami patted her stomach gently and encouraged her to go to sleep, to which she gave a small nod. Her face relaxed and her breathing deepened as she fell into a deep slumber. Shinonome had finally managed to put her to bed for the day and earned himself some alone time.

"Who you calling Shinomeme? My name's *Shinonome*, silly," he muttered, slowly removing her fingers from his sleeve so as not to wake her.

He stood and heaved a sigh. A fair amount of time had already passed since the black cat started the search for Kaori's mother, but something was off. It seemed to him that the cat wasn't putting in as much effort as she could to find the woman she was seeking. Maybe she had her reasons, but right now he wanted nothing more than for the child to return to where she came from.

He peered down at the sleeping Kaori. The temperature was moderate, and yet she was sweating so much that her hair was now damp. If he left her alone, she would probably catch a cold. As he wondered whether he should change the towels that had been laid out, he frowned.

What am I doing? I'm not even her father, he thought. *That's enough of that.*

He sighed and turned his gaze to his desk. He'd swept it clean for fear of Kaori messing with any of his things, but guilt began to creep in as he stared at its empty surface. He'd given writing no thought at all since the girl's arrival. All his available brain capacity had been dominated by taking care of her.

How am I supposed to become real like this? he scoffed dryly at himself.

Well, a fake was a fake. He was born one and would probably die as one too.

"I want to be real," he whispered. "I'm so tired of being fake."

He curled up and hugged his knees to his chest. His heart stung. The anxiety of his unknown future was like a crushing weight on his shoulders.

He released another sigh and realized that Kaori was locking eyes with him through the darkness.

"Wanna pee," she said.

Shinonome felt the blood drain from his face. He'd failed to put her to sleep, so he was back at square one. His posture sagged, and he scratched his head.

The days of trouble continued. Shinonome spent every waking moment desperately trying to calm the crybaby Kaori, cleaning up the mess she left at mealtimes, taking her out to unwind and look at the stars, and buying little treats and candies for her that he'd never have considered purchasing otherwise. The more time they spent together, the fonder Kaori grew of him, and she would follow him around like a smiling duckling.

"And what about when you first started living with Bakin? You were just like a duckling then too," people would laugh.

As time passed, Shinonome started thinking about things differently. He even began to think that taking care of Kaori was fulfilling in its own way. Something about it made him feel more alive than when he was sitting at his desk and unable to do anything but get frustrated at his inability to work.

"Shinomeme! Look!" Kaori announced proudly, holding out the plate she had cleared, even though her face and the dining table were smeared with ketchup.

"Wow, you're such a good girl! You did great," Shinonome smiled as he wiped the sauce away. The girl had grown with each passing day, and she was also more comfortable living in the spirit realm now. The one thing that remained the same was that she still preferred to cling to his side.

"Where Shinomeme go?" she whimpered.

"Jeez, at least let me go to the bathroom in peace..." he sighed.

The Tsukumogami would find himself crumbling under the smallest of things, but at some point it started to become enjoyable for him. Unbeknownst to himself, he'd begun to look for

Kaori whenever she was out of sight. It turned out that he even wanted to cling to her side too. Whenever she smiled at him, his heart would melt. He could stare at her playing joyfully all day and never get tired of it. He loved seeing her picking up small or pretty rocks that she liked, and he even grew a little shy whenever she handed him a picture she'd drawn of him in black and beige crayon. The stars above seemed to shine brighter when they gazed upon them together, and he marveled at the tininess of her hands when he held them in his.

Shinonome's time—and world—had been completely taken over by Kaori.

He had basically no time to himself, and there were days where he felt suffocated by all the things that didn't go the way he wanted. But the strangest thing about being ruled by this tiny tyrant was that he was smiling more and more every day.

Sometimes, Noname would jokingly tease him by telling him that he was "just like her real father," but these words stung more than she realized.

"Kaori doesn't need a fake for a father," he muttered.

Her real parents were probably waiting for her in the human world, anyway. Whenever the thought crossed his mind, his heart would twist into a knot, and it would get tighter still whenever Kaori looked at him with her eyes full of trust.

One day, the black cat returned with some final news.

"Kaori has no parents or reliable relatives. Basically, there is no one in the human world who can take care of her," she said.

Noname seemed to take the news badly.

"What do you mean? I thought you said you found some leads!" she exclaimed.

All the spirits present knew that the cat had gone to Akita, and she'd even found posters searching for a child. However, the fact was that this human girl had no parents to call her own.

"Yes, I did have some leads, but there's no mother. That's all I can say," the cat reiterated, and her tone suggested that she was not going to expand on that. She walked over to Kaori and rubbed against the girl.

"I'll do everything I can to protect her, but we can't exactly have a cat taking care of a human. So please, can we leave her at the bookstore?" she said, peering at Shinonome sincerely.

"Nyaa-chan?" Kaori said, tilting her head.

"That's Nyaa-*san* to you," the cat replied, her ears twitching. Her tone had become much gentler than before. Shinonome realized that something must have happened to cause the Kasha spirit to change, but unfortunately, he could not see into the depths of her mind.

He looked at Noname, who looked right back at him. She shared the burden of looking after Kaori, so this decision would affect her life significantly as well. Plus, her apothecary took a lot more energy to run than the bookstore.

"Right," she whispered.

Then she shrugged. "That means we'll have to keep playing family, I guess."

Playing family... Meaning it was all a charade. It wasn't real. This entire relationship was fake.

Noname swooped her green hair up into a ponytail, took a deep breath, and flashed a bold smile.

"All right, bring it on!" she declared, excitement flooding into her cheeks in a shade of red.

"I accept this challenge. I've always wanted a family, anyway. I've going to give this child aaaaaall the love she needs and raise her into the loveliest woman the world has ever seen. I'm always going to be there for her when she needs me. If she falls, I will be there to catch her. When she's going through hard times, she'll always have a shoulder to lean on. I'm going to be a mother who Kaori can be proud of!"

She squeezed Kaori tightly in her arms and showered kisses upon the child, whose eyes darted about in confusion.

Noname then pointed a daring finger at the Tsukumogami.

"And you'll be the father, Shinonome!"

"What? Me?!" he gasped.

"Yes, you! Who else would be her father besides you?" Noname said. "And you'd better put in one hundred percent too. Sure, we might just be playing family, but it's up to us to raise Kaori properly. We need to take this seriously."

Shinonome fell silent, at a loss for words.

"Be a real father for her," Noname implored.

She seemed to be the only enthusiastic one in the room, though.

"Hey, cat..." Shinonome said, hoping for some guidance.

"My name isn't *cat*, it's Nyaa," the Kasha spirit said.

"I thought you hated being called that," Shinonome said.

The black cat huffed and turned away, then struck up a conversation with Noname. Shinonome, having missed his chance to join in, was left all alone. He chewed on his lip in silent solitude, uneasy about what the future had in store.

A few days later, on a night when Noname was absent, Kaori was acting especially restless. It was well past her bedtime, yet she would not stop crying. She refused the picture book Shinonome had offered to read her and kicked and screamed when he tried to hug her, so he thought that taking her outside the store might switch up her mood.

"I don't wannaaaaaa! Aaaaaahhh!!!" she wailed, her screams echoing in the stillness of the spirit realm. A few glimmerflies flew toward her, gathering around the child as though they were checking up on her.

"Calm down, calm down..." Shinonome begged.

A nice, gentle rocking was normally enough to get her to stop crying. He could also play the waiting game and let her tire herself out with her sobbing. But today, she showed no sign of stopping. It had been a few months since Kaori had come to the spirit realm, so perhaps she'd gained more stamina in that time.

"Mamaaa!" she howled. "Mama, Mamaaa!"

Oh, not now, please...

Although he was racked with exhaustion, Shinonome continued to comfort the girl. It was hard to tell when it was all going to end, though. He wanted nothing more than to rest, to spend some time alone, but Kaori cried on and on. The Tsukumogami could feel his patience wearing thin as the girl bawled for the mother who was never going to come for her.

"Mamaaaaaa!!!"

"Oh my God!" Shinonome growled. His dark emotions were bubbling over. He'd had enough of the endless catering he had to do for this child, and he hated himself for his inability to become real no matter how hard he struggled.

He couldn't hold himself back any longer.

"Give it up! Your mama's gone! You've only got me!" he shouted.

Kaori's crying stopped for a second. Shinonome thought that the screaming was finally over, but she started again, and louder this time.

"Aaaaaaaaahhh!!!" she shrieked.

Although Kaori was still only three years old, by now she was at a stage where she could understand what was being said to her. It was no surprise that she would suddenly explode after being told that her mother was gone.

Oh, I've gone and done it.

Filled with guilt, Shinonome shifted Kaori in his arms. Noname's words came back to him.

"Be a real father for her."

His face crumpled, and he gnashed his teeth.

Be a father? When I can't even calm a single child down? We're not related—or even the same species! I was born a fake anyway, so there's no way I can be a real anything to anyone.

Suddenly, the little girl in his arms felt like a ton of bricks.

He stumbled, overwhelmed by the weight. He tensed his arms, afraid that he was going to drop her.

What was going on? Was he just tired because he had been holding her for so long? Or was it something else?

"Waaaaaah! Mamaaaaaa!"

It was as if Kaori was saying that someone like him could never fill her mother's shoes. She squirmed like she was trying to escape Shinonome's clutches.

I can't do this anymore. I can't raise a child.

Hot tears slowly pricked at his eyes as his vision blurred. His heart felt like it was going to buckle in on itself.

What can I even do? I'm not her real father. I'm a fake. I'm worse than a real person in every single way. I have no value. I can't... I can't do anything.

He wanted to throw everything aside and run somewhere far away, but he couldn't bring himself to mercilessly abandon a child.

I really can't commit to anything, can I?

He couldn't write properly. He couldn't take care of Kaori properly. He was the polar opposite of the real ones out there who could stick to their vision and achieve their goals. He could neither give up nor accomplish things. All he could do was live as a sham and slowly sink to the bottom of the swamp of his regrets.

"Dammit."

How did things turn out like this?

"Dammit...!"

I just wanted to be real!

"Goddammiiiiiit!!!"

The emotions he'd been holding back had finally come to a head, and he cried like a child throwing a tantrum. Hot tears rolled down his cheeks, making even Kaori, who was still in his arms, damp.

"Shinomeme?"

The girl had stopped crying and was staring at the Tsukumo-gami with wide eyes. She blinked, unable to grasp what was happening. She finally reached out a tiny hand, slick with the sweat from her earlier wailing, and touched it to the spirit's face.

"Don't cry," she said, trying to pat him. "It's okay. Don't be scared."

Those were the very same words that Shinonome had offered her countless times. She must have been trying to copy him, perhaps because it had worked so well in calming her down. It was so adorable that Shinonome felt his heart clench.

He gritted his teeth, trying to hold back his tears. He hugged Kaori closer to his chest, his face a wet and crooked mess.

"Sorry I can't be a real father for you. I'm sorry. I'm sorry..." he whispered.

"Ngh," Kaori squirmed. "Shinomeme, I can't breathe."

But despite her struggles, the spirit just couldn't bring himself to let go. He feared that if he did, he would transform into something that was beyond all help.

"Jeez, you're still as inarticulate as ever, huh?" said a familiar voice.

Shinonome's heart leapt in his chest, and he turned around to find an old man wearing a conical hat and a shimagappa cape.

"Bakin!" he shouted with a definite wobble. The author stretched his suntanned face into a crooked grin.

"How's your writing going, my student?" he asked.

Shinonome gulped and shook his head.

"Terribly. I don't have the slightest idea of how to do anything," he said.

"I figured," Bakin answered, laughing silently.

Kaori looked at Bakin, then back at Shinonome.

"Who is this old man?" she asked with a tilt of her head.

Kaori fell asleep straight away once Shinonome returned her to their room, perhaps because she had now well and truly tired herself out from crying. The Tsukumogami slumped his weary body against the wall, and Bakin, who had changed out of his travel clothes, sat opposite him.

"What happened?" he asked.

Those two words made Shinonome spill everything that was on his mind—his writer's block, his lack of motivation, and the little girl who was dropped on him out of the blue.

"Time just flies by when I have to look after a kid. I don't even have a moment to spare for my own thoughts, and the sun sets before I can do anything at all. I'm panicking because I'm not getting any writing done, but I don't have the time to pick up a brush, either. At first, I thought this would be temporary and all I'd have to do was ride it out, but..."

"But it turned out that you had to raise her permanently?" Bakin guessed.

"Yeah. We couldn't find her parents anywhere!"

The old man's expression darkened, and he looked over at the sleeping Kaori with heartbroken eyes.

Shinonome clenched his fists.

"All I do is half-ass everything," he choked, his voice strained like he was trying to squeeze all the pain out of his throat. "How did I get here? All I want is to become real."

Bakin raised an eyebrow. He let his eyes wander and then asked quietly, "I've been wondering this for a while now. Why are you so obsessed with being real?"

The Tsukumogami's cheeks flushed red. He swept his head downward and gripped his hands more tightly. It had only just hit him that he'd never told Bakin he was a forgery. In fact, the truth also remained unknown to Tamaki, Toochika, and Noname, as he'd always tried to hide this source of deep shame.

His nails dug into his palms. When he released his fingers, his hands had turned white. He took a deep breath. He'd sworn to protect his secret till the day he died, but maybe, just maybe, it would be all right to tell Bakin. After all, the author was the one who had shown him what a genuine soul was like, given him a name, and served as his master in the craft of writing.

"I'm... I'm a forgery," Shinonome admitted after mustering all the bravery he could.

Bakin's eyes widened slightly.

Shinonome quickly began to ramble about his history, trying to bury his shame and terror. He told Bakin about his birth in the run-down shack during the Edo period, the forger who painted

THE HAUNTED BOOKSTORE

him, and the reputation that various swindlers had built for him by pretending he was a Maruyama Okyo piece and a scroll of good fortune.

"Somewhere along the way, I became recognized as a real work of art, all because some appraisers were bribed to lie about me."

He swallowed. He was too frightened to raise his head, afraid to see what kind of look Bakin was giving him.

"I should have just faded into obscurity as a forgery, but here I am as a Tsukumogami, all because a bunch of people decided I was a real piece worth being treasured."

That was why Shinonome wanted to be real. His obsession stemmed from the fact that he was a forgery that had been falsely sold as the genuine article.

"Pffhah!" Bakin burst out.

Shinonome whipped his head up in shock and saw the old man's shoulders shaking from the chuckle he was holding back in his throat.

"What's so funny?" groaned the upset Tsukumogami. "Am I really that stupid?"

He felt like he had been stabbed by the one he trusted so wholeheartedly. However, when Bakin saw the tears well up in his student's eyes, it was his turn to be shocked.

"No, no," he clarified, wiping his tears away. "I was just impressed by what an amazing man your artist must have been."

"What?" Shinonome's jaw dropped.

Bakin drew a pipe out of his clothes, stuffed it with tobacco, and lit it.

"So you don't like being a forgery that was treated as something real? It's not as unreasonable as you make it out to be. When something like this happens, it just means that the fake has surpassed the real."

He sucked on the pipe, savoring every smoky note on his tongue, and gave a mischievous grin.

"Maruyama Okyo was amazing. He drew the artwork you were based on, right? He's what you would call real, no doubt. And you said that the artist who drew you was a forger, correct? If something is fake, the truth will always come to light. Suspicion is cast at the very first sign of uncertainty, after all."

Shinonome sat unmoving, not saying a single word. Bakin suddenly looked off at an unseen horizon, as if he had remembered something.

"Do you remember the day you were brought to my house?" he asked.

"Oh, yeah, of course!" the Tsukumogami answered.

"A man called Ozu Keiso gave your scroll to me. He had a real eye for art. I knew I could trust him as both a merchant and a writer. He was...a very dear friend of mine," Bakin said with fond eyes.

He exhaled a soft puff of white smoke and grinned again. "There's no way he would ever bring me something fake, so I'd say you are real."

"No, wait!" Shinonome protested. "I just told you, I'm a fake that was created by a forger—"

"Oh, quiet!" Bakin exclaimed. "Or are you saying that you know art better than Ozu does?!"

The Tsukumogami jumped at Bakin's sudden rise in volume. As he was still trembling, Bakin continued matter-of-factly.

"Honestly, it doesn't matter who drew a piece of art. What matters is how good it is, and I trust my eyes," he said. "Shinonome..."

The corners of his eyes crinkled as a gentle smile pushed them into crescents. His lips curved, and his eyebrows relaxed. It was the first time Shinonome had seen such a surly face look so peaceful.

"Your artwork is amazing," Bakin said.

Shinonome gasped.

"I am positive that your creator was someone quite incredible," the author continued. "I can't say I've ever seen the original piece before, but I can still confidently tell you that it won't come anywhere close to how stunning you are."

The memory of his artist came back to Shinonome again. The forger was a man who moved his brush with such intensity that he would forget to blink and breathe. He knew better than anyone else that his works were fake, yet he still refused to compromise on their artistry. And now, for the first time in history, his hard work was being recognized even though he'd never had the chance to leave his name behind.

The Tsukumogami sniffed, and his tears returned. He couldn't stop the sobs from welling up from the burning heat in his chest.

"B-Bakin..." he said, quaking. He was doing his utmost to hold his head up high, even as the tears kept falling. His teacher was giving him an important lesson here. He had to keep his back straight and listen well.

Bakin continue to speak calmly but firmly, as though acknowledging Shinonome's bravery.

"As I see it, your main body is as real as it gets. But it's the inside that really counts, you know," he said. "You're still so immature. What a waste of a perfectly good piece of art! You became a Tsukumogami because everyone loved you so much, so don't let them down now!"

"But... But..." Shinonome sniffled, wiping his face with a sleeve. His expression drooped like that of a lost child. "I don't know what to do. I can't even write a proper story, and I've failed to gain an interest in anything else."

"Jeez, you really are clueless. Just look around you," Bakin sighed as he glanced at the sleeping Kaori. "You've planted a good seed here."

"A seed?"

"Yep. One that will grow big and strong," the old man chuckled, peering at his student. "You have to raise her either way, right? Then just do it."

"Me? Raise her?" the Tsukumogami asked.

"Sure, your scroll looks amazing, but you need a major overhaul on the inside and more experience too. This girl looks like she's still quite young, with the life experience and mentality to match."

"What are you trying to say?" Shinonome frowned.

"Since you need experience, just focus on raising her," Bakin said casually. "If you still think you're a fake, then put in all the effort that a real father would. Build on your experience with her.

If you do that, you'll find things that you want to write about, and you'll be reaching for your brush like it's second nature in no time."

The author then recommended that Shinonome keep a diary as well. Recording his days would make for good practice in turning his thoughts into words, he said.

"You were really diligent in keeping your own diary, huh?" Shinonome recalled.

"That's right. I was pretty shocked to see it get published as a book in the human realm, though," Bakin admitted with a merry laugh.

When he saw that Shinonome still looked lost, he said, "You'll be all right. I know you can do it."

"Oh!" the Tsukumogami gasped. "Really? You think so?"

He nodded to himself. Just hearing those words was enough for him. He was already amazed to hear so much praise for the parent-artist whom he'd tried to forget for so many years, but Bakin had also set him on a new path that he'd never considered before. He realized all over again just how much impact the author had had on his life and how lucky he was to be a student of someone so wise.

"Can I actually become real on the inside too?" he asked meekly. Even though he now had a new path to walk down, he was still scared to set foot on it.

Bakin laughed softly and looked into his student's eyes.

"It'll happen when it happens. You might just find your answer when this girl grows up and is able to leave the nest."

Shinonome nodded. There was still a long way to go before Kaori would mature into an adult. A very, very long way to go, in fact. When he thought of what would happen if he strayed from the path Bakin had given to him, Shinonome felt the fear trickling in, but this was it—he had no choice but to just do it.

Especially because Kaori didn't have anyone else in her life.

"Looks like you've found the courage you need," Bakin said, picking up his conical hat.

The Tsukumogami began to panic as he saw his teacher putting his traveling clothes back on.

"Wait, you're going already?" asked the flustered Shinonome. "Why not stay and relax for a while? I want Kaori to meet you, and I've also made some new friends. The bookstore has more customers than ever, and Noname and Toochika miss you too!"

But Bakin ignored his pleas. Once he was dressed, he flashed Shinonome a grin.

"Sorry, I've just got too many things that I want to write about," he said as he spun on his heel.

He paused for a moment and said, "Oh, but maybe I'll come back for a little visit once the girl's grown up."

Then he left.

That had been eighteen years ago, and Bakin still showed no sign of returning. No doubt, he was somewhere out there absorbed in a world of his own creation.

After that meeting with Bakin, Shinonome devoted all his energy to raising Kaori. They passed their days laughing and crying together, and Shinonome also learned to get angry at the typical things a father would. He made sure to write in his diary every day after Kaori had fallen asleep, and he would occasionally read back on his entries deep into the night to ponder whether he was being a good father and think of anything he might need to improve on.

Around the time Kaori turned ten years old, Shinonome began to grow increasingly concerned for the spirits whose links with the human world had grown thin. More and more spirits were passing away without anyone ever knowing about them, and he wondered if there was anything he could do to help. As he mulled over this question and reflected on it in his diary, he realized that he no longer felt afraid to write. Maybe now he could finally pen something. That was why he approached Tamaki with the idea of writing *Selected Memoirs from the Spirit Realm*.

"Are you sure?" Tamaki had asked. "I know you said you wanted to write it yourself because there was no one else doing the writing, but..."

"I'll just be recording things instead of making my own stories, so I think I'll be fine," Shinonome assured him.

They decided to go forward with it. While Shinonome drafted *Selected Memoirs*, he also practiced creative writing on the side, bit by bit. Even after so much time, he still found it difficult to create a whole world and cast from scratch and struggled greatly with his work. However, this time, he felt at peace. After all, there was no need for him to rush.

Until Kaori grows up, huh?

He just had to foster his love for Kaori and the seed of his creativity with a bit of patience.

"I'm not sure what you want to become, but whatever it is, I'll do anything I can to help!"

One day, at the end of summer, Kaori took Shinonome off guard with those words. She must have unconsciously sensed his desire to become something real. As her offer sank in, he became overwhelmed by his daughter's adorable and considerate nature. The sense of fulfillment flooded through his entire body, and he almost started to cry.

"Sure. The moment I find something I want to be, I'll be sure to come to you."

I hope I didn't seem like I was going to cry. Did I sound like a proper father to her?

He wanted to ask Kaori one day, once she was older.

With the flow of time, Kaori matured from a helpless child to a fine young woman who was now capable of taking care of both herself and Shinonome. She had grown tall and beautiful, and she was well on her way to building her own life experiences, even finding someone to fall in love with.

Little by little, the distance of independence grew between her and Shinonome. Anyone could tell that she was now a mature adult who no longer needed the protection of a guardian, and she would surely start her own family someday too. Shinonome knew all of this, which was why he didn't feel much shock at all when Karaito Gozen told him that his main body couldn't be fixed. He'd had an inkling that would be the case, but more than that, he knew that the seeds he'd sown in his heart had blossomed fantastically. With a bit more nourishment and time, he was sure that his own unique story would grow too.

And, if he were to be honest, his thirst to become real had also subsided, because Kaori considered him to be a real—and *her* real—father. Of course, he felt sad that he was going to leave his beloved daughter behind, but above all he was excited for the story he'd been fostering within himself. There was nothing more...more *cool* than giving birth to a new story the moment the roaring flames of his life extinguished.

After Shinonome finished his lengthy story, Kaori spoke with a trembling voice.

"Is that why you don't want immortality?" she asked.

Shinonome's gaze fell onto the brazier, and he nodded with a single "Yes."

"In my closing moments as a Tsukumogami, I'm going to create an exceptional story," he said.

Kaori gripped his arm.

"Stupid! Stupid, stupid, stupid!" she wailed, shaking her father, who could only chuckle dryly in response.

"Am I the only one who wants to stay with you forever? Am I the selfish one here?" she whimpered, her voice tight and strangled.

Shinonome's face fell. With Kaori's gaze cast downward, he couldn't tell what kind of expression she wore, but he didn't need to see it to know that she was hurting more than she ever had.

"No, I'm the selfish one," he said, reaching out a hand to gently stroke Kaori's hair.

Pat, pat, pat.

With each touch, the heaving of Kaori's shoulders grew stronger. She grasped his sleeve, so hard that it seemed like the wrinkles might set in forever.

She looks just like she did when she was a kid, the Tsukumogami mused.

After that, Kaori didn't open her mouth again for the rest of the night. The loungeroom, which was usually filled with the most festive of clamors in the spirit realm, became enveloped in a silence so thick that not even Noname and Suimei could break it. The only thing that disturbed the air was the sparking of the fire, each of its soft pops as clear as the feelings that Kaori and Shinonome held close to their hearts.

Crackle. Crackle.

That night, as Shinonome was preparing for bed, Kaori came to visit him. He was pleasantly surprised since he couldn't remember the last time she'd done so.

She held out a well-loved picture book to him and asked, "Can you read this to me, Shinonome-san?"

Kaori was already well past the typical age for a picture book, so he didn't quite understand what her intentions were, but he nodded nonetheless and laid out another futon beside his. They both flopped onto their respective mattresses, and Shinonome began the tale of the mouse brothers who were on a mission to make pancakes. The pages had been leafed through so many times that they'd been worn smooth. He read the words on them just as he'd done when she was still a little girl, and Kaori listened as intently as a curious child. The glimmerfly light danced in her eyes as she hung on to every syllable, and Shinonome felt like he was looking into the entire universe when he glanced at them. He paused at the breathtaking sight.

Finally, the mouse brothers finished cooking their pancakes. The Tsukumogami glanced at Kaori again and noticed that her back was turned to him.

"I guess I'll go to bed too," he said. He lifted the lid of the lamp, watching as the glimmerflies fluttered out. He cracked open the window to let them escape, and he heard a small sniffle from behind him as they disappeared into the night.

I'm sorry, he thought. He opened his mouth to apologize but decided to shut it. He had his own wishes to fulfill, to go out how he wanted to. An apology would mean that he thought he was doing the wrong thing, and he couldn't let himself pour cold water all over the faith he allowed himself.

He looked out the window and into the darkness of the spirit realm. There was nary a spirit outside, and seeing the emptiness of the world out there made him feel slightly despondent.

He crawled under his covers without a word.

When Shinonome woke the next morning, he noticed that the second futon was completely empty. He scratched his head and folded it up until it was tidy enough.

"All right, let's get to work," he said as he began to grind some ink at his writing desk.

CHAPTER 3
A Tale for Eternity

EVEN IN THE EARLY MORNINGS of the spirit realm, the merry voices of spirits doing their shopping can be heard. However, I found myself walking the streets alone in silence after leaving the house before Shinonome-san had even woken up.

"Good morning, Kaori-chan! I've got some very fresh veggies in this morning. Come have a look!" a spirit called out to me from a shop.

I paused for a split second, but my mind remained completely blank. I couldn't think of an adequate response, and so I simply continued on my way.

"Huh? Maybe she didn't hear me," the spirit wondered.

When I heard the comment, it sent a pinch of pain into my chest.

I'm sorry, I did hear you, I mentally apologized, trying to ease the guilt I felt. I didn't have the energy in me to make small talk, only enough strength to keep my head down and pass through the lively street.

I didn't even have any destination in mind; I just wanted to get away from the bookstore. Being there brought back too many memories of my adoptive father, which was more than I could bear. I didn't want to see Shinonome-san, either.

He'd finally shared all the secrets he'd been keeping locked away. But, like always, he'd been so clueless and constantly beat around the bush. I could sympathize with his hesitation to bare his innermost thoughts, but I wished he'd also consider what it would be like to be on the receiving end of it all.

"In my closing moments as a Tsukumogami, I'm going to create an exceptional story."

I pulled a face as Shinonome-san's words rang in my mind.

"Why are men so obsessed with being cool or going out with a bang? I don't get it," I muttered.

My vision began to blur, and I hurriedly wiped my eyes with my sleeve. The dry air had rendered my skin more frail than usual, and the fabric stung as it dragged across my cheek. Out of the corner of my eye, I could see a bunch of glimmerflies fluttering about as if they were trying to catch my attention. As was always the case in the spirit realm, the day was dark as night, and the cloud of glimmerflies that were attracted to my human self stood out like a sore thumb. Among the spirits that passed by me on the street, I could spot a few that I recognized. However, they continued on their way without stopping so they could pretend they hadn't seen me crying, which I was grateful for. I sniffed and moved on.

The whole world didn't seem real. It all felt like a mirage.

Sometimes I wished that this was a nightmare I could wake up from. Deluding myself into thinking that I was just living a bad dream helped dull the pain, but in my moments of clarity, I would feel like a vacant hole had been punched out from my chest. I was running out of strength, lost and uncertain about what I should do.

A single coat couldn't fend off the unforgiving cold of the spirit realm, and I was feeling every bit of it. All the trees had already shed their leaves, and the scenery seemed to have a film of gray over it wherever you looked. I entered a side street covered in dead leaves that crunched under each step. As I walked, I spotted something black standing in my path.

"Where are you going?" it asked.

It was Nyaa-san. She was glaring at me with her sharp, multi-colored eyes.

"Nowhere," I answered and tried to walk past her.

But she simply stepped in front of me and leaped onto my shoulder with an agile bound.

"Take me with you," she demanded.

"Oof!" I gasped, surprised by her mass. She wasn't exactly the most lightweight cat on the block. "You need to go on a diet!"

Nyaa-san huffed and continued to glare grumpily at me.

"Oh, quiet. We've got more pressing matters at hand," she replied, waving her three tails about as if to tell me that I wasn't going to escape her anytime soon.

"I'm not going to do anything drastic," I told her to try and ease her worries, although I did appreciate that she was looking out for me.

The cat spirit twitched her whiskers.

"Are you sure about that? You don't exactly have the cleanest record, you know," she pointed out. "Once you've got your heart set on something, who knows what you'll end up doing?"

"You don't trust me?" I asked.

"No, I don't," she said. "You're too much like Akiho for me to do that."

I fell silent and stiffened when she brought up my mother's name. She had left me all alone at the age of three when she died, and I'd been too young to even see her off.

I felt the hot tears rise again, distorting my world. I was becoming convinced that crying so much in the past few days had broken my tear glands because they were turning on faucets for even the tiniest reasons. I automatically wiped the wet drops away, and my fragile skin protested as the friction stung it. It was unbearable, even though it didn't particularly hurt.

Ugh, I'm so weak now. Get a grip, I thought to myself.

Suddenly, I felt something soft and warm lapping against my face. When I looked up, my eyes connected with Nyaa-san's own worried ones.

"Well, it doesn't matter what you have in mind because I'll be there to stop you if I have to," she said with a slow blink.

"Nyaa-san..." I mumbled.

"You'll always have me, no matter how tough things get, and

no matter how much sorrow fills your heart," my best friend said. "It's my duty to bring happiness to you, after all."

"...Because you promised my mother that you would?" I asked.

"Well, there's that too, but..."

Nyaa-san rubbed her head against my cheek and mewed.

"...it's mostly because I love you. I'll always stay by your side, even as you take your last breath," she swore.

I gulped as I felt my emotions welling up again.

"Thank you," I whispered with a trembling voice, and Nyaa-san sighed.

"Jeez, save those precious tears for another time," she mumbled.

"Huh?"

"Nothing!" the cat spirit said. "Anyway, let's go somewhere. You want to get away from the bookstore, right? I totally get it. Like, who wants to see Shinonome writing anyway? Are we sure he's working hard and not just lying around on his butt? Eugh."

I spat out a laugh I couldn't hold back, and Nyaa-san seemed to relax when she saw me smile through my tears.

"Think back on all the tough times you've had to endure. You've made it through all of them, right? We're all here to lend you a hand. Remember, you're never alone," she reassured.

I sniffled and nodded, and my best friend showed me a rare smile.

"But, you know, we can't reach out to you if you shut yourself away. Now that you're finally out here with us, let's go vent your heart out. Sometimes you have to compromise because the world isn't black and white."

She looked off into the distance, but at what?

"We spirits don't fear death, but it's not like we want to see our loved ones pass away, either," she said.

I didn't know how to respond to her.

The leaves rustled as Nyaa-san hopped off my shoulder. She sat on the ground and glanced up at me.

"Jeez, this weather is miserable. No cat should have to endure this cold," she complained. "Hey, let's go to Noname's and buy a treat on the way. Can't run on an empty stomach!"

She walked off, and I followed. I noticed someone on the side of the road selling giant, round roasted chestnuts that were making my mouth water.

I noticed Nyaa-san's eyes lingering on the stall.

"Oh, did you want to get some?" I asked.

"I..." she faltered. "I mean, not really! I'm just looking!"

She hissed at me, and I giggled. I still wasn't feeling the best, but I did have the sense that a weight had been lifted off my shoulders.

I thought about Nyaa-san's suggestion of talking to someone. Maybe it would be a good idea to do that instead of stewing over my thoughts in solitude. If I did, would I finally be able to come up with an answer that I could accept? Would I be able to someday calm my stormy emotions and wash away the pain that was tormenting me?

Wouldn't that be the day I forget about Shinonome-san...?

I felt my mind grind to a halt. I wanted to squeeze my eyes shut and fling the truth I was facing into the darkness.

But I couldn't.

Shinonome-san wasn't going to change his mind, so what should I do as his daughter?

I looked up at the sky, watching the soft puffs of my breath dissolve into its expanse. Maybe it was because I'd shut myself away for so long, but somehow the sky of the spirit realm looked more beautiful than ever today.

With our bag of giant chestnuts in hand, Nyaa-san and I gaped at the sight before us.

"Hey, how much longer are you going to make us wait?! I'd like to get home by evening, if that's all right with you!" a spirit yelled.

"I placed my order first! Why are these others getting served before me?!" another protested.

"Waaah!" a child began to cry. "I'm tiiired! Moooooom!"

The apothecary had been transformed into a battlefield with an endless, snaking line of spirits who were out to get their remedies. When I peeked inside, I could see Noname and Suimei rushing around.

"I think this is the first time I've ever seen the apothecary so busy," I commented.

"Same," the cat spirit nodded. "I wonder if something happened?"

As we tilted our heads in confusion, we caught a snippet of a conversation between Suimei and a customer.

THE HAUNTED BOOKSTORE

"Hey, I heard that your formulas work so well because you used to be an exorcist," a sunakake-baba whispered with her hand over her mouth. "Is that true? They're saying that you know what makes a spirit tick because you used to kill them for a living."

Suimei almost rolled his eyes.

"Haven't heard that one. I just do whatever Noname teaches me. The results are all the sa—"

"Ah ha ha! Yes, yes, I suppose you can't tell the truth here!" the spirit cackled in high spirits, much to Suimei's chagrin. "Tell me some other time, I promise I won't tell anyone else. Oh, and one blend for cold sensitivity, please."

The young man sighed.

It seemed that there was a flood of spirits that wanted to see Suimei, and that was what had caused the size of the crowd to blow up.

"They look swamped," I said. "Should we try again later?"

"I guess we can't just go barging in either," Nyaa-san replied.

And so we left the apothecary, but that didn't stop Nyaa-san from sulking on the way back.

"Now our chestnuts have gone cold! When you have guests, you need to welcome them. They have a lot to learn about hosting!"

I chuckled in sympathy. It was our fault for visiting when we knew that this was a rush period for them.

I wasn't expecting it to be that bad, though, I thought.

I wanted Noname to wrap me in her warmth. I wanted to see Suimei because he always managed to calm me down. I knew

272

there wasn't much we could do under these circumstances, but I also couldn't help feeling a bit sad. Who else would be able to lend me an ear?

A potential candidate suddenly popped into my mind, and a burning sensation zapped inside of me. I gripped my fist, unconsciously crushing the paper bag of chestnuts in my hand.

What would she do in this situation? I wondered.

"Kaori? Are you all right?" Nyaa-san asked in confusion.

"Oh, yeah! Sorry," I answered, trying to laugh it off.

I fell silent again immediately, but the person in question wouldn't leave my head. I would need a lot of courage to visit her, though, because I wasn't sure I would be able to stay calm.

My gaze fell to the ground, and I gulped.

Nyaa-san, who had sat down, glanced up at me. Her blue and gold eyes were clear as crystal, and they were the perfect complement to the mountains of Akita that were preparing to enter winter. My mother had once pointed that out, a very long time ago.

As I stared deeper into her eyes, I started to see my mother. Unconsciously, I reached out to Nyaa-san. She usually didn't like being touched, but today she didn't seem to mind. I gently curled my arms around her and tried to imagine how soft and warm it might have been to hug my mother. I told myself that I was going to be okay, because I had the best, most trustworthy cat in the world by my side.

All right, let's go.

"Nyaa-san, I thought of someone I want to talk to. Will you come with me?" I asked.

She nodded. "I'll go wherever you want."

"Thanks, Nyaa-san. I love you."

I gave her a gentle pat on the head. The cat spirit dropped her usual haughty attitude and flattened her ears so I could pet her some more, which made me understand just how deeply she cared about me.

Would I be able to resolve my feelings if I talked to the person I had in mind? I wasn't sure, but something told me that I had to go and see her, no matter what.

The glimmerflies scattered with a whoosh of the wind. In their glow, the underground prison looked like it was beckoning mysteriously. As I stared at it from the bridge on top, I could just make out a small number of red fish swimming above it as well. A few rows of lanterns shining dimly in the dark lit up the home of the trapped souls below.

This was the place where the souls who had rejected reincarnation came to gather and rest. It was a strange place, even by the spirit realm's standards.

"Have you come here to bemoan your circumstances? Or are you here for revenge?" asked a woman who was leaning against the railing with obvious displeasure in her voice.

"No, I'm here for neither of those things," I smiled back.

"Don't lie to me," she scoffed, wrinkling her nose.

The woman wore a Buddhist nun hood and a purple rakusu, and her name was Yao Bikuni. She was the one who had damaged Shinonome-san beyond repair, about a year ago.

"I'm the reason why Shinonome is dying right now. I was the one who set fire to his main body. You must feel nothing but rage toward me," she said, stabbing her pipe at me.

I blinked. Something sinister began to bubble within me, and I only got angrier as the seconds ticked by. I opened my mouth to let my feelings spew forth, but suddenly Nyaa-san rubbed against my leg.

"Hey," she meowed, and my calm returned to me.

I took a deep breath and exhaled.

"I think you've already paid for what you did," I said with a glance at her left sleeve fluttering in the wind. "How's living without your arm?"

"Ha!" she laughed. "Is that what you've come to ask, you horrid, cheeky girl?"

"Cut the attitude," Nyaa-san hissed. "You want me to eat your other arm too? It's not like you'll die from it."

The color vanished from Yao Bikuni's face, and she looked at me awkwardly.

"If you're not here to get revenge or deliver books, then what other business could you possibly have?" she huffed.

"Um... I was just looking for someone to eat some roasted chestnuts with?" I tried, but the words got caught in my throat and came out as more of a mumble than I intended.

The nun clicked her tongue. Although the immortality she'd gained from eating mermaid meat had given her all the time in the world, it seemed that she had no time for jokes. I breathed in and tried to pep myself up.

"Who told you about my father?" I asked.

Yao Bikuni scrunched her face in disgust.

"Shinonome himself. In fact, he was all smiles when he came to report the news to me," she spat.

Apparently, he had said, "All Tsukumogamis break sooner or later, so don't worry too much about it."

It was so like him to say that, but it didn't make me want to face-palm any less.

"Did he forget that I was the one who wrecked his scroll?" the nun grumbled on. "Telling me not to worry just made me feel worse about it! What an awful man."

"Y-yeah..." I nodded. "I'm sure he didn't mean to do that, though."

"Pure types like him drive me crazy! Ugh, I want to throw up."

I guess Shinonome-san did get his own justice, in a way. As I thought about how funny it was, Yao Bikuni looked straight at me.

"Just say what you came here to say. I don't have all day," she scowled.

"...Okay," I said.

I tried to calm my racing heart, but being under the spotlight of Yao Bikuni's dark, piercing stare didn't help. She took no prisoners with her savage honesty, so the prospect of being vulnerable with her was nerve-racking.

I took a few steady breaths before opening my mouth.

"I don't know what to do," I admitted.

I could feel fresh tears streaming down past my wobbling lips as my face crumbled from the weight of my emotions. I felt oddly at peace, probably because my mind was already so filled with sorrow, but it didn't make the tears seem any less real.

"Everything just happened so suddenly, and I feel totally stuck. I can't seem to find a way out of the maze in my head. I don't even know if I should throw a tantrum or try and find peace with my father's choice."

I looked at Yao Bikuni with wet, unfocused eyes.

"What do you think I should do?" I whispered.

She clicked her tongue and raised an eyebrow.

"What are you asking me for? Go ask Noname or something. Isn't she your mother?"

"Yes, but I want your opinion," I said. "Because I appreciate how honest you are."

And that was the truth. I didn't agree with everything she did, but her role as the guardian and savior of lost souls made her worthy of trust. Behind her harsh words was some of the strongest compassion I'd ever seen, and I knew that she would be able to offer me some guidance.

She made a strange face, produced a handkerchief from her sleeve, and shoved it at me.

"Jeez, you're way too soft. You're giving *me* a headache," she muttered.

"Ah ha ha. Yeah, I kinda need to work on that," I laughed as I dabbed my eyes. "And you've had to say goodbye to a lot of your loved ones, so..."

Yao Bikuni grimaced.

Despite everything, she had a lot of love to give. Her immortality meant that she outlived all of her family and partners, and the love that she poured out from her heart became a sorrow that drowned her.

"You are really annoying, you know that?" she shot back.

Her appearance was that of a young eighteen-year-old, but she had more life experience than I could ever imagine. Every word from her mouth carried an immense weight, which was something I needed right now.

She knitted her brows and glanced at me. I looked back at her anxiously.

"Let me just ask...you're not expecting some happy miracle to happen, are you?" she sighed.

"No," I replied. "I'm an adult now. For better or for worse."

I might have been able to cope better if I were still innocent enough to believe in magic, but I'd already had reality knocked into me for a long time now. I knew the ways of the world. I was aware that death was merciless and it stopped for nobody, including the cicada siblings whose short lives ended in my arms.

"Good," the nun said with grief shining in her eyes.

"People lead many kinds of lives," she said as she gazed out at the lake, folding a finger down every time she listed one. "Lives that end with no regrets. Lives that are taken away without warning. Lives full of displeasure and regrets. I don't have to tell you which one is most common, do I?"

"No," I replied.

"Our most intense emotional experience comes when we're on the verge of death, and that goes for both humans and spirits. If a life is cut short, it doesn't matter how fulfilling it was. The person would still feel unsatisfied, and vice versa."

"So you're saying that as long as we're happy in our last moments..."

"You'd be able to say that you lived a good life," Yao Bikuni nodded.

"So you're saying I should make sure he dies as happy as possible?" I asked with an aching heart, trying to come to terms with her suggestion of accepting Shinonome-san's death. At least, that was what it sounded like she was saying.

"Is that what you think?" she questioned. "Or is that what your ego as a living person is saying?"

"My ego?" I asked in confusion.

"Well, that's what it is, isn't it?" she replied. "How can you tell whether anyone was satisfied when they died? You're not the one crossing the Styx with them. Same goes for funerals. No matter how much the mourners grieve, no matter how much incense you burn, how can you ever know for sure that it reached them? It's all just for self-satisfaction. For yourself."

"For myself..." I murmured.

Now she seemed to be saying that nothing anyone did would matter, which stung even more.

As my tears threatened to spill again, Yao Bikuni suddenly said, "But that's fine."

My eyes widened in surprise.

Yao Bikuni continued as she watched the glimmerflies in the sky.

"Death splits the paths of our lives in two. The living must continue on while the dead stop at their destination. The ones who are left with regrets and remorse are the living, not the dead, so you should just do whatever you want."

The light glowed softly in her peaceful eyes, a mark of the roads she had wearily walked.

"I'm sure Shinonome worked himself to the bone trying to be your father, but what about you? Have you ever thought about how much you let him spoil you?" she said.

I gulped. She had seen right through me.

The nun watched me quietly and said, as bluntly as ever, "Why are you still wasting time here? It's time for you to put in the work now, and I don't want to hear any complaints. Go think about what you would do for yourself until Shinonome's last moments, think long and hard about it. Are you his daughter or not?"

After leaving Yao Bikuni, I mulled over what she'd said as I aimlessly wandered the spirit realm. Once I realized where I was, I saw that I had arrived at a small hill on the outskirts of town. It was where I used to stargaze with Shinonome-san, and where I'd brought Suimei to admire the fields of nemophilas. But during this season, the blossoms had already wilted, and not a petal was in sight. I climbed the hill, crushing the dried leaves under my feet.

"What a beautiful color," I murmured as I looked up. The sky in the spirit realm was a blanket of autumnal purple, tinged with scarlet on the horizon. Winter, the realm's quietest season, was just around the corner.

I'm not sure what you want to become, but whatever it is, I've got your back!

I really missed the simple times I spent with my adoptive father.

"You know, I always thought he wanted to become an author."

A thought occurred to me as I stroked Nyaa-san's head beside me.

Shinonome-san was forged, so he tried to create his own story in an attempt to become something real.

I had once asked him, "So if I grow up, I can become anything?" and now I finally understood why the question made him falter. He was still in the middle of pursuing his dream—in the middle of growing his life experience through me.

He devoted himself to raising me, even though he didn't know if it would even help him become real. He shared so much of his time with me, for which I was forever grateful. I had only come so far because he showered me with all that love and charity.

"I want to become Shinonome-san's real daughter."

From the moment I gained self-awareness, that was the one hope that stayed with me.

It still did, because no matter how hard I tried, no matter how many times Shinonome-san told me that I was his daughter, the truth was that we were not related by blood. To be his daughter, I had to put in more than double the effort of any blood-related child.

I took a deep breath and looked inward. What was my duty as his daughter?

To support my father, I thought.

Shinonome-san had already accepted his death. Then shouldn't I make the best of whatever time we had left together? He was trying to create a story unique to his life, so supporting him was probably...no, supporting him was *definitely* the best choice to make.

"Hey, Nyaa-san? I'm his daughter, so I shouldn't spend all my time sulking and crying, should I?" I said.

Suddenly, the cat spirit slinked out from under my hand and dashed a short distance away, staring at something behind me. When I turned around, a voice called out to me.

"Kaori!"

It was Suimei. He looked out of breath.

"What's up?" I asked.

"What do you mean, what's up?" he gasped. "I heard you left the bookstore, so I came looking for you!"

"Oh, you shouldn't have!" I said. "Weren't you pretty busy at the apothecary? I saw a huge line there."

"What? You came to the store? You should've said hi or something," he said and sat beside me, still huffing and puffing. I felt a sting of guilt for making him worry so much.

"So, what's on your mind?" he asked.

The gaze of his light brown eyes made me feel exposed. I broke eye contact to try and save myself from the discomfort, looking up at the stars instead.

"I was just thinking about what I should do as Shinonome-san's daughter," I explained.

As I spoke, I tried desperately to move the muscles of my face that had frozen into an emotionless mask.

"I talked to Yao Bikuni and decided I had to stop being so negative and start thinking positively. Shinonome-san doesn't have a lot of time left, so I've got to do whatever I can to make sure I don't regret anything later."

I managed to pull my lips into a smile. It felt like a smile, anyway. I couldn't just...keep crying forever.

An unexpected warmth enveloped me, and I blinked. Suimei had swept me into his embrace, and I caught the smell of his sweat and the medicines he surrounded himself with. It was a special and calming scent that I could drift into for eternity.

"What is it?" I asked as I wrapped my arms around him, pressing his tender warmth against me.

He tightened his hug and grumbled, "You don't have to pretend you're okay around me, you know."

My breath stopped.

"You can share your tears with me," he whispered into my ear as he stroked my hair. "And you don't have to think you're being annoying or anything, because I swear you're not. I know everything there is to know about you, including your scatterbrained tendencies, how much you like to eat, your deep love for books, how hard you try to be a good daughter for Shinonome all the time, and how you're actually a crybaby."

"S-Suimei..." I mumbled.

"I think I said something like that last summer, didn't I?" Suimei asked.

The cries of the cicadas sprang from my memory. I realized that Suimei was hugging me the same way now as he did when the cicada siblings died.

"Just cry, silly. There's no need to hold it back," he said as he squeezed me. His embrace was so strong that it would have bordered on pain any other time, but today it was just what I needed.

"Ah..." I whimpered.

Then I could feel the hot tears welling.

"Waaah!" I wailed as I scrunched my face, letting the droplets roll down my cheeks. When they dripped off my chin and onto Suimei's clothes, the emotions that I'd been pushing deep down inside of me came bursting out.

"I hate this, Suimei! I hate everything!" I screamed like a petulant child. "I hate that Shinonome-san's going to disappear from my life! I want to spend more time sharing our happiness and sorrows together! I wish I could keep telling him off for making so much trouble!"

My emotions spiraled out of control, but Suimei stayed still and listened to everything that poured forth. I balled my fists as my frustrations and misery continued to boil over.

"I don't want to be positive anymore! I don't care about trying not to sulk anymore! To hell with giving him the support that a good daughter should. Who cares about what's best or whatever? I don't! I can't do this anymore!" I wailed. "I just... I just want to be with Shinonome-san!"

I would do anything to keep seeing him grumble over his writer's block and tell him off for lazing about the house. I wanted to keep feeling that he would always do whatever he could to protect me in spite of his sloppiness.

Was it so much to ask for our lives to keep going the way they always had?

"I'll do anything to make him stay with me. I'll stop nagging him so much and I'll never complain about him ever again. I swear I'll be a better and more thoughtful daughter. I'll try even harder at running the bookstore, so please..."

I sank deeper into Suimei's arms as my strength gave out.

"Please, don't leave me. I don't want to lose anyone else. I can't take this anymore."

My birth mother and father were both dead, and there was no one else left for me in the human realm. It had been that way since I was a child, so I'd always felt like I belonged more in the spirit world. And in that realm, my home was wherever my adoptive father was.

"Help me," I pleaded. "Shinonome-san's going to die. I don't want to see him die! I don't wanna, don't wanna, don't wanna!"

I continued to bawl like a child and thump my fists into Suimei, but he didn't even flinch and continued waiting for me to settle down. My desperation only grew stronger, though, and it seemed to have no end. The only way I could calm down was by accepting my father's death, but that didn't seem possible. There was no way that my heart would do it, and I didn't want to.

"Aaaaaagh!!!" I screamed. "I hate this!!!"

"So just make him eat some mermaid meat," came an airy voice from behind me.

My heart jumped at the sound. I turned around nervously and saw the mermaid butcher slither out from the shadow cast by Suimei and I. The casual outfit he'd worn when I last saw him was gone, and instead he was wearing a traditional fisherman's outfit, like a typical depiction of Urashima Taro.

The butcher stuck a hand into his fishing basket and pulled out a writhing mermaid.

"I'm sure you already know this, but mermaid meat can grant you any wish you want," he said with a grin. "And that includes restoring a Tsukumogami to perfect condition. I can give you a few slices if you want, and all you'd have to do is mix it into Shinonome's food."

I felt a chill run down my spine as I stared at the mermaid butcher's serene smile.

"Didn't you say that you'd have to get permission from whoever's eating this stuff first before giving it to them?" I asked hesitantly.

"True, but do we really have time for that?" he shrugged. "Plus, I think Shinonome would be okay with this if he knew that you were the one who wanted it!"

His green eyes creased with his smile, a smile that exuded goodwill.

"Eternity can cure anything! I'm sure he'd be fine with immortality if he knew that the alternative was to hurt his daughter this much. I promise I'll help you find a way for everyone to be happy. At the very least, this would make all your pain disappear," he said.

His voice—the voice of the man who was doomed never to meet his true love again, bound by the chains of eternal life—echoed in my eardrums. If the devil existed, then surely this was what his sweet whisper would sound like.

But...

I cupped a hand to my mouth. I could feel my own desires and Shinonome-san's wishes boxing me in, squeezing the air out of my lungs.

"Stay out of this," Suimei said in a steely voice. I looked up and saw him glaring at the mermaid butcher. "Nobody asked for your opinion. This is for Kaori and Shinonome to decide."

"That's uncalled for," the other man pouted. "I just want everyone to be happy..."

"Shut up," Suimei said, cutting him off.

The butcher stuck his lip out even further and furrowed his brows. Suimei lifted me away from him by my shoulders and fixed his eyes onto mine. A few glimmerflies fluttered between us, their hazy glow shining a golden light in the young man's irises.

"I understand how much you're hurting," he said, his eyes filling with a glistening sorrow. "When I heard that my mother was going to die, I felt the same kind of pain too."

Suimei probably knew the torment of loss more deeply than anyone else. On top of losing his mother at a very young age, he'd also been so brutally disciplined by his father that his hair had turned permanently white.

"I, um, I'm sorry," I hastily apologized as I tried to acknowledge that I was not the only one who was going through a hard time.

Suimei shook his head softly and brushed away the tears on my cheeks with a finger.

"We all have our share of sadness," he said. "It's not a competition."

He beamed at me with a smile so warm that I felt like I was being bathed in the sunlight of spring.

"So, what do you want to do?" he asked. "You and Shinonome are the only ones who can make this decision."

We had two choices: either give Shinonome-san eternal life or let him see the end of his life as he wanted.

Suddenly, Kamehime's words came back to me.

Make the right choices, Kaori. There is nothing more soul-crushing than a life of regret.

Her own choice had resulted in a thousand years of anguish and left her a stranger to the one she loved most.

This is too much for me. I just can't make this decision.

My chest twisted itself into knots, but it loosened when Suimei squeezed my hand.

"Just calm down and think it through. I'll support whatever you choose," he assured me. "If you can't stand the idea of seeing him go, I'll help you convince him to eat the mermaid meat. But if you feel ready to see him off, I'll stay with you and make sure you don't get hurt any more than necessary."

I looked up at him slowly. Hearing him say that made me feel safe.

"So let me stay with you when you feel like you're at the end of your rope," he said. "Let out everything that you're feeling. Don't just swallow it and push yourself into a corner. Whenever you're hurting, I want you to be able to share your feelings with me. Please."

He exhaled slowly and gazed into my eyes.

"After all these years, I've finally found somewhere I can truly call home...and it's wherever you are. So leave some space for me next to you, okay? I promise I'll always be with you."

"Oh...!" I gasped. I was suddenly aware of all the places where I was feeling the warmth from Suimei's body, and my heart felt like it was trembling as its scars were soothed by a comforting heat.

Suddenly, Nyaa-san meowed.

"Hey, why do you get to hog Kaori all to yourself?!" she protested. "I'm her best friend, you know! Yeah, the final decision is up to her and Shinonome, but I can offer some great advice too! So ask me any questions you have and tell me anything you want, Kaori. It's not like you to keep festering over these kinds of things!"

"That's right!" came another familiar voice. It was Noname, with Kuro in her arms.

"You can ask me anything you want too!" the Inugami piped up. "Not that I think I'll be much help. Heh heh."

I looked toward them, and when I saw my adoptive mother looking back at me, I noticed that she had been crying too.

"Kaori!" Noname cried, setting Kuro down and running toward me. She brushed Suimei aside and flung her arms around me, rubbing her cheek against mine. I was thrown off guard by how hard she squeezed me.

"I heard that you went to see Yao Bikuni," she whispered weakly. I'd never heard her speaking in that voice before.

Her face crumpled. "Wasn't I good enough? Didn't you trust me?"

I shook my head quickly, trying to comfort her.

"No, that's not it," I clarified. "It's just that I rely on you too much, so I thought that if I went to see you about it, then everything would be solved without any self-reflection on my end. And...that wasn't what I needed."

She smiled once she knew that I hadn't thrown her aside, but there was still a sliver of doubt in her eyes.

"Oh... Really?" she asked.

Then it hit me, way too late, that Noname had been worried about the same thing as I was. She'd been trying her hardest to be a real mother to me too. Her efforts were clear to me, as her daughter, and I'd been saved by her warmth and generosity countless times. I put my head to her sturdy chest as I welled up with love for her.

"Yeah," I said. "I promise I'll come to you next time. I mean, you *are* my mother."

Overwhelmed with joy, she gasped and squeezed me harder.

"Jeez! You're so... You're so...!" she sniffed. "Promise me that you won't keep whatever's stressing you out to yourself, okay? We're family, after all!"

"I can't...breathe..." I choked.

"But... But..." she cried. "Oh, gosh, I've still got such a long way to go as a mother!"

Noname burst into tears, and I managed to wiggle out of her grip. Then more cheery voices called from the bottom of the hill.

"Heeey! I heard that Kaori was sulking around the spirit realm! Is she there?" Ginme called.

"Jeez, did you have to say it like that?" Kinme sighed. "Oh, hey, Kaori! We bought a bunch of meat buns. Eat up! Hunger is one of the biggest reasons why people start spiraling, you know," he said with a lax attitude that seemed almost out of place for the atmosphere at hand.

Everyone had come together before I even knew what was happening. When I looked past the Tengu brothers, I saw that even more spirits were making their way to me.

"Kaori-kun! Are you all right? I just had to come over here as your most dependable and trustworthy uncle!" Toochika-san yelled.

"Ho ho, would you like to go for a walk with my jellyfish? That could turn your frown upside down," Nurarihyon said.

"My, my, my, what do we have here? What have you all been up to while I was gone? A woman must always reserve her tears and only show them in discussions of love!"

"Oh, you are so beautiful even when you're grumpy! I must thank the heavens for the opportunity to gaze upon your visage like this!"

Fuguruma-youbi and Kami-oni were here too, along with Yamajiji, Goblin, Karakasa-niisan, and even Konoha and Tsukiko.

"Kaori!" they cried, waving at me. I was surprised to see them all gathered here, bringing more merriment to this quiet hill than what was going on in town.

"Pfft," I laughed. "Gosh, you guys. What happened to your jobs and training?"

"Forget about work. This is an important time for our dear Kaori-kun!" Toochika-san said, and everyone nodded in unison.

"Ah ha ha ha!" I burst out. The knots in my chest were being slowly unraveled by their kindness.

"Jeez, can't I even cry alone in peace?" I joked.

I inhaled deeply until I felt my lungs strain and then let all the air out gently. I raised both my hands and slapped my cheeks with a loud *bam*, then straightened my back and cleared my tear-streaked face.

"Kaori?" Suimei said in confusion, and I flashed him a smile.

"Sorry for making you worry!" I said.

He remained stunned.

"Hey, did you know that death splits the paths of our lives in two? The living must continue on while the dead stop at their destination," I quoted.

"What do you mean?" the young man asked.

"Oh, nothing. Just something that the harshest but kindest person in the spirit realm told me."

I grinned and scanned my eyes over the crowd. I knew that after seeing Shinonome-san pass away, my heart would feel like it was mortally wounded. It would bleed itself dry and leave me a hollow shell, but even so, I had everyone here with me. I had Suimei, Noname, Nyaa-san, Kuro, Kinme and Ginme, Toochika-san...

There were so many spirits that loved me here, and they would make sure that my heart would not bleed itself out. They'd prepare remedies and words of encouragement, and they'd tell me off when I needed it. They would support me so I wouldn't crumble. After Shinonome-san was gone, I would still have my own path to walk, and it would not be an easy one. It was sure to have its ups and downs, and I would come across all sorts of challenging life events that would drive me to the end of my rope. But I knew I was going to be okay, because my loved ones would pick me up if they saw me falling, and I would do the same for them too.

That was life. And we all had to walk our own paths to reach our own ends. But, even as I told myself that, the pain still remained.

I couldn't shake off the shock of my adoptive father's impending death so easily. But I wasn't scared of what was to come— despite everything, I was going to keep moving forward. I didn't have to walk alone, because I was surrounded by so many people who loved me.

"Thank you, everyone," I said.

All the spirits relaxed when they saw me smiling at them, and I tried to compose myself too. What could I do for Shinonome-san? Although it hurt to think about, I still had to make a decision. There was probably no right answer to this question, but I wanted to fulfill whatever conclusion I arrived at to the best of my ability.

The mermaid butcher stared at me in silence. When I caught his eye for a second, his face darkened and he immediately looked away. He knew that even though he believed immortality to be the best solution, his offer had no part to play in my plans.

"I promised Shinonome-san that I would help him become whatever he wanted, but he's gone and made all his decisions himself without leaving any room for my input. What should I do?" I asked the crowd.

Everyone looked at each other. Noname heaved a sigh, her groan rattling in her throat.

"Shinonome's just the type to focus his tunnel vision on what he wants to do and charge full steam ahead," she said.

"That's true," Toochika-san piped up. "Pretty rich of him to put off telling Kaori-kun about how little time he has left, when you think about it."

"Not only that, but he got me involved in this too! It's enough to make *me* anxious," Nurarihyon cackled.

The other spirits followed suit and burst into laughter. Shinonome-san had a bad habit of going in roundabout ways to convey what he meant. On the outside, it seemed like he had already made his final decision, but he was probably struggling with hesitation. I was happy to learn that he had this vulnerable side.

"He always turns tail and runs during the important stuff, even though he's already shown that he's perfectly capable with all the effort he puts into being my father," I laughed softly.

Noname's eyes flashed.

"That's it!" She grabbed my hands and pulled me toward her. "That's what we need to do!"

I blinked at her, not sure what she was trying to say.

"We just need to let him feel the joy that comes with being a father!" Noname gushed.

"Joy...?" I frowned.

She giggled.

"Yep. That's it, that's it! I just remembered the thing that Shinonome spent a lot of money getting the folks in the hidden village to make!" she said, jumping up.

My eyes widened at the unexpected mention of the hidden village.

"Wait, what do you mean?" I asked. While I puzzled over Noname's words, she continued to hop around giddily.

"Now that you mention it, there *was* that thing. Hmm, good idea!" Toochika-san piped up cheerfully.

He hooked his arms over Suimei's and my shoulders and looked at us both as he whispered into our ears to fill us in on the plan.

"What?!" we sputtered when he finished, and our faces grew a bright red. We couldn't find anything else to say, and our mouths hung open like goldfish.

"It's all gonna be okay. Just leave it to us," Noname said.

"All right, show me some moxie now!" Toochika-san cheered. "We're going to make this the best present that my best friend's ever had!"

Suimei and I looked at each other, stunned by the two spirits' excitement and confidence. However, when our eyes met, we couldn't help but look away in embarrassment.

That night, I returned to the bookstore. When I opened the door, I was met by a worried Shinonome-san. The room was filled with the smell of the tobacco he had lit in an attempt to calm himself down.

I sniffled and smiled at him, my face still red from crying so much.

"I'm home," I said.

When he heard me greet him like usual, the Tsukumogami lightly relaxed.

"Welcome back," he said.

I took a seat beside my father and looked intently at him. He appeared slightly sickly, a sign of his shortening life.

"We gotta hurry to make sure I have everything I need to take over the business, right?" I whispered.

Shinonome-san's face crumpled.

"Are you sure?" he asked.

I scooted closer to him and tugged at his sleeve. He was wearing his best kimono.

"I'll be with you until the very end," I promised.

My father's pale blue eyes grew damp, and I could feel my own become watery too. Still silent, I prepared to brew some tea, just as if it were any other day. But nothing lasts forever, including the days I had thought of as so average. That was one of the painful truths I had been confronted with, one of the facts of life that pushed me another step into adulthood.

The winds in the spirit realm changed from cold to freezing, and the trees completely shed their autumn garb.

During any other year, this would be the time for the bookstore to enter its end-of-year break, but there was no time for that this year. We had to visit all the corners of Japan so Shinonome-san could introduce me to his clients and let them know that I would be taking over.

At the same time, I was meeting with Noname and Toochika-san to iron out the details of our plan. My body screamed for rest, but I urged it to keep moving. Everything had to be perfect, no matter what.

Day by day, Shinonome-san grew weaker. He ate less, and eventually even walking became a feat of colossal effort for him. We renovated the bookstore to make it as accessible for him as possible, allowing him to get around with a wheelchair. Even with his failing health, he never abandoned his desk, but he would never tell me what he was writing.

As his writing continued in silence, the spirit world was painted white with snow. The soft frost fell endlessly and blanketed our home, muffling every sound.

All of our customer visits finished around that time, along with the preparations for our secret plan. Shinonome-san wrote on, and I immersed myself in reading. He didn't have many days left, but I chose to act as though each one was just any old day to savor the important feeling of normalcy. With every flip of the page, I dove deeper and deeper into the story I held in my hands.

Flip. Flip. Flip.

It was a calm and quiet winter, but one that I would never forget. For the rest of my life, I would remember the days that ticked by as we approached the end of a long tale.

Eventually, spring arrived once again. The flower fields rustled as the warm breeze billowed through the spirit realm, carrying with it fresh hopes for the new season.

Shinonome was confused. Kaori had been missing all morning, and now Noname was taking him on an impromptu trip to who knew where. He stared out into the expanse of nemophilas with a frown creasing his brows.

The nemophilas were in full bloom this year too, blanketing the hills in a field of blue and waving with each whisper of the wind. The scenery was stunning—it was one of Kaori's favorite views for a good reason. He felt like he was at the beach looking into the deep azure of its waters, and for a moment he was almost confused at the lack of a salty scent in the air.

But there was something different about this landscape today. Someone had set up a row of glimmerfly lanterns among the flowers, their yellowish glow wavering with the flutters.

And that wasn't the only odd thing—a large group of spirits were also gathered on the hill, each one of them holding their own lantern. They were all wearing black and headed for the top.

"Noname? What is all this?" Shinonome asked, just as confused as before.

The other spirit smiled at him knowingly as she pushed his wheelchair along, her amber eyes glinting.

"Oh, it's nothing," she said. "Just be quiet and let me take you where we need to go."

"You want *me* to be *quiet*?" the Tsukumogami protested. "Real nice of you to take advantage of a guy who can't walk."

Shinonome had grown so frail that he even struggled to stand up from his wheelchair by himself. He was grateful for all the help he received, but it didn't leave his pride unscathed, especially because of how annoying Noname could be.

"Where's Kaori? I want to see her," grumbled the irritated Shinonome. He didn't have the strength to complain any louder.

"You're getting more and more like old man Bakin," Noname said, and Shinonome grew even more annoyed. He pulled a sour face, and Noname peered at him in response.

"C'mon, smile now. Kaori's going to be very sad if she sees you like that," she said.

"What's Kaori got to do with..." Shinonome began before he noticed that the other spirit was pointing into the distance. Puzzled, he followed her finger, and what he saw nearly stopped his breathing.

"A bride...?"

Surrounded by the sea of blue blossoms stood a figure clothed in pure white. It was a woman with her back turned, and she wore silk bridal robes that shone like the moon.

Shinonome only noticed when he was closer that the woman's face was turned slightly toward him, although it was obscured by her headdress. However, even without seeing it, in his heart he already knew who it was. After all, he had been with her nearly every day since she was three years old.

It was his precious little girl.

"Kaori!" he called, and his daughter slowly walked toward him in all her resplendence. Her skin glowed, and her lips were accentuated with a vibrant red. It was like she had shed her young, childish cocoon and emerged a woman who had slipped into adulthood as the very definition of beauty. She was exactly what that word had been created to describe.

"Surprise! Thanks for coming out here," Kaori smiled as Shinonome's wheelchair came to a stop in front of her.

There she goes, trying to force her smile again when all she wants to do is cry, Shinonome thought.

Understanding his daughter's mood was second nature to him. It was difficult seeing her like this, but he had to know.

"What is all this? Tell me what's going on," he demanded.

It came out sounding much more severe than he had intended, and he silently cursed at himself. When he glanced at the top of the hill, he could see someone else waiting there, and he already had an idea of who it was.

"It's my wedding with Suimei. Noname and Toochika-san helped us prepare it," Kaori answered.

"Hey, who said you could..."

A tickle in his lungs stopped him from finishing his sentence, and he hacked and coughed, scrunching his face as he tried to breathe.

Noname chuckled from behind him.

"Aw, here come the mixed emotions! But you knew this was going to happen sooner or later, didn't you?" she teased.

Still unable to speak, the Tsukumogami shot his deadliest stare at Noname. But she was completely immune to it, as wives tend to be.

"The fine folks at the hidden village said this is their magnum opus. They spent many sleepless nights to complete it. Doesn't she look wonderful in it?" Noname sighed fondly.

Kaori was simply dazzling to look at. Shinonome had placed an advance order for fabric to be used whenever his daughter's special day eventually came, and the result was the custom-made bridalwear she had on. When Karaito Gozen told him that he didn't have much time left to live, the Tsukumogami had been saddened by the fact that he would never see his daughter be wed, and he'd never expected this surprise.

Once the itching disappeared from his throat, Shinonome gazed at Kaori and whispered, "Yes."

Their eyes met. Kaori's were tinted with a shade of worry, but when her father finally said "You are so beautiful," her face crumpled. She darted away, trying desperately to hold the tears back.

Shinonome laughed lightly. It would be a disaster if her makeup were ruined before the ceremony.

Suddenly, he realized that something had been draped over his shoulders. It was a black haori decorated with a family crest.

"Can't have the bride's father looking so shabby on such a big day, can we?" Noname said.

"You..." he growled.

"Oh, save it. I promise I'll let you complain all you want later," she giggled.

"Shinonome-san?" Kaori called. Then the Tsukumogami realized that his daughter was standing right beside him with her hand out, and he took it on reflex.

"Will you come with me?" she asked.

He presumed they were going to meet her groom. He cleared his throat and looked at Kaori, who returned his gaze with a serene smile.

"...Yeah, sure," he agreed reluctantly.

Kaori beamed in delight. Up the hill they slowly went, with Noname pushing Shinonome's wheelchair.

A spring breeze swept across the land, brushing the nemophilas with the warmth that blessed the earth with so much life. A few shining glimmerflies flitted across Shinonome's field of vision and led his eyes to his radiant daughter.

She looked like a work of art, and her eyes glittered like the starry sky above. Her crimson lips suggested a charm that

Shinonome had never known before today. There was no doubt that everyone present was stunned by how gorgeous she was. She was brimming with a zest for life, as if she were the embodiment of a hopeful future. Shinonome smiled to himself. He had no future, and that was supposed to be a very sad thing, but...for some reason, his heart burned with enthusiasm.

Once they arrived at the top of the hill, Shinonome saw Suimei's father, Seigen. He was dressed similarly in a crested haori, complete with a hakama.

And...the mermaid butcher.

"You..." Shinonome muttered, narrowing his eyes.

The butcher took a step forward and spoke.

"This is...your last chance, Shinonome."

He took a mermaid from his fishing cage and held it out, his green eyes wavering uneasily.

"Would you like some mermaid meat? It can grant any wish you want."

Shinonome remained silent and still. Then he shook his head.

"No," he declined. "I have no need for the eternity that mermaid meat offers."

The other man bit his lip and mumbled "I see" before turning away. He jumped into a nearby shadow and vanished completely.

Seigen, wearing his best outfit, stepped out to greet Shinonome in his place.

He gave the Tsukumogami a firm nod and said, "Leave the young'uns to me."

"You think you've got what it takes?" Shinonome raised an eyebrow.

"Ha ha! Harsh," Seigen laughed. "I don't blame you, though. I realize now that I've done a lot of awful things to my son. But unlike you, at least I have all the time in the world to make things right."

He was indeed different from Shinonome, as he was one of the many in this world who had chosen the mermaid meat's immortality.

"I'm going to take the time to earn his trust back. I'll show everyone that I can be a good father."

Shinonome stuck his lip out at Seigen's sensible words.

"Fine," he grumbled. "I believe you."

He offered his hand, and the other man shook it with a smile.

"I promise I'll do a good job," he said.

Then came another voice.

"Shinonome."

The final person to greet him was Suimei, who was staring at him with clear, brown eyes. He was completely cool and confident. Shinonome inwardly laughed to himself, impressed at the young man's bravery in planning this wedding behind his back.

"You can hit me if you want," Suimei said.

Shinonome spat. He wasn't expecting that at all.

"Ha ha!" he guffawed. "Giving me cheek, eh?"

"I'm serious. Go ahead, if it'll make you feel better."

"It really just might," the Tsukumogami said.

He glanced at Kaori, who was fidgeting at the tension between the two men.

The corner of Shinonome's lip rose. To be honest, he didn't even have the strength left for a single punch.

"No, let's drop it. My daughter would hate me for the rest of her life if I hit her groom on her big day," he chuckled, trying to be nonchalant about it.

Suimei smiled and went down on one knee.

"I have to thank you, too, for being the first one to find me when I collapsed in the spirit realm."

He was talking about the night he had fallen unconscious in the rain, surrounded by glimmerflies. Even for someone like Shinonome, who had lived in the spirit realm for years, it had still been quite a shocking sight.

"I never thought the young man I picked up would go on to marry my daughter," the Tsukumogami said.

"Neither did I," Suimei said.

The two laughed together. Then the young man's face suddenly grew serious as he focused on Shinonome once more.

"I swear I'll make Kaori happy," he declared, his voice full of conviction.

Shinonome pursed his lips and looked away.

"You'd better, or I'll haunt you for the rest of your life!" he grumbled.

"You're welcome to," the young man nodded reassuringly. But soon after, he was overtaken by an inexplicable and complicated feeling, and his head drooped.

Noname took this as an opportunity to hurry things along.

"All right, it's time to get going," she said. "After all, the bride has to leave her father eventually."

Shinonome's face shot upward. The distance between him and Kaori was starting to grow. A sting of loneliness pierced him, and his hand stretched out as if it had a mind of its own.

"Kaori..."

The young woman was now standing beside Suimei. She turned to the Tsukumogami and smiled.

"Shinonome-san... No, Father..."

"Ka... Kaori..."

"Thank you for raising me," she said. "Thank you for always being by my side and for loving me."

"Kaori...!" Shinonome cried before another cough derailed him.

"Spirits eventually return to the cycle of life after they die, right?" Kaori continued, the tears now streaming down her face. "So I'm going to wait for when you finally come back."

Shinonome's eyes flew open.

"Wait, don't tell me *you're* going to eat the mermaid meat?" he gasped.

Kaori shook her head.

"No," she said. "I'm going to do everything I can to make the bookstore last long enough for my children to inherit it, and for them to pass it on to the next generation. That way, it'll still be here when you return. Well, I guess that technically means I won't be the one doing the waiting, then."

She and Suimei exchanged looks, and Suimei spoke next.

"We're going to continue your work. We'll deliver stories to spirits all over Japan and publish more books like *Selected Memoirs from the Spirit Realm* so spirits don't fade into obscurity when they pass away."

Kaori nodded. "We think that publications like *Selected Memoirs* are very valuable and should be preserved for eternity."

"It's not going to be easy, and I'm guessing we'll fumble with a lot of trial and error, but..."

"We're going to give it our best. We'll never give up, even after you're gone. If we can do that..."

The two of them smiled.

"...then all the feelings and memories that we put into this work will reach you wherever you are in the future. It'll be our version of immortality."

They linked hands, their gazes full of faith and confidence.

When they met, she was just a spirit's daughter to him and he was just a young exorcist to her. But, as they went on to have their own experiences and grow their own seeds within themselves, they'd changed into something different. There was no one more fit to take over the bookstore than the two of them, and Shinonome felt relief spreading over him.

Ah... Kaori's a fully mature, independent adult now.

A few silent tears began to fall. As they traced warm trails down his cheek one after another, snapshots from his life with Kaori flashed through his mind. There were many difficult times, some that had almost made him give up, but they were only a few drops in the wide pool of joyful memories they'd created together.

"Get up, Shinonome-san! How many times do I have to ask you to shave your stubble?"

"That was a lot of writing you did today. Do you want a beer? I can get one for you."

"Heeey! I got this super rare book today! Isn't it just awesome? Let's read it together!"

Kaori was always full of energy, and her eyes spoke of the safety she felt with him. She smiled innocently at him, she got angry at him when she needed to, and she turned to him whenever she needed help.

He climbed further and further back in his memory to Kaori's earlier years. To when she was a sensitive teen. To when she was an innocent child. To when she was only three, the age at which they met. Shinonome's hand moved instinctively, reaching out to his daughter.

"Mama..."

Poor little Kaori looked so anxious. Back then, she and Shinonome were still a fake family.

It's all right. You're all right now, Kaori.

He ruffled her hair. Her head was so small that he could cup it comfortably with one hand. He swept her into a big hug, and Kaori blinked in surprise, her eyelashes batting against her tears.

You're going to be such a beautiful bride when you grow up, and you'll have a husband you can trust with your life too. And look at all the friends you have! The path ahead of you shines with the light of a future filled with hope, so there's nothing you need to worry about.

Little Kaori's face lit up as her cheeks bloomed with a rosy pink.

"Thank you, Shinomeme! This was all because of you. I love you!"

She squeezed him back as hard as she could with her tiny arms.

"And now, the bride and groom will exchange rings."

Seigen's voice snapped Shinonome back to reality. He hadn't realized how far the ceremony had proceeded. It was different from the type of ritual you would see in the human world. Spirits didn't swear eternal love to a god during their weddings; instead, they would make a promise of happiness to all their loved ones present.

And then, when Suimei slid his ring onto Kaori's finger...

With a great whoosh, the spirits all released the glimmerflies from their lamps. They fluttered around the bride and groom in a gleaming flurry before trailing off into the sky like a ribbon of light, shining with blessings for the newlyweds wherever life might lead them.

It was mesmerizing. In their glow, Shinonome spotted a distant figure. It was an elderly man, dressed in an old-fashioned conical hat and shimagappa cape. His eyes sparkled as he watched the glimmerflies. Then, as quickly as Shinonome had spotted him, he turned his back and left. He must have been struck by a bolt of inspiration for his next story.

I did it, Bakin. I've fulfilled my purpose as Kaori's father.

His heart swelled with pride, and a smile began to tug at his teary face. He could feel the seeds of experience that he had sown waiting eagerly to burst into bloom.

But one question remained: Was he able to become something real? His true trial was right around the corner.

But all he wanted to do now was take in the beautiful sight before him. He grinned as though the sun had finally come out after a long storm.

Shinonome-san passed away without a chance to greet the new summer.

The spirits knew that when souls passed on, they would eventually cycle back into life. As most of them could live long enough to see that happen, mourning wasn't really a part of their culture. However, after Shinonome-san died, the bookstore was filled with spirits coming to offer their condolences. They shared their memories of him and borrowed books in his honor. I was so busy that I didn't have the time to grieve, but I honestly preferred the distraction. By the time the visitors thinned out, the colors of fall had already settled into the spirit realm, and my hands became full again as I took stock and aired out the books.

At the same time, we were preparing for Suimei to move in with me. The house was a bit on the small side, so I had to organize Shinonome-san's room appropriately. I wanted to leave it as it was so I could preserve his presence, but while he had arrived at his final destination, I still had my own road to walk. The room couldn't stay the same forever.

Did Shinonome-san ever become something real, like he wanted?

The question weighed on my mind. I knew that he had been fervently writing something before he passed away, but I came across nothing resembling a manuscript when I went through his things. Had he ever been able to craft a story from scratch? When I asked his closest friends, they said they didn't know anything either, and so the truth remained shrouded in mystery.

One day, when I was tidying Shinonome-san's room with Suimei, we came across an old wooden box tucked away in his closet. Curious, we opened it.

"Whoa! I haven't seen this in forever," I gasped.

Suimei nodded. "Not since the Daidarabotchi incident."

Inside the box lay a copy of *Tale of the Bamboo Cutter*, the only edition in the world whose pictures floated in the air when it was opened. Shinonome-san and Noname had created it once upon a time to calm little me down during my bouts of crying.

"I was wondering where this went! I can't believe he had it tucked away in here," I said as I took the book out. Then I saw that there was another volume hiding underneath it.

"What's this? *Tales of the Spirit Realm Bookstore?*"

I ran a finger down the cover of the curious book. It appeared to be newly bound, since the paper was still a sparkling white and I could smell the glue. The binding was tight, and it even had a color cover. I stared intently at the illustration, then snapped my head around to meet Suimei's eyes.

"Hey, isn't this the store?" he said.

"Yeah..." I nodded. On the cover was an old, intricate, traditional Japanese house whose walls were lined with shelves full of glimmerflies flitting between them. It felt exactly like the store I had spent my life in with Shinonome-san. And we *were* a bookstore in the spirit realm too. So could it be...?

That wasn't the only thing about the cover that stood out to me.

"Hey, look at this," I said, pointing at the illustration.

"Now I've definitely seen *them* before," Suimei said.

There were three figures, two human and one not. There was a girl with a book in her hand sitting next to a smug black cat. The last figure was a young man with white hair, staring into the distance as he stood still.

"That's gotta be us, right?" I whispered.

"Probably. The cat's even got three tails and multi-colored eyes."

So...that means...

I lifted the cover, my heart thudding and thumping in my chest. A soft light spilled out from within.

I watched in shock as the illustrations drifted in the air and moved. It was just like *Tale of the Bamboo Cutter*, even though Shinonome-san had said he would never be able to make anything like it again!

Suimei and I stared in fascination, our words failing us as we were sucked into the tale of a girl who worked at a bookstore and a boy who wandered into the spirit realm.

The girl and the boy traveled all over Japan to deliver books to spirits who needed new stories in their lives. It was a difficult journey filled with many obstacles, but they were able to overcome whatever came their way by supporting each other.

Then, as the story neared its ending, a black cat and a black dog joined the boy and girl, and they all walked toward a light ahead of them. They were grinning ear to ear as they strode into the bright unknown.

When the story ended, I realized that my cheeks were soaked with tears.

"Shinonome-san..." I whispered as I stroked the colophon at the back. The date printed on the page was a few days before Shinonome-san's passing.

He did it. He finished his story.

I began to cry again out of pride.

"You did so well..." I murmured.

But there was a loneliness in my heart that I couldn't ignore. It was so clear that this book was based on our story, and yet Shinonome-san did not appear even once. But why? He was such a vital part of my life. Was he too embarrassed to put himself in his own book?

I hugged the book to my chest and sobbed.

Suimei suddenly pointed to the back cover, his eyes wide.

"Kaori, look," he said.

Wondering what had caught him off guard, I turned the book over.

"Oh!" I gasped in delight.

The back cover illustration continued from the front, featuring two crows and a black dog with red spots. They were together in a familiar room...the very one we were in, in fact. And seated at its desk was...

"Dad..."

There was Shinonome-san, brush in hand, writing quietly.

"I can't believe he's still writing even in this drawing," I giggled. All the emotions in me broke like a dam, and my shoulders trembled as I bawled.

Suimei hooked an arm around me, and I sank into him, gazing at the illustration with blurry eyes.

Who drew this? I wondered. Then, as I stared more closely at it, I saw a single handwritten letter: "T."

"Tamaki, huh? Of course it was him. Sneaky guy," Suimei mused.

Tamaki-san must have been working on this before he passed away. It couldn't have been easy, designing and drawing a cover for a story that was not yet complete.

"This is amazing... Shinonome-san is amazing. Wow," I breathed.

"Yeah, he is," Suimei agreed.

I linked my hand with his and squeezed, and he squeezed back. Just as Shinonome-san had written in his book, there was a path ahead of us that we would have to walk with our heads held high, hand in hand.

We closed our eyes and let our minds take us back into the story my father had written us—back into the treasure that two of my precious loved ones had left for us.

The Haunted Bookstore
Gateway to a Parallel Universe

TIME WAITS for neither man nor spirit, and so on it marched. The human world saw the birth of many new lives and the passing of many old ones. A hundred years could change cities and towns into completely new metropolises and turn current values into outdated ideals. Such inevitable changes push humans to make the most of the time they have.

However, in a universe only a shimmer away from the human world, it was quite the opposite. The spirit realm reveled in its stasis, and change plodded through its towns so slowly that even a few centuries could pass without any major transformations. The world whose sky was perpetually dark cycled through yet another day similar to the one before it and the many that came before that one.

"Welcome! Come on in!"

"We've got the lowest prices on fish today! How 'bout it, ma'am? I'll even throw in something extra!"

Winter had just broken, and the streets were filled with lively shouts as the crowds milled about. The snow was finally beginning to melt, and the spirits had taken the first possible opportunity to crawl out of their cramped quarters and shake off the hibernation blues.

The cobblestones clattered with the clip-clopping of a man's geta as he made his way through the clamor with a relaxed gait, smiling to himself and taking in the nostalgic landscape. The spirits who caught sight of him whispered excitedly among themselves, but no one made a move to speak with him. They simply looked on, each of them knowing that his first conversation should be saved for others.

Finally, the man arrived at a store located past the hustle and bustle of the main street. However, that did not mean the place lacked a commotion of its own. In fact, it was packed with a veritable crowd. Curious, the man peeked over the tops of their heads and saw a wagon piled high with new books sitting at the front of the shop.

"Hey, everyone! The new volume of *Selected Memoirs from the Spirit Realm* is finally here! Come and get your copy!" yelled a lively voice.

The surprised man looked up to see a young girl shouting at the top of her lungs over the din.

"Get your hands on the thirtieth volume! And since thirty is such a special number, we've got an exclusive interview with the big boss of the human and spirit worlds, Toochika the kappa, and Nurarihyon, whom I'm sure you're all familiar with! Come on and get your copy now!"

Then a spirit spoke up.

"Hey, what if I just want to borrow it instead of buying?" he called out.

The girl shook her head.

"Sorry, but reservations are already backed way up. If you'd like to put your name down on the waiting list, we can do that for you at the apothecary!" she said and pointed to the shop next door.

The man let out a small *ooh!* when he saw that the bookstore and the apothecary had combined into one business. That made sense.

He rubbed his stubble and stared into the bookstore. He could see two black furballs nestled in a corner—a cat and a dog with red spots. They looked to be happily cuddling, at least until the cat decided she wanted to shoot a vicious paw punch at the dog.

Then he looked toward the apothecary, where he spotted a figure with a head of luscious green hair making small talk with the customers. Beside her was a young man earnestly mixing a medicinal blend, who seemed to resemble the girl touting *Selected Memoirs* at the bookstore. Were they siblings, perhaps?

The man smiled to himself and approached the girl. When she noticed him, she smiled back.

"Hey, I haven't seen you around before!" she greeted him, immediately friendly and welcoming. "Have you already borrowed from us, sir, or would you like me to run you through how things work here?"

She looked up at him eagerly, her chestnut eyes sparkling. Her cheeks were rosy with enthusiasm, and she seemed ready to leap into action at a moment's notice, aching to give this newcomer a tour of the shop.

"You know, every spirit is reading mountains upon mountains of books these days. You don't want to fall behind, do you?" she giggled.

The man's eyes widened at her words. His gaze moved to the back of the store and made contact with the fuzzballs. The two of them stood up with a start, their fur immediately puffing out.

Suddenly, an irritated voice rang out from the back of the crowd.

"Move, please! I haven't got all day! When a gentleman is in a hurry, stay out of his way!"

"Oh, look. It's the big boss of the human and spirit worlds."

"Ugh, don't call me by that stupid nickname. Hey, you twins over there! Come give me a hand!"

"Yes, sir!"

A loud *bang!* thundered through the space, knocking a few spirits off their feet with its sheer force. The young girl seemed unfazed, though. It probably happened so often that she'd already grown used to it.

The man chuckled and patted her on the head.

"I'd love to know more about this store. Would it be too much of a bother for you to show me around?" he asked.

The girl's face lit up, and she cleared her throat.

"This is the one and only bookstore in the spirit realm, founded by Kyokutei Bakin and succeeded by Shinonome and Muramoto Kaori as the second and third generations of owners.

And, of course, we boast the largest selection of books in the spirit realm! We've got all you need to laugh out loud and have a good cry. Or if you want a way to pass your sleepless nights, we've got you covered there too," she declared proudly with a sunbeam of a smile.

"So, is there a specific book you're looking for? Any time you need anything, call on the haunted bookstore!"

Ah... She used to say something like that too, didn't she?

The man laughed happily as he mused, and then he turned to the girl with a wide grin.

"I'd just like something good, thanks."

~Fin

THE
HAUNTED
BOOKSTORE
Gateway to a
Parallel Universe

Afterword

H EY! It's Shinobumaru. Thank you so much for reading Volume 6 of *The Haunted Bookstore*.

Here we are at the final installment. To be honest, I never thought I'd write this many when I started. It was my first ever chara-bungei work, which is a genre aimed toward readers in their twenties that feels more "anime." Back when it was first published, it was also the series that my publisher used to launch their new Kotonoha Bunko label. I remember being so nervous when we first started selling it! I still can't believe that I was able to publish six entire volumes. I have all of you dear readers, my editor Sato-san, the illustrator Munashichi-sensei, and everyone else who helped me on my journey to thank. You all have my eternal gratitude.

I fumbled quite a bit with my editor in the early stages of this book, but I think I was able to write everything I wanted to, more or less. Now that I think about it, this little old bookstore really has soared through so much hard work right from the first volume. I also used the Side Story chapters to really dig into the characters' backstories and their ups and downs. They certainly went through a lot in this series. I hope you all enjoyed getting to know more about Kaori, Suimei, Nyaa, Kinme and Ginme, Noname, and Shinonome. And if their stories spoke to you, that's all I can ask for as an author.

To me, novels are what a writer produces when they cut a slice from the lives of their characters and turn it into something that they can show to other people. We started when Kaori and Suimei met and ended with the climax of this volume, but all I did was borrow a few bits and pieces from their lives. There are still so many more escapades from their time in this world that I didn't get to write about.

Even though the story ended here, Kaori and her friends still have so many more exciting things waiting for them. No doubt, they have a tough road ahead of them filled with laughter, tears, bitterness, and sleepless nights. Like Toochika said, we all get our share of life events that we must face. Even as Kaori hits the hurdles that make her want to drop everything and run away, I'm sure she's going to grit her teeth and keep moving forward into the future filled with the light and hope that awaits her, just like it was outlined in the climax of the story Shinonome wrote.

I'm sure you dear readers will have your own share of life events. Whenever it gets too tough or painful to carry on, or when you want to give up, I hope you'll think of Kaori and her friends and let them fill you with the strength to keep going.

Nowadays, we're all a lot more forgiving with ourselves during hard times, and we don't want to just force ourselves through them. Still, there will come days where we have to keep pushing ourselves whether we like it or not. Kaori was able to stay true to herself and keep moving even as her tears flowed, but did she make the right decisions, or will she end up leading a life of regret like Kamehime? The only one who knows the answer to that question is Kaori herself, but if any of you guys ever find yourself in a similar situation, I hope Kaori's determination can become your helping hand.

Anyway, I guess I should proceed with the usual acknowledgments of gratitude now.

Sato-san, where would I be without your editing expertise? You've done so much to help me round up my ideas into something cohesive. I really appreciate that you gave me the space to let me do my own thing while also offering me much-needed support when I was going through tough times. The time we've spent working together since the establishment of Kotonoha Bunko is some of the most precious experience I've ever gained. I promise I'll keep polishing my skills as a writer so we can work together again. When that day comes, I hope you'll offer me the same kindness as you always have.

Sato-san was also the one who helped me brainstorm the subtitles for each volume of *The Haunted Bookstore*, and I can never thank him enough for that. He's so good at foreshadowing things in a succinct way. Be sure to look out for the clues we've dropped when you reread the series!

And, of course, Munashichi-sensei also returned to illustrate the cover of this final volume. It's the perfect culmination of all the stories that happened in *The Haunted Bookstore*. I got so emotional just seeing it! Thank you for your fantastic work, Munashichi-sensei!

I'm sure some of you have noticed already, but yes, the cover of Shinonome's final book—*Tales of the Spirit Realm Bookstore*—is indeed Munashichi-sensei's illustration for the first volume of *The Haunted Bookstore*. She once commented that it looks like we're peeking into Shinonome's workplace, and that observation has always stayed with me. And now it's made its way into the series too! This series would not be the way it is without her wonderful drawings, and I'm forever grateful for that. It all started with that first volume, and I'm happy that I was able to incorporate its cover into the story. I really can't thank Munashichi-sensei enough for her work.

I have the awesome sales team of Micro Magazine to thank for supporting this series too. I would never have been able to write so much if not for their convincing pitches to all the bookstores they visited. So, thank you all!

And to all the bookstore workers and readers, you also have my gratitude. I've already long since lost count of the times I was motivated by all the comments written on NetGalley (a review site). This series is filled with my desire to give back to all of my fans and supporters, and I hope you've all received it loud and clear.

Anyway, I know I said that this would be the final volume, but...that's technically not true. I've actually got a collection of short stories in the works! It's scheduled to come out next spring, and it's going to share with everyone what Kaori and company get up to after the events of this volume. I hope you guys will all be looking forward to it!

> From an autumn of twice-
> bloomed sweet osmanthus,
> Shinobumaru